WESTFARROW ISLAND

WESTFARROW ISLAND

PAUL A. BARRA

The Permanent Press
Sag Harbor, NY 11963

For information, address:
  The Permanent Press
  4170 Noyac Road
  Sag Harbor, NY 11963
  www.thepermanentpress.com

Library of Congress Cataloging-in-Publication Data

Barra, Paul A., author.
  Westfarrow Island / Paul A. Barra.
  Sag Harbor, NY: The Permanent Press, 2019
  ISBN: 978-1-57962-569-6
    1. Spy stories. 2. Suspense fiction.

PS3602.A8363 W47 2019
813'.6—dc23   2018057838

Printed in the United States of America

To Joni Lee
Who thinks my work is brilliant;
I think she is brilliant.

"The gray sea and the long black land;
And the yellow half-moon large and low."

ROBERT BROWNING
"Meeting at Night"
1845

CHAPTER ONE

People who drifted in a certain stratum of Bath society knew the sailorman named Joshua White, a man whose face was gullied by salt air, coarsened and darkened by sun, and whose life was a solitary pursuit. He had never married—had never even had a serious girlfriend as far as anybody knew—and was most often seen alone except for the company of his wee dog, an ugly brute that snuffled and groused as it trotted at White's heels, stuffing its bent muzzle into whatever flotsam had washed up from the Kennebec River. Sometimes the dog rode on the man's shoulder. It did that when it tired of waiting for its master to leave one or the other of the bars that huddled along the cracked sidewalks of Front Street.

When he laid off the booze, White was functional enough to serve as mate on *Maven*, Big Anthony Tagliabue's coastal freighter. He and Tagliabue were friends, although many thought Anthony put up with him on his boat rather than needed him. Whatever the case, the captain was unhappy when Joshua White didn't show up for a scheduled trip to Westfarrow Island on that cold April morning. They were supposed to get underway at two, to make landfall at first light.

Tagliabue liked sailing at night. He liked to ride down to the harbor slowly, the voices of a Cherubini *missa* drifting out the windows of his Jeepster. He liked to suck in the smells of the waterfront

as he rolled onto the rocked lot of Cronk's Pier, the tarry, salty,
rotting odors of life in a salt-river town.

None of what he liked was happening forty-five minutes after
one A.M. PBS was playing Tchaikovsky on *Music Through the Night*
and the car windows were closed to a late season chill. The harbor
was keeping her smells beneath the surface of dark, gelatinous
water supporting broken bits of kelp, feather weed, and sea let-
tuce. The water lay across the Kennebec like a used painter's tarp.

Anthony Tagliabue looked around the parking area for his
mate but saw no one. He waited. Ten minutes later, he hoisted
his sea bag with a sigh and walked down to the boat. *Maven* squatted in the water next to one of the weak-bulbed bollard lamps,
their frailty protected by pitted brass frames. The sixty-foot former
buoy tender was a hulking presence in the shadows, a big, solid
mass, a Percheron waiting in the stall for harness and a way
forward.

The old Director smelled as it always did: of damp bedding
overlaid with the bite of fuel and the faint odor of paint. The
sensory impact of the boat's interior, along with the motion of
the hull at its berth, put Tagliabue in seagoing mode. He didn't
descend the ladder but swung the bag on a near bunk and went to
the conning station to prepare for getting underway. The Detroit
diesels cranked and coughed and caught with a rumble. Tagliabue
listened to them for a minute. He left them burbling beneath the
surface while he loosed the hawsers fore and aft, hustling back
to the con in case the wind shifted while she was untied. Joshua
would have handled the lines had he been there.

Tagliabue watched the black void alongside widen as *Maven*
drifted from the pier. He inched both shifters ahead and eased
the boat out. Red buoy Alpha showed to port; the channel was
otherwise clear. Barely glancing at the stars blinking above him,
he flipped the toggle switch for his running lights and peered hard
into the darkness ahead.

Maven moved slowly through the harbor. Tagliabue had seen
and spoken to no one. He guided the beamy craft around errant

pot markers using the conning spot. Twenty minutes later they were past the Fastend anchorage and out into open water. The boat took up the swaying of the sea as she churned through the black-green depths toward Westfarrow, where they waited for his arrival. He sat in the wheelhouse, felt his body begin to roll with the ocean rhythms. In his mind he strove to suffocate the premonition that had intruded on the start of the voyage, a vague feeling that something wasn't right. Why didn't Joshua show at Cronk's? The mate was usually reliable. He could do this deal without Joshua, but he didn't like it. A solo transit at night could be hazardous. He decided not to worry about his absence until he had more data to analyze. He blew out a breath, sat back, and increased speed.

Tagliabue checked the corners of the blackness forward, moving his eyes constantly, hoping he could react fast enough in an emergency. His belly rumbled like *Maven's* big engines at idle, reminding him of the coffee he'd made at home. The starboard lamp turned the spray green when he tossed the dregs over the leeward side. He stared at the empty cups. He missed Joshua. By now he would have had a fresh pot going. The salty old bastard had plenty of knots in his personal lifeline, but he could sail and was loyal. The two of them often anticipated problems when they talked over contingencies at sea. Joshua could be a contrarian in his opinions but always agreed with their final decision. Tagliabue needed someone to talk to but he kept off the radio. It was too early in the morning.

Cursing Joshua's absence under his breath, he moved to the navigation table to take a LORAN fix. He noted his position on a plastic-covered chart then stood quietly, eyes closed, feeling and listening as the wind from *Maven's* forward motion misted the air around him with seawater. Was the boat's motion just a bit sluggish? Probably not. Probably he was a little keyed up knowing what he had committed to do, looking for things that could go wrong. He sat back down at the wheel. The steady rumble of the diesels calmed him. Time passed.

A different noise stole into his consciousness and sat him up. What was that hum? The waves were still moderate, the gauges steady. This was not a sound he expected to hear on the *Maven*. He could not identify it. Pulse quickening, he scanned the cargo behind him with his flashlight and saw nothing amiss. When he recognized that it was the bilge pump at work Tagliabue released the breath he'd been holding.

But why would the pump start? The ocean wasn't coming aboard, not topside, and the bilges were dry yesterday. It had to be a leak below deck.

Tagliabue twisted the dial for autopilot and slid down the ladder. His boots hit the cabin deck with a splash. His heart jumped. *Maven* was miles from shore and taking on water. He bolted back topside, slowed the engines, pushed the gearshift to neutral.

Below again, he slapped the wall light switch. The water sloshing around the interior of the cabin looked rusty when the twelve-volt lights bounced off it, but he didn't take the time to analyze that yet. He had to find the leak and plug it. Bending at the hips he scanned the deck, looking for telltale bubbles. Something dark, large and dark, showed along the starboard side forward, almost in the V of the bow. A mattress from one of the bunks had somehow become wedged into the framing of the narrow space. There was movement in the water around the shape.

He sloshed closer, realized he was not looking at a mattress. The shape was wrong, there were appendages trailing from it, like broken limbs of a felled tree. Some of it appeared puffy and had risen to the surface. He refused to believe his eyes, pulled the flashlight from his jacket pocket, and trained it on the object. He was standing over a human body, in foul weather gear with a watch cap pulled low on its head. The body was partially submerged, so it had to be dead. What was a dead person doing in his cabin?

The corpse was jammed into the space head first. Tagliabue had to use both hands to pull it out. Bubbles burst to the surface. The side of the boat was holed and the dead man had been keeping the sea out mostly.

He turned the body over—God, was it Joshua? With a burst of strength, he heaved it up on a bunk. Its clothes were torn and ragged across its chest. Lacerations decorated the skin beneath like a tracery of solar flares. The wounds were washed clean. Some were deep and puckered at the edges. They began to suppurate blood as he stared at them. Blood plopped into the bilge water. It was hard to recognize the wan and flaccid face in the repose of death. The muscles weren't knotted as they were in life, but it was Joshua's face. There was no doubt in his mind that his friend was dead, and no doubt that his boat was sinking.

Tagliabue sucked in a breath, closed his dead mate's eyes, and turned back to the gouge in his boat where the sea was flowing in. It was a jagged affair, about a foot wide and half that tall, most of it above the waterline. He pulled gear from the bosun's locker. He grunted like a sow in labor as he worked. He stuffed fiberglass batting into the rupture and lay planks across it. He set his hip against the planks and tried to drive eight-penny nails through them and into the hull of the boat. One bent, another flew off into the bilge water. His hands were stiff with cold; his legs felt numb. Despite the frigid seawater he was working in, his upper body was warm. Sweat stung his eyes. He concentrated and tried again. One nail went in, then another. By the time the wood was secured, he felt exhausted. Work was something he was used to, hard work, but this frantic race to save *Maven* used up the adrenaline that had squirted into his bloodstream and left him deflated. He staggered to the ladder and hauled himself up into the night air. He breathed deeply and willed his heart to slow.

The patch would hold at slow speeds, he figured. Once the pump lowered the water enough, he could effect a more permanent repair, permanent enough to get him to Westfarrow Island. He'd beach her there and fix it with tar and glue and strong screws, if he could make it on the falling tide.

There was nothing to be gained by worrying about that now. The boat was still on course, steaming at a knot or two toward the island. It remained black outside, a late moonrise producing only a sliver. It seemed that half the night had passed but he knew it was probably less than an hour since he discovered the body. His own body felt washed out, the big muscles trembling as he sat and let the weariness seep from him. His head nodded to his chest; he was tired. Normally, he and Joshua would take turns napping once their course was clear at sea, so he hadn't tried to sleep before setting out for Cronk's earlier that night.

He roused himself with an effort of will, went below to check the patch. It was bleeding water around the edges but not as fast as the pump was pushing it over the side. Joshua's body had kept the hole nearly plugged until *Maven* started carving the waves at speed. Once the pressure of the incoming ocean shoved the body out of its niche in the forward bulkhead, the hold began to flood. Joshua had saved his boat, and his life, with the mass of his mortal remains. The mate lay on the bunk now. One arm had fallen off the edge, its hand appearing to play in the bloodied water as it was drawn to the pump drain in the cabin decking. Tagliabue turned abruptly and went up the ladder.

Forcing himself to stay above deck and let the pump work, Tagliabue tried to imagine what had transpired below. What had killed Joshua? What made a hole in the hull? It had to have been some sort of explosion, based on the pattern of wounds on Joshua's torso and the jagged hole in the boat. Be patient, he told himself, wait until daylight. Mysteries that careened around in his head would settle out then.

The nearest transmission tower for cell phones was located at the headland on Westfarrow Island, but it was not emitting a strong enough signal to access yet. He dialed 911 on his cell, hoping to pick up a signal from the mainland. A dispatcher answered, sounding as if she worked in the spray of a car wash. She kept asking him to repeat himself, her voice drifting in and out. Slowly and loudly, Tagliabue told her that he had discovered a dead body on his boat and that he would report it to the Westfarrow PD once he arrived at the island. The splintered voice of the 911 operator was still asking him to "Say again" when he disconnected and turned off the phone.

He reached down and hauled his sea bag out of the cabin. After changing his jeans, he massaged feeling back into his feet. With dry socks on, he rested, surprising himself by nodding off. A crackling of the PRC-25 woke him. He heard a low voice, one he recognized instantly.

"*Maven* here," he answered.

"What's your ETA, Tony? Over."

"I can just make out Pepys Light. Over."

"You loaded?"

"Aye. Pretty much. Over."

"Good. I'll be happy to see you."

"Likewise. Switching to Zebra. Out."

Zebra was their personal code for a channel they used for private communications. Switching to it would alarm Agnes Ann, but broadcasting his predicament over an open band could be dangerous until he figured out what had happened to Joshua. Normally, once he sighted Pepys on a clear night, he was an hour from the island. At the *Maven's* reduced speed, it would be daylight before he made landfall.

On Zebra, he told her about the damage to his boat but said nothing about Joshua's body or the likely cause of the damage. He was reluctant to alarm her when she could do nothing. Agnes Ann was conscious of radiotelephone discipline and Tagliabue knew she would wait to see him for the details of his troubles.

"You staying afloat, Tony?"

"Aye. Slowed but not sinking. I'll contact you if anything changes."

"All right. I'll prep the Dunphy and have Jesse set up a block and tackle on the beach."

The Dunphy was her lapstrake runabout, a small boat her teenage son, Jesse, could maneuver quickly in tight spaces.

"Roger that. I'll need rollers too. The tide will be falling by the time I get there."

"Okay. I'll be waiting . . . stay on this channel, okay? Don't be afraid to call."

"I'm never afraid. Out."

She laughed, tittered really, before he broke the connection, a tiny, bright laugh that caught somehow the exact expression of her pleasure at his remark. Joy pushed at his chest.

It was a short-lived emotion as the thrum and wallow of his limping boat reminded him of his current predicament. He hoped to ease her fears with his joking braggadocio, but he was afraid, afraid his patch wouldn't hold and afraid of who had killed his mate. He could do something about the former immediately, if not the latter. Pulling on his boots he went below once again.

CHAPTER TWO

Tagliabue sighted the island not an hour after the fiery red sun had lifted off the horizon. His eyes were gritty and salt in the air made his skin feel tight against his face. Westfarrow was a substantial coastal land mass situated some fifty nautical miles from the mainland, usually a five-hour transit at *Maven's* cruising speed. It seemed as if he'd been at sea for weeks this time, he was that wrung out. The trip hadn't taken too much longer than a normal passage; it was the stress from the damage and being alone the whole time. He shook his head and pressed the mic button.

"Westfarrow, Westfarrow. I'm approaching your location. Over."

Seconds passed.

"Yes. I can just make you out in my glass. We're ready. Over."

He could sense the relief in her voice. He wanted to reassure her, reinforce her feeling of relief, but piloting the boat single-handed meant concentration. Agnes Ann knew that and kept her radio talk brief. She advised him that the tide had just turned and was still nearly full. He could see the outboard floating peacefully at the right side of the pier; he made for the left side.

He came into the dock at Westfarrow slowly and reversed the engines, twin screws churning the still water to a creamy head. Agnes Ann and her son tied him off. Tagliabue swung out to the worn dock and shook hands with both of them. Their hands were smooth, leathery even. Lines radiating from the sides of the woman's eyes caught the new-slanted sun as she smiled at Tagliabue. Her barn coat couldn't conceal her slender leggy body, at least not to his mind's eye. She wore a wool cap, like the one Joshua was wearing when he died. Brown hair straggled out from the back of it and lay flat against her neck. The boy, Jesse, tall as his mother at sixteen, was already looking in *Maven*, ready to begin unloading her cargo.

"How many bales you got, Mr. T?" he asked.

"Forty. Two hundred fifty dollars, total."

He mentioned the cost because he didn't want Agnes Ann to have to ask. She said she'd get her checkbook, but he suggested they unload first and lay the *Maven* on the shingle beach. She agreed, knowing the boy was ready to get this early work done before he fed and watered the animals. He already had driven the flatbed to the dock. Tagliabue didn't want to break the news about Joshua to Agnes Ann in front of Jesse; he felt it was a mother's choice when and how to break bad news to her child, so he said nothing about the body in the cabin as he rigged the winch and started hoisting the bales ashore. Mother and son moved them into stacks on the back of the truck.

"Phew, are these bales extra heavy or am I just getting old before my time?"

"They're heavy, Mom. It's a good sign, means they're packed tight so we get more hay in each one."

She smiled in admiration at her son's growing maturity as she drew in deep breaths and shucked her jacket. Tagliabue tried not to look at her body. In less than a half hour they were finished. Tagliabue retrieved a heavy line Jesse had rigged to a tree. He tied it off to a bollard on the bow of *Maven* and started the port engine. He backed her away slowly from the dock. He dropped an anchor over the stern and eased the boat forward as Jesse took up the slack in the hawser until the boat ran aground. Steadying her with the engines, Tagliabue tightened the aft anchor line and heaved a rope ladder over the side. He killed the engines and climbed down. They left the boat like that, tied off forward and anchored astern.

Agnes Ann said. "You'll soon be stranded on the beach, Tony. You'll have three or four hours before you can refloat her."

"That should give me enough time."

"Us."

"How's that, lady?"

"Us. I'll be helping you with repairs."

Tagliabue nodded as Jesse drove off to unload in the barn. He would do that himself while his mother and her friend had coffee in the kitchen. They walked up the dirt path to the house. The island hadn't seen rain for five days so the ground was loose. They went through the blue door to the kitchen, the man leaving his boots in the mudroom and ducking under the lintel. Agnes Ann pushed the button on a Bunn. They sat at an enameled table.

"The hay smelled good. What kind were you able to get?"

"Fescue and timothy mix."

"Oh, that's perfect. Decent price too after last week's warm spell. That should do us for a while."

"Yeah. We'll be getting spring grass next time we need to load up," Tagliabue said.

"If there is a next time."

He looked at her. "You thinking you might stay on the mainland for the season?"

"Well, you know . . ." She reddened a touch. "Francine could do well at Saratoga. A couple of decent finishes there and at Aqueduct would pay for a lot of feed."

"I guess it would."

"Old Mr. Hammet will take care of the other horses for as long as I want him to."

They sat quietly. Tagliabue knew this was the time to tell her about Joshua's death and the explosion that had holed his boat. But her features softened as she thought of something entirely foreign to death and destruction. He caught the look and said nothing yet about his mate. He reached across the table, put his hand in her hair, and kissed her lips gently. She closed her eyes and returned the kiss. Agnes Ann got up to pour. With her back to him, she asked: "Will you stay awhile, Tony?"

"We need to get off before dark."

"I'll take that as a yes." She smiled as she put the mug down in front of him. She combed stray strands of hair from his forehead with her fingers before she turned to her chair.

"No new gray ones."

He smiled this time, teeth showing bright against his sun-darkened skin. They drank coffee and took care of the cargo business. Jesse came in with a burst of salt air and youthful energy.

"Francine doing all right?"

"Yessir. She's feisty now. We keep her away from the other horses in the morning, so she don't get hurt bossing them around. Been like this since the weather turned. Ready to run, I guess."

"Nobody ever recognized her?"

"Nossir. We exercise her early, about now in fact. People around here don't carry stopwatches with them anyway. They know she's a thoroughbred and a looker, but I don't think anyone realizes how fast she really is."

The man turned toward the boy's mother. "Why is it so important to keep Francine a secret?"

"Well, first there's Jack, y'know. I can't get free of the suspicion that he still might try some devious trick to get her back, whether it's a legal ploy or something else. I know that sounds paranoid. Besides that, we don't want the filly to have a reputation for being fast before she even gets to the racetrack. We'd like to kind of sneak up on the opposition."

"How fast is she?"

"She breezed four furlongs in forty-seven and change Monday." She sounded like a proud mother, her body taut with controlled excitement.

"That's a half-mile, right? And that's a good time."

"Real good," the boy said, "especially this early in the year. She's going to astound folks in Saratoga this summer. Including your grumpy friend Joshua White."

Tagliabue kept his face bland and didn't look at Agnes Ann. He would have to tell them about Joshua's death soon. Not yet. Tagliabue couldn't see any reason to darken the teen's ebullient mood before he had a chance to show off his racing filly. Jesse moved about the kitchen, not doing anything, just moving, fiddling with the Bluetooth headset and mic he would wear under his helmet. He wanted to exercise the horse, Tagliabue knew, show his mother's friend how well she ran. Tagliabue pushed his chair back. The boy headed for the door.

"She's already tacked up."

Agnes Ann smiled and went with them, shrugging on her barn coat as she walked. Francine was waiting, tied to a verandah post, head and ears up, muscles rippling under her glossy red coat in the early sun. The boy vaulted into the small saddle and walked her out to the training track as the two adults followed on foot along a weeded-over trail. The chestnut pranced and blew and shook her head, as anxious as her rider to run.

"She looks good, Aggie."

"Yeah, she's in great shape, eating well and training well."

The horse and rider moved ahead of them.

"You hearing anything?" Tagliabue asked.

"Only an e-mail confirming my registration for an $80,000 maiden race on July 29th."

"Nothing from Jack?"

"No. Thanks be to God."

The boy warmed up the filly on the dirt oval.

"Joshua didn't show up this morning at Cronk's."

Jesse took her up to a slow canter, her feet scooping sprays of the dry track behind her.

"Oh, my. I hope he's not in the drunk tank again."

"He's not."

Francine ran by them for the first time, still throwing her
head as her rider kept a hold on her. Agnes Ann smiled at Jesse.
When the horse was past and the pounding sounds of her gait
had abated, she turned to Tagliabue for the first time since they'd
taken up their positions at the track fence.

"Have you heard from him, you mean?"

"Not exactly."

Her smile faded at her friend's tone.

"What's wrong, Tony?"

"He's dead, Aggie."

"Oh, God." She shut her eyes. Tagliabue figured she was
saying a prayer for his mate's soul. She did things like that. The
filly was stretching out by then and came by in a blur of thunder-
ing hooves that rattled the fence rails.

"The poor man," she said into the silence that followed the
horse. "What happened, do you know?"

"I'm not sure what happened. I think someone killed him."

"You mean murdered?" Her mouth was open slightly as she
looked up at his weathered face, crow's feet outlining blue eyes that
avoided hers as they looked out at the running animal. She took
his jaw in her hand and turned it to her.

"You'd better tell me what you know."

"As soon as we're finished this training session. Let Jess have
his moment."

Agnes Ann accepted that wisdom with a quick nod. They
watched Jesse and his horse circle the track again at speed, the
beast's muscles bunching and stretching as she ran in long strides,
the boy's lips cracked open at the pleasure of it all. Jesse slowed
Francine and walked her one more lap.

Agnes Ann left Tagliabue at the rail. She walked out to the
middle of the track and gave instructions to her son as he close-
hauled the panting, prancing filly around her. Horse and rider set
off again in a light canter. Trainer and rider spoke to each other
on their electronic devices. Agnes Ann gave instructions, the boy

talked about the horse's breathing, her stride, her attitude. When the animal started showing signs of tiredness, they moved to a two-stall starting gate and practiced loading her into the contraption, the boy sitting quietly on the filly's back. Agnes Ann closed the back flaps of the gate and let the filly stand in the enclosed space. She climbed in and led the horse out again, then back in. After three times doing this, she said to Jesse: "Tomorrow we begin with some fast starts." He tapped his helmet in a one-fingered salute and rode off slowly toward the barn.

She came back to Tagliabue: "He'll be a while brushing her down and feeding her. Come to the house."

Seated again at the kitchen table, Agnes Ann asked about the death of Joshua White.

"We were supposed to meet at one forty-five. He didn't show. I was pissed. I was out to sea an hour or so, the bilge pump lit off. When I went below to find the leak I found Joshua's body. His chest is a mess."

Agnes Ann spoke in a small voice: "We'd better look, do you think?"

"Aye. We've got some decisions to make."

They walked down to the beach to find the boat grounded forward, its stern still afloat. They climbed aboard. The cabin deck was mostly dry although they could hear the pump kick on once in a while as it cleared water from the aft bilge. Agnes Ann walked over to Joshua White's body and looked without touching it. Tagliabue pulled a coarse blanket from another bunk and handed it to her. She covered the corpse.

"I'd better call Constable Fletcher," she said in the same small voice.

"And tell your son."

"Yes. Yes, I'll have to do that."

Westfarrow's sole police presence arrived at the horse farm in forty-five minutes. He was a stout, graying man with a belly and a lugubrious manner. He greeted Agnes Ann with a smile and a peck on the cheek, and he remembered Tagliabue. He seemed in no hurry to view the body.

Ian Fletcher accepted a cup of tea. They sat in the kitchen, joined by young Jesse, as Tagliabue told of finding his mate's remains in the cabin of his boat earlier that morning. Jesse seemed quiet but not surprised; his mother had talked to him.

"His body was jammed up against the hole in the hull, I guess, but I actually did not see it until it had been pushed away by the force of the water when I went to cruising speed. I don't know why else the boat didn't flood sooner."

"Did you notice anything else when you discovered the poor man?" Fletcher asked. "Any smell, for instance? Any weapon?"

"No, nothing. We'd been underway for nearly two hours by then. Everything in the cabin had had a good wash."

"When was the last time you were on the boat? Before you set sail this morning, I mean."

"Yesterday afternoon. The hay truck met me at about two thirty. I'd been through the boat by then. I was looking to be sure everything was dry so the hay wouldn't get wet. I think I can say for sure that there was no damage at that time, say half past one or so."

"Is there anyone you can think of—any of you—who would want to damage the boat?"

They all looked at the policeman. Tagliabue and Agnes Ann harbored vague suspicions about her ex-husband, Jack Brunson, who lost the filly to her in the final divorce decree and who suspected even then, two years ago, that she might develop into a special racehorse. Their suspicions were unformed and nowhere near ready to be aired to the police. Jesse knew nothing of these suspicions. All three shook their heads at Fletcher.

"How about Mr. White, the victim? He have any known enemies? Anyone with a reason to want him dead?"

"Joshua was a rough character. Hung around waterfront bars and did his share of drinking. I guess he had a fight or two, but nothing serious enough to kill over, I don't think. He was my mate for a decade or more and I never saw or heard any threats."

Constable Fletcher sighed once, said: "Well, I guess we better view the body."

CHAPTER THREE

They set off, the cop making a call on his cell to the island satellite hospital as they crunched down the beach to the boat. *Maven* was completely aground. Fletcher and Tagliabue went aboard. Tagliabue hated having to look at his old friend's corpse again, even though it didn't much remind him of the man who had sailed with him hundreds of times. Joshua had a snarly voice and a face that moved like an ensign rippling in the wind as he argued or cajoled or laughed, until it finally came to droop as a flag did in calm conditions when he settled in for a glass of scotch at the end of a trip. The body on the *Maven's* bunk held no resemblance to Joshua White anymore. His spirit was long gone.

Fletcher, the Reluctant Cop, as Tagliabue had taken to thinking of him, gestured vaguely with his hand at the blanket covering the body. Tagliabue peeled it back. Fletcher looked at the body, at its ruined chest and wrinkled face, the cop's Adam's apple working like a Lilliputian elevator. Standing two feet away from the corpse, he made no move to touch anything.

"Er, how'd the poor lad come to land on this bunk?"

"I put him there. When I saw the hole in the hull of my boat and realized he would be in the way of repairs."

The two men were speaking in near whispers, even though mother and son were out of earshot. Constable Fletcher took out his smartphone, began snapping some pictures of the body *in situ* and taking random shots around the cabin. He picked up shards of what may have been some kind of plastic, tiny lengths of wire, and random bits and pieces that lay about the decking and put it all in a large baggie he had pulled from his pocket. They peered at the body some more and then Fletcher nodded. Tagliabue floated the blanket over Joshua's remains again and they went topside. They waited in the fresh air until an ambulance puttered slowly down to the dock.

"There's not a coroner on the island, Anthony. We'll ship White's corpse to the mainland."

They helped two EMTs move the draped body—Jesse looking on with an ashen sheen to his face—and watched it driven away before Fletcher spoke again.

"I'll e-mail a report. They'll want to visit with you when you get back to Bath."

Jesse went off to school while Tagliabue and Agnes Ann gathered material and tools to patch the hull. They worked side by side for almost two hours, speaking only about the work. A thin sun was out and they both began to sweat freely by the time they finished the job. Tagliabue had his shirt off. Flecks of glue and sawdust stuck to his chest. They went back to the house and showered together before spending another two hours in her darkened bedroom.

Later Agnes Ann sat in the living room wearing a flannel robe and slippers. It was an old house; the thick walls kept it cool in the spring for most of the day.

"It feels good to just sit. I'm not used to so much work."

"Work was it?" Tagliabue asked. He was stretched out on the couch, drowsy from his night at the helm.

She dipped her head, a hint of color coming to her face. He thought she looked ten years younger, and innocent.

"I'm talking about the boat repairs, big man, not you ravishing me."

"Ravishing?"

That brought a chuckle from Tagliabue and got him to a sitting position. She giggled into the mug she held in both hands. He stretched and groaned, smiling broadly. The smile slowly faded as reality intruded again. They had another risky voyage facing them, and more work to do. They also had to face the mainland police, bury Joshua, and get Francine safely stabled a long way from her home.

He wondered, not for the first time, at the vagaries of human nature. Despite the violent death of a friend and danger he had faced at sea—or maybe because of it—he and Aggie had been wanton in their sex. They'd been apart for two weeks, so that may have had something to do with it, but it occurred to him that he should be feeling some guilt at enjoying life so much when Joshua lay in a hospital morgue.

"Jesse will be home in a minute," Agnes Ann said. "I'd better get dressed."

She walked over to Tagliabue and straddled his lap. She let the front of her robe fall open as she held his head to her breast. He felt a stirring, but then she was gone, closing the bedroom door behind her. He shook himself and took the mugs to the kitchen.

When the boy drove the pickup home from school, and after he consumed what seemed to be as many calories as the horse ate following her workout, they found *Maven* refloated on the second high tide of the day. They moved her back to the pier and made her ready for the most important voyage of her long career. The *Maven* was an old Coast Guard buoy tender that Tagliabue had converted to a carrier boat. At sixty feet long and beamy, she had a deck winch and cargo space, drew a bit over five feet and was maneuverable inshore with Tagliabue at the helm in the covered conning station that snugged up against her snub nose. He had built a half-sized makeshift stall in the aft section of the open hold; they had to get Francine into the stall for her journey. The entire evolution had to be done away from public scrutiny. If Constable Fletcher had recognized the stable for what it was he had said nothing. Tagliabue blew out a breath and got ready to face a difficult loading and a secret journey.

Jesse walked the horse down. Agnes Ann had administered a sedative to her but she was skittish walking out on the worn pier decking. Mother and son calmed her by stroking her face and muzzle, talking in a constant low-pitched flow. The woman slid a blindfold over the beast's eyes. Tagliabue fit a double-strap harness around her belly, watching her sharp hooves as he worked even though Francine was used to being saddled and handled. She moved her feet but did not otherwise protest. He clipped the harness rings to the winch cable and took up the slack slowly. The filly started when the winch engine cranked up and stood twitching when the straps pulled tight. The humans all kept their distance.

"She seem comfortable enough, Aggie? If she starts kicking in the air we could have a mess in a hurry. I don't know how much strain this old rigging can handle."

Mother looked at her son, who answered Tagliabue: "Maybe give her another minute, Mr. T. I think she'll be all right."

Tagliabue kept the winch motor running. The horse began to rest against the straps as the barbiturate kicked in. Her head slowly drooped. At Jesse's signal, Tagliabue worked the winch lever slowly and the horse lifted off the pier. He upped the power and the three of them began to move quickly, mother and son steadying the animal while Tagliabue swung the winch aboard and lowered it. The horse was soon standing on the boat deck. When he slackened the cable, she swayed. Jesse put his shoulder to her flank and took some of her weight. Tagliabue dropped the straps and the three of them forced the horse into the stall, he and Aggie linking hands around the horse's buttocks and hauling her forward while the boy pulled her by the halter. Dragging her hooves, Francine clopped into the structure and rested against one wall. She nickered softly.

Tagliabue had fitted a rubber mat designed for a pickup's bed to the floor and covered it with a thick layer of straw. Jesse stayed in the stall with his drugged filly while Tagliabue and Agnes Ann secured the winch and made the vessel ready for sea. They had less than an hour before the sun went down.

They set off into the gloaming on a falling tide, *Maven* rolling easily on long, reaching swells. When Tagliabue turned his cell back on he saw two messages from a sheriff's detective in Bath, both asking him to call. The second seemed a bit more testy in tone than the first. He saw the blinking lights of a small plane heading into the regional airfield on Westfarrow and wondered if that could be sheriff's investigators. Calling the number on his cell, he left a message saying he was at sea and would call in at the sheriff's office when he put ashore, about midmorning.

Agnes Ann went aft to check on her son and her horse. She was smiling when she returned.

"Both of them sleeping the sleep of the innocent," she said. "Ain't life grand?"

"Amen, sister."

Hours passed. Tagliabue kept the throttles moderated so the noise and motion of the boat were easy. He and Agnes Ann took turns napping in the conning chairs. It was unsatisfactory sleep, often interrupted and uncomfortable. Neither wanted to go below to a bunk.

When the sun came up to a clear cool morning, Jesse scuffed his way into the wheelhouse scratching his unruly curls. The sedative was wearing off, he said. Francine was beginning to move around. He ate the remaining two sandwiches for breakfast while the adults smiled and settled for a third pot of coffee.

"How long before we put ashore?" Agnes Ann asked.

"Maybe an hour."

Armed with that estimate, she and her son went back to the stall to give the horse another shot, one that would last through the offloading procedure. Leaving Jesse with the horse, Agnes Ann went farther aft and stood on the fantail, watching the churning wake *Maven* carved through the pool of molten bronze made by the early sun. Tagliabue saw her standing there and wondered to himself what she was thinking.

CHAPTER FOUR

AGNES ANN

I was thinking of the long night voyage from Westfarrow, the way my mind wandered during the hours while Tony drove the boat, needing nothing from me but my company. It's as if I can relive the time in the present, it's so real to me.

Sitting in the wheelhouse of *Maven* as she plows through the dark sea in the hours after we left the island, the motion of Tony's old boat a steady roll and drop as she lumbers along, the rumble from the engines already part of my consciousness, I start to drift into a state halfway between wakefulness and sleep. It's the cadence of the sea and the infinite absence of color that makes a person's mind drift away on a long night voyage, according to Tony. My mind drifts into a haze of sensuousness.

I remember the session with Tony in the bedroom before Jesse got home from school, the bright sun brightening the edges of the pulled drapes, his big hands on my skin, hot and slick from the shower, my body taking on a motion of its own, rolling and dropping like the boat. The thought brings me back awake. I squirm to upright in the seat.

"What're you smiling about, Aggie?"

"Oh, just some pleasant dream is all."

"You can go below if you want to sleep. The bunks are fairly clean. There's a blanket on one of them."

Joshua's body had been on one of them. I know he died from an explosion, had no disease and had not been aboard long enough to rot, and I am not some silly girl who lets her imagination run off with her mind. Even so, I don't want to sleep where his body had been so recently.

When I was still in high school my father told us kids a story of his navy days, how a sailor went over the side during a refueling operation at night and drowned. When they recovered his body from the frigid ocean, the boatswains wrapped it in canvas and placed it in the walk-in freezer. Since they'd been at sea for a few weeks by then, there was a space empty of food. They sailed for two days back to Norfolk. When they made port, the ship's pork chop (the navy's delightful idiom for a supply officer) had to give all the frozen food on the vessel to other ships in the squadron because the sailors on my father's ship refused to eat anything that had been in the locker with the dead body, even though the body had touched nothing and was itself soon frozen solid.

"And there was nothing wrong with the sailor's body, except that it was dead," my father went on. We thought he was making a joke, so we laughed. But he was making a point instead.

"Compare that with the tale I read of whalers back in the nineteenth century. Two years into a three-year journey, the captain of one of the whaling ships died in his sleep one night. No one on board knew what killed him. Since he was part owner of the ship the crew put him in a tun of rum to preserve his body for burial ashore. When they got back to Nantucket a year later, the cask was empty of liquor. When the other rum on board had eventually run out on the long voyage, the men had drunk the rum from the barrel with the captain's pickled corpse inside."

Dad thought the story was about the force of need overcoming imaginative fears. I thought he was telling us not to be ninnies. I always try hard not to act like a ninny, but I don't want to nap in the bunkroom where my friend Joshua had lain dead. Although I said nothing to Tony, he seemed to understand. He didn't go below to nap on a bunk either.

I put my feet up on the bulkhead in front of me. I think about Joshua's death and the way Tony was able to control the urge to tell me about it until he thought the time was right. He's a deep man, my Tony, making it hard to know him. In some ways, intimate ways, I know him better than anyone ever has, but he has a depth I'll never plumb. Not that I need to. I am willing to accept him as he is, accept that he has a life apart from mine, and accept that everyone has a right to a private inner being.

So I wasn't surprised that he kept his mate's murder from me temporarily or that he didn't appear to overtly grieve for him. Tony's life has been difficult. He has probably seen other friends die. He has probably killed other men. I don't know for sure, but if he doesn't want to talk about the things he's done and seen, that's okay with me too. Whatever he is internalizing doesn't seem to have an impact on his integrity or his stability. I can abide the strange scars on his body, the long ones and the small punctures. I don't fuss over them; I don't ask about them. He offers no explanations, although he might if I did ask.

Tony was gone from Bath for my formative years, first off to college and then into the navy. He was one of the older guys who we teens found so intriguing, but nobody ever seemed to know much about him. And it sort of stayed that way. Just before I really met him, for instance, when I came back to Westfarrow, he was doing something overseas that he never talks about. He never talks about his parents either, so I really don't know him all that well.

I know him well enough to believe that he is what he seems to be: a hard-working, bright, and generous man who means well and treats me as his partner and lover. I do hope to marry him someday. The impediment to marriage is mine. I need to annul the sacramental covenant I agreed to many years ago with Jack Brunson, to free myself morally to enter into another one, binding this time, with Anthony Tagliabue.

The problem with my marriage contract with Jack Brunson is that I was ignorant. Jack was all he seemed to be at first, a vibrant, popular, and handsome third-year at UVA Law when I got to the university as an undergrad. We married too early—it is obvious to me now—but he seemed to love me and was so attentive that I probably overlooked some of the subtle signs of his shallow nature. When I turned up pregnant in my junior year, the subtlety disappeared as soon as my belly began to appear. Some men find a pregnant woman attractive. Jack liked his women slender. There were many of them, I found out, so we separated before I gave birth, when he was in private practice. After Jack left me, my mother hired a man who took photos of Jack with his mistresses, not that his infidelity was hard to prove. When I confronted him with what I knew, and told him never to touch me again, he laughed and poked at my huge belly. But he moved out. He saw his son only once, when he came to what had been our apartment in town to tell me that he was no longer able to pay the rent for me to live alone. I took my sheepskin and Jesse and went home to momma. She was widowed by then and we settled into a comfortable life together on her horse farm near Bath, more like close friends than mother and daughter. I worked the stock as she grew old. We needed each other.

I didn't divorce Jack until fourteen years after my college days, when I had uncovered a new dimension to living in the person of Tony. By that time, Jack Brunson was busy making a sumptuous living as a partner in Gaines, Livvy, and Brunson and might have been meaning to wrangle a divorce from me eventually. Or he might have thought I was never going to seek redress for the wrongs he had done to me. I had never asked him for money in those fourteen years, so really, he never had any motivation to seek a divorce. He was obviously not meant for marriage and was just as obviously enjoying his bachelor lifestyle. When I finally did hit him with papers, it turned into some nasty divorce proceedings. He was forced by the filings to recall how I had thrown him out. Jack Brunson wasn't used to being turned away. He was used to winning.

Jack had been wolfing up piles of money in his law practice
and was not happy with the settlement my lawyer negotiated. He
had begun treading in some dark alleys and I was happy to be
shed of him. He had tricked me, he thought, with another sleight
of hand move that eventually worked against him: he bought a
weanling filly at a sale in Kentucky, hoping to race her. First she
needed to mature and be trained, so Jack had a friend of his pretend to be her owner and bring the horse to my farm to be raised
and broke to race, thinking no doubt of the extra insult to my
pride when she turned out to be a champion running under his
silks. It was the kind of nasty ploy Jack Brunson would try to work
on a person who had rejected him. He acted as if he had never
loved me, not even in our college days, as if he only married me
to get me into bed with him. Marriage to him was just another
legal rule to be exploited with his genius.

I didn't know Francine belonged to Jack until my lawyer found
out during the discovery phase of my divorce trial months later. By
then I had come to like the animal and could see her potential, so
I insisted she be part of my settlement. Maybe I was being vindictive. Jack hated losing the horse more than anything. It wasn't as
if he loved her, any more than he loved his son, but he was a man
committed to having his vengeance and wanted still to punish me
for throwing him out.

Deep in my belly I am afraid that he works every day to figure
a way to get even with me.

In the immediate aftermath of the divorce, though, I had other
scary visions ruining my sleep. Mom became weak and dizzy suddenly and within weeks was no longer able to tend the farm. By
the time the specialists diagnosed a high-grade brain tumor called
a glioma, it was too late to stem its progress and she was dead in
a few months. Those months and the ones just after were as bleak
and soulful as any I had ever experienced. The stock dispersal sale
was the low point. I kept only Francine, two older geldings we used
for riding, and two mares I hoped to breed.

We carried my stock and my teenage son (and a bundle of Jack's money) to sea on the *Maven* one calm, sunny day and moved to our family summer home on Westfarrow Island. I named the acreage Seaside Stables, since it sits on a small cove in the Atlantic off the coast of Maine. Part of the name was for subterfuge purposes—for I hoped to keep the talents of my filly secret for as long as possible so that Jack wouldn't plan some ugly scheme to get her back. A stable gave me an excuse for erecting a training track—and part was because that is my ultimate goal, to have a breeding farm on the island. Tony visited often. We kept our sex life away from Jesse, a decision that caused us both to exercise a good amount of constraint—and probably didn't fool my sharp-eyed son for a minute. I learned a lot about Tony on Westfarrow.

Now we are sailing back to Bath for some new adventures. My filly is ready to go racing, but mostly we have to find out who killed Joshua on *Maven* and why. Was the boat supposed to sink? None of these questions make sense on the surface. I realize as I roll with the seas on our long slow voyage to the mainland that I am about to find out things I never suspected, and that is okay with me. It's an anticipatory pleasure, expecting to learn more about Anthony Tagliabue, an opportunity to look further into his character and uncover talents and maybe even secrets of the man I love. There is no dread apparent in my anticipation, nothing to worry about. That can't be true, of course. The cops in Bath would be looking for answers, and looking for someone to blame. How is Tony tied up in this murder and bombing? That alone should worry me, but it doesn't. Not yet, at least. Maybe I'm still immature, but I feel excitement in the air as *Maven* slows where the Kennebec River pools into the great ocean. It's first light.

Jesse comes forward—eating the rest of our food—and I go aft to sedate Francine again. She's calm, munching hay, ears up, and steady. She has learned to trust humans. That's fine, as long as Jesse and I are there for her to trust. We are entering the river mouth where Jake Collier is supposed to meet us, so I give the horse some more barbiturate and talk to her quietly until she grows sleepy. By then we are docked at Heal Eddy and Tony has the winch in position to offload her.

CHAPTER FIVE

Johnny Coleman was fresh-faced and wiry, dressed in a shirt and tie with the butt of a Smith & Wesson M&P 9 semiautomatic peeking out from a shoulder holster near his heart. It reminded Tagliabue of a moray in its cave, ugly and dangerous. A gold badge, rimmed with "Sagadahoc County Sheriff's Office," was clipped to his belt. Tagliabue thought the detective was trying hard to control his anger about the twenty-four-hour delay in his investigation of the suspicious death of one Joshua Peter White. Detective Coleman scrubbed his hand over the flattop bristle of his fair hair. Tagliabue spoke to release some pressure from the interview.

"I thought it might be easier for your work if I was here instead of on Westfarrow," Tagliabue said.

Coleman grunted at that. He said: "Not bad thinking, all right. I just didn't expect radio silence for all day yesterday. You coulda called. You coulda called when you discovered the body."

"I tried but got a bad 911 connection."

"You try again?"

"No."

"This delay makes me think you're avoiding the police here, Mr. Tagliabue. It makes me suspicious, you get that?"

"I do. Try to remember I had a stricken vessel on my hands on the high seas. At the time I'm worried more about me than

Joshua. Then I was intent on repairing it and getting back here on the mainland where the murder had to have taken place. I'm sorry my phone was off. I often turn it off when I have serious work to do in a hurry."

"Those are all bullshit excuses for not calling the police when you discover a body."

"We did alert the constable on the island."

"There are no forensic people on Westfarrow. I fly a team out and what do they find? The fucking scene of the crime is gone. In the middle of the night."

Coleman's voice was rising. Tagliabue spoke in an even tone.

"I thought about waiting but the cabin of the boat was pretty well washed out by then. Plus the Westfarrow PD had checked it out and taken some pictures."

"Constable Ian Fletcher ain't hardly qualified to conduct a forensic investigation. He might as well be a rent-a-cop for all he knows about police work."

Tagliabue did not argue the point.

Coleman went on in a softer tone. "I don't mean that. Ian's okay. They just don't get much more than traffic problems and teen drug use on the island, although I gotta say the place does get thousands of visitors a day in the summer. It can get pretty wild. We probably need more of a police presence out there. Having said that, I gotta tell you that I don't think Ian gets to handle too many homicides out on the island."

He paused, probably thinking of the damaged relationship with the Westfarrow PD if Tagliabue mentioned his attitude toward Constable Fletcher. He continued, gruff again, "And what about the woman? She's a witness and she ain't home. We can't locate her."

"She came with me, figuring the police will want to talk to her."

"Okay, okay. What's her name, address?"

"Agnes Ann Townsend Brunson, Seaside Stables, Westfarrow Island. You should know also, detective, that she's my fiancée."

Coleman looked at him in surprise. He cleared his throat and said, "You're gonna marry her. Any other witnesses besides her?"

"Her son, Jesse Brunson."

"They kin to the lawyer Brunson?"

"Jack Brunson is Agnes Ann's ex-husband, and Jesse's biological father."

That distinction precipitated some rapid scribbling by Coleman in his little notebook. Along with some indecipherable murmuring. He stuffed the notebook into a pocket and clipped his pen to the same pocket.

"Let's get us down to your boat so I can see what's left of the crime scene. You might as well ride with me."

The two of them drove down from the Bath county seat to Cronk's Boatyard and Marina on the Kennebec River where *Maven* was tied up. Agnes Ann and Jesse were ten miles away at a horse farm that was boarding Francine. After dropping them off with the owner and his trailer at a boat ramp near the mouth of Heal Eddy, Tagliabue had motored another hour to Bath. He did not stop to eat before he reported in to Coleman. Now he wished he had. His stomach was making a few unhappy noises and he seemed to have lost his energy, the long nights at sea and the hard work on Westfarrow undoubtedly contributing to that. He longed for a lobster roll and a soft bed. It was unlikely either was in the immediate offing.

The sheriff's detective wanted to look at the actual hole the explosion made, so Tagliabue removed the temporary patch inside the cabin. He needed to take it off anyway to effect a smooth repair, he told himself, as he labored to jerk out the nails and pry off the boards. With bright sun streaming through the cabin hatch, he could see a few shadowy marks here and there around the splintered edge of the hole. Coleman touched his finger to them and remarked: "Powder burns. Amazing there's any left after flooding and repairs."

With a penknife he scraped some of the residue into a small glassine bag. He took a Nikon digital SLR from a black carrier he brought with him and snapped a few photos.

"Our plane brought the body back with it last night . . ."

"So the trip wasn't entirely wasteful."

Coleman shot him a black look and continued: "The ME thinks the vic was pressed up against the bomb when it went off, based on his wounds."

"You think he was knocked out and stuffed in there or something?"

"There's a gunshot wound in his back. He may have been killed by that, although the doc don't think it was a mortal wound. More likely your friend saw the perps set the explosive device and crawled into that corner to try to dismantle it or something after they left. Maybe they wounded him first, I don't know. If the bomb goes off without his body in the way, I'm thinking the cabin fills up fast once you start making a bow wave and the sea gets above the waterline. You maybe don't get the water out in time. Some of the pieces the island constable found mighta been a timing device. It was maybe set to go off when you're out on the ocean a ways. White sets it off early trying to defuse it or whatever the hell he was doing in the cabin. Plus, my guy tells me the damage to the boat could have been greater without his body shielding the blast."

Tagliabue stared at the cop. Coleman said, in a slightly quieter voice: "At least, that's my working theory."

"Jesus, Mary, and Joseph," Tagliabue whispered.

"Amen to that, pal. It's good to have friends like Joshua White."

They looked around the cabin for a while longer and then went back to the station house where Coleman interrogated him. Tagliabue told him about Agnes Ann, the divorced wife of John "Jack" Brunson, a mob lawyer.

"I know that mutt. You think he's a mob lawyer?"

"He'd like people to think so," Tagliabue answered. "He represented Carlo Netherton in a civil case once and does his drinking at Pelham East. Y'know, D'Annunzio's place? I've never seen him on the television speaking for any gangsters, but he wears shiny sort of suits and smokes cigars and acts like he's connected.

Same as Peter D'Annunzio. He's purported to be close with Al Delgado and his bunch over in Portsmouth."

Seeing that Coleman was unconvinced, he went on: "First time I met him, he says, 'Hey, how ya doin', pal?' People don't talk like that around here. At that same cocktail party where I met him I overheard him tell a man that he knows a guy and maybe can find out something. When Agnes Ann filed for divorce he made some veiled threats."

"What kind of threats?"

"She won a racehorse in the settlement, a yearling filly. He saw the potential of the horse and wanted it badly, but so did she. He told her after the decree came down to, quote, check her feed bag every day."

"Mrs. Brunson told you that?"

"Aye."

"Still," said the detective, scratching at his head with the balls of his fingers, "be hard to prove that he meant it to threaten her, or the horse."

"Agnes Ann took it as a threat, serious enough to move out to the island with her horse and her son."

"She got a house out there?"

Tagliabue nodded. "Her mother left it to her."

"She still live there?"

"She does, although she's on the mainland just now like I said."

"I probly need to talk to her."

"I'll bring her over. You got a sheet on Jack Brunson, by the way?"

Coleman looked as if he wasn't going to answer, but then said, "The word is he's dealing but we ain't never got a thing on him."

"Why are you suspicious?"

"He seems to have a lot of dough, got a cabin up in the Adirondack Mountains, and just bought a new big, expensive boat, but he never seems to be doing any work. He don't even have a secretary at his office. How many cases can he be taking on?"

Tagliabue thought about that while the detective hunched over his computer screen adding to his incident report.

"You releasing my boat?"

Coleman looked up. "In the morning. Forensics will be done with it by then. Just don't take off on a world cruise or nothing. Bring the lady in tomorrow morning too."

Tagliabue ate a bowl of fish chowder and a hard roll at a kiosk on the square near City Hall before he Ubered down to Cronk's to retrieve his Jeepster. He drove back to his apartment, arguing with his eyelids all the way. He made coffee and read his e-mail and cleaned the place a little, wasting time. It was too early to sleep. He heated a can of soup for supper, but by seven P.M. he gave it up. He fell into his own bed and slept for eight straight hours, dreamless every one.

It was still dark when he woke up. It was disorienting at first, until he lay there replaying his day and thinking of the things he still had to do. He made coffee and went out into the cool damp street. Tom Sharkey's blue television light was the only break in the darkness. Sharkey was his retired neighbor, a widower who filled his days and nights with the company of soaps and series. His slumped silhouette filled the shade on his living room window as Tagliabue got into his car.

Navigating the quiet streets slowly in his Jeepster, Tagliabue made his way back to Cronk's. The boatyard was silent in the still early morning. Gulls sat on bollards with their feathers fluffed against the chill, workboats rested in their berths, the dew on their superstructures shimmering in the yellow lamplight. He walked down to *Maven* and noted her tight lines and clean deck. He went below and observed that just a little water had splashed in through the holed hull. Back topside, satisfied all was shipshape, he stared at nothing for a while. He thought about Joshua, about the missing tooth behind his left canine, a gap that showed only when he smiled, and about the constant growl of discontent that issued from his mouth as he went about an onboard task. It was going to be a different life without him.

He conjured up a scene when the mate arrived on the dock at Cronk's Wednesday night and found someone in the cabin. Did Joshua try to escape when he was shot? Had he already discovered the explosive and was trying to disarm it when he was shot?

Somebody must have heard something. Cronk's was a commercial dockage and yard facility. People didn't live aboard their boats as some did in marinas that handled pleasure boats, but it was practically in the city. Houses and businesses surrounded the place.

"What the hell happened, Joshua? How'd you find the bomb?"

Realizing he'd spoken aloud, Tagliabue left the docks. He started the Jeepster and listened to its soft, powerful, and even rumble. He put it in first and drove to Chad's Deli, parking around back and thumping on the kitchen door. It was still an hour before the place opened to serve breakfast. His cousin Maurizio opened the battered tin door to his knock, letting out a cloud of damp heat smelling of baking bread and frying bacon.

"Hey, Anthony. Come in, come in. Damn, it's hard to believe it's halfway through April already and this fucking cold at night still."

"Forty-five hardly qualifies as cold, Maury."

"Then why you rubbing your hands together, eh?"

"Well . . ."

"Hey, it don't matter, Cuz. Good to see you, cold or not. Come in and talk to me."

Tagliabue sat in a wooden chair at a butcher's block table while his cousin went back to work kneading and chopping, his hands moving constantly, surely.

"You hear about Joshua, Maury?"

"No, what?"

"He was killed, on my boat."

Maurizio's hands stopped: "You mean that was *Maven*? Your fucking boat was blown up?"

"Not quite."

"It was on the radio this morning, but they didn't have no names or nothing. What's going on, Cuz?"

Tagliabue told his cousin about the hole in his boat and how he found his mate's body while he was steaming out to Westfarrow.

"Holy shit. The radio said there was a casualty but didn't give no details. The dead guy was Joshua, huh? That poor old bastard."

Maurizio went back to work, still shaking his head from side to side, thick hair wobbling like Moses's burning bush.

"Who did it, you got any idea? That shitbag Harris, I bet. That sounds like something he'd do, the piece of shit."

Marvin "Magpie" Harris was an associate of local wannabe hood Peter D'Annunzio who flogged some weed and stolen cigarettes, protected pool halls and waterfront bars, and ran a few prostitutes out of a tablecloth restaurant called Pelham East. D'Annunzio owned three Pelham restaurants, the main one in Bath, one in Portsmouth, and one on Westfarrow Island. Magpie was known for his quick temper and quicker fists but had never been associated with murder. In fact, murder was rare in Bath, the occasion usually a domestic dispute that got diseased. Still, Tagliabue knew, Marv Harris liked to play the ponies and had been upset when Jack Brunson lost the promising filly, Francine, in his divorce to Agnes Ann, especially now that she had reached racing age. A friend of Tagliabue had overheard Magpie bitching about missing out on a piece of the horse. It sounded to this friend as if Brunson planned to syndicate the racer and had invited Harris to get in on the ownership, as an inducement to maintain the relationship between the two men. At the time it hadn't sounded serious enough to Tagliabue to warrant his intervention.

People on the dark margins of Bath, the Magpies of the area, knew that Tagliabue and Agnes Ann were a couple—and they all respected his boundaries. But as far as anyone knew, *Maven* was merely supplying feed to her barn on Westfarrow Island when he sailed over to see her. Tagliabue couldn't work out a connection among Marv Harris and the boat and the horse that would be worth trying sabotage. To say nothing of murder. Motives seemed in short supply.

"You hear anything about Magpie getting into something new?"

"Naw," Maury replied. "He's still pushing a coupla whores and running his book, far as I know. He's a fucking mutt though. I don't know what he had against poor old Joshua."

It sounded to Tagliabue that his cousin was convinced that Marv the Magpie had killed Joshua.

Maurizio was back working, his chin wobbling, face dark. He took out a tray of plump chickens and began separating the joints with a cleaver. Tagliabue moved his chair back from the chopping block.

～

An hour later Agnes Ann and Tagliabue ate bacon biscuits from Chad's that Maurizio had made up for them. They sat in the tiny kitchenette of the motel where she was staying.

"Jesse still in the bunk?"

Agnes Ann made some muffled humming noises and moved her hands around in circles, long fingers floating in the air, until she finished chewing. "No," she said. "Mr. Collier took him over to the regional airport yesterday afternoon once they got Francine settled. He still has a couple of months of school left. Auntie May-belle's place is not far from us, as you know." She smiled at him. "He's a good kid, so she doesn't mind looking out for him for a time. She may wonder what's become of Francine though."

"What's the cover story?"

"Cover story? This ain't Watergate, young man. It's all legal and it even makes sense. Jacob Collier is a fine trainer."

"You don't have to convince me."

"I know. Well, we are telling anyone who expresses an interest that we have taken the filly to Mr. Collier for training, which is true enough. Since we don't know how well she'll respond we are understandably vague about the timing. The meeting at Saratoga starts in three months, and the track is three states away, so I don't expect too many people will link her training with that racetrack. What do you think?"

"I agree. It's all going to turn out to be an expensive proposition, but it has to be done sooner or later. You can't expect to get the animal to top readiness on Westfarrow Island."

"Please let me worry about the money angle, Tony. It's actually kind of fun spending some of Jack's ill-gotten cash."

He nodded at her, relaxed and comfortable, returning her easy grin. Money issues were not something that bothered Anthony Tagliabue much. He made a fair and honest living hauling material in his boat, and he augmented his income with highly remunerative side work no one else knew about. No one who wasn't involved, that is. He lived simply and paid most expenses in cash. The fact that Agnes Ann had land and a big bank account meant only that she could spend more than she usually did if she wanted to. If spending some of the loot from her divorce was fun for her, his only hope was that she enjoyed it.

She looked at Tagliabue, her smile fading slowly. He was dressed in jeans and sandals under a blue fishing shirt that highlighted his eyes. His long legs were stretched out in front of him. He needed a shave but he often did. Her tongue slipped out of her mouth and licked her lower lip.

"Speaking of fun," she said. "Let's go to bed."

"Thanks, but I had a real good sleep last night."

Agnes Ann got up smoothly and grabbed him in a headlock. The two of them went to the bed that way, him laughing quietly and pretending to resist.

They spent the rest of the morning naked and in the bed. She made an omelet for lunch before they departed, he for work and she for the sheriff's office to see Detective Coleman and then over to Collier Stables to work out her filly. He offered her a ride but she had already arranged a long-term lease of a car. She seemed a bit defensive about the expense. Maybe money issues bothered her more than they did him.

"It was not expensive and will be easy to just return it when I'm finished here and can get back to the island. It's going to be cheaper than hiring taxis and the like, certainly more convenient."

She tootled off in her two-year-old Kia Soul and he drove to the Pelham East.

CHAPTER SIX

"I got ten pallets of canned food and other supplies for the Pelham Island Restaurant. Nothing needs refrigeration. I also got a load of lumber, loose. You gotta tie it up."

The speaker looked at Tagliabue with his bushy brows up, waiting for affirmation. Tagliabue nodded: "Sounds okay, Max. Can you get it to the loading dock today?"

"Yeah. We got Timmy O'Brien gonna pick it up at four, after work. That okay with you?"

"I'll be waiting at four thirty."

"Good. You going over to Westfarrow tonight?"

"No, I think I'll catch the early tide and be at the town dock by noon or so. I'll radio Peters when I'm close."

Harry Peters was the kitchen manager of the Pelham Island Restaurant, a seasonal establishment on Westfarrow Island that catered mainly to visitors. The place was loading up for the summer business.

"That's done then," said the other man, Max Shertzer. "Let me buy you a beer."

They went in through the kitchen and out to the bar. The lunch crowd was thinning out. The bartender was Timmy, the young man who would moonlight driving the cargo down to Cronk's for the transit out to Westfarrow Island on *Maven*. He raised a palm.

"Say, Anthony."

"Hullo, Tim. How's the family?"

"All doing fine, thanks. You okay?"

Tagliabue nodded as he and Shertzer took stools at the kitchen end of the long glossy black bar. Glassware twinkled in the glow from hanging lamps. The carpet and the wall panels were a rich blue. The place was highlighted by gilded mirrors behind the stick and hundreds of gallons of salt water in aquaria dividing the bar from the dining room. Blue and yellow angelfish glided through the electric turquoise of the tanks. Timmy served Tagliabue a draft Stella and Shertzer had his usual seltzer and lime.

"Magpie been around, Max?"

"You know me, Anthony. I just work here, run the kitchen, keep all the joints supplied. I don't know who frequents the place."

The Pelham East was Peter D'Annunzio's flagship restaurant, entirely different in motif from the Pelham Island on Westfarrow where Tagliabue was headed with the supplies. That was mainly a summer business, open, airy, and done in weathered wood. It was closed in the winter. The third D'Annunzio establishment was a French bistro in the Portland business district called Pelham Paris. Pelham was the name of the first subdivision D'Annunzio ever built, twenty years ago, and the original source of his wealth.

Shertzer drank in silence for a minute and then made his excuses. Tagliabue hadn't expected any serious response to his query; he knew Max pretended his job was an ordinary managerial position in a fancy restaurant. It paid well, according to local scuttlebutt. There was no way he was going to jeopardize it by getting involved in any of D'Annunzio's unsavory side efforts, and that included Marv Magpie Harris. The word was out now that he had asked about Harris, though, and sooner or later it would filter down to the street that *Maven's* skipper was looking for Marv.

The beer made him sleepy. He went back to his apartment for a nap that lasted less than an hour. At two thirty he drove to Cronk's and moved his boat over to the commercial dock area where he repaired the bomb hole again. It still looked like repaired damage, but it would hold and would have to do until he could afford the time to have it professionally done by Cronk's boat builders.

His dockage fees included use of the loading dock and equipment. Timmy O'Brien came in a flatbed and the two of them offloaded the freight Max Shertzer had ordered for Island Pelham and stacked it in *Maven's* cargo hold. They sat on the gunwales of the boat afterward, resting from their exertions.

Timmy, aka Timothy O'Brien, was a strapping lad of twenty-five with a wife and two young boys. His father was Bronc O'Brien, a hulking offensive lineman on the Morse High team that had preceded the one Anthony Tagliabue played for. Bronc had started out like Timmy after him, marrying early and working hard. His Sunday bouts with 'Gansett Bock bled over into Monday mornings with a hit of vodka to get him through the day. Soon he was drinking cheaper beer most nights, adding shots of rye on the weekends. His drinking habits got worse. By the time he was thirty-five, Bronc O'Brien was the town drunk. He was a maudlin sot, who hardly ever caused trouble. Local cops drove him home and protected him from any serious episodes with the law, but no one could protect his liver. The alcohol ate holes in it until there wasn't enough organ meat left to function. He was dead when Timmy was still a Morse High School Shipbuilder.

Bronc's son, Timmy, was that rare bartender, a complete teetotaler. He worked only day shifts except in the summer, pulling beers, mixing a few drinks, and opening bottles of wine for the lunch waitresses and setting up the bar stations for the busy night crew. He made mixers, cut lemon peels and lime wedges, filled ice bins, and stocked product and glasses and napkins. And he cleaned. The night bartenders appreciated his setup so much they cut him in on a piece of their tips. He worked every day but Sunday and left before happy hour. He never touched a drop of the alcohol he sold. Sitting on the side of the boat next to Tagliabue, sweat staining his undershirt and darkening his fair hair, he looked as if he wanted a beer more than anything just then.

"Something on your mind, Timmy?"

"Yeah, actually."

Tagliabue said nothing. He waited. The younger man went on: "You know Josh White, he was a helluva guy. A born story-teller. Always had a sea story once he had a few in him, y'know?"

Tagliabue nodded. Joshua was taciturn sober, loquacious drunk. Timmy went on: "I'm sorry about him dying. Heard he saved this boat by shielding the blast. That true?"

"Pretty much," Tagliabue agreed. "Nobody knows exactly what happened, but if old Joshua's body hadn't been where it was, this baby may have sunk."

"Damn. I hate that."

Tagliabue waited some more.

"I heard you ask Max about Marv Harris. He ain't going to say nothing because he worries about his job. I'm behind the stick every day so's I see all the regulars anyway and sometimes he don't cause he's in the kitchen or his office. I seen Harris coupla three days ago. He was right agitated."

"You not worried about your job, Timmy?"

"Not like Max." He laughed. "I'm a hard worker and can always find work if I need it. Course, I don't make sixty grand like Max is supposed to make. Besides, it's not like I'm gonna reveal state secrets or nothing. All I seen was Harris grab holt of Red Fowler and head up to Mr. D's office. When I seen them leave the restaurant it was an hour later or so."

"They leave together?"

"Yeah."

"What day was that, you remember?"

"I'm thinking it musta been Wednesday. We get our Coors deliveries on Wednesday and I was restocking the coolers."

"Thanks, Timmy. That's good to know."

And it was. Wednesday was the day before *Maven* left on her ill-fated voyage to Westfarrow Island, the day Tagliabue loaded forty bales of hay. Was there a connection between the meeting of Harris and Fowler in Peter D'Annunzio's office and the bomb going off in *Maven*? The timing sounded significant and Timmy thought the meeting was unusual enough to mention it to Tagliabue. He knew their habits as well as anyone, since he was at the Pelham East most days. Tagliabue decided to have a talk with Fowler, to see what he made of the meeting.

Red Fowler was a big man, massive chest sagging a little as age and booze worked their damage on him, but still a force to reckon with. He had been an intimidator for so many years that his flagging strength didn't concern him as much as Tagliabue thought it should have. He confronted young bucks with an air of invincibility; he acted quickly, instead of talking, so most drunks learned to fear him. The bar at Pelham East turned into a popular party venue as soon as the dinner hour faded out and Red was its unofficial bouncer, seated at a corner stool every weekend night and most others. He ended fights before they started, separating would-be combatants and removing them with little fanfare. The Pelham East enjoyed a reputation as a safe place to drink and socialize, thanks in good measure to Red Fowler's presence.

He lived near the bar in an old fisherman's shack with a black woman named Hannah, a pleasant-faced former prostitute with a big smile and an easy nature. Because of Red's kinky red-orange hair and wide nose, people thought he was part black, even though his skin was pale and freckled. No one dared ask him about his racial makeup.

He was the constant companion to Marv Magpie Harris, a startling contrast to his smaller, swarthy friend. He was Magpie's muscle in the many small-time nefarious deeds cooked up by Harris: selling stolen cigarettes and, sometimes, whiskey; insurance scams in staged car accidents; and some minor protection rackets along the waterfront. They also ran a few call girls, according to the contacts Tagliabue maintained in the village, and might have begun dabbling in pills. Both men had short rap sheets. Fowler had been arrested for a violent assault in 2010 that he pleaded down to a misdemeanor and six months in jail. He also paid the victim

$25,000 as part of his punishment. The vic took his money and left Maine before Red's jail term was up.

Like his lawyer, Jack Brunson, Peter D'Annunzio fancied himself a mobster even though he had never had trouble with the law. In Tagliabue's mind, the rich developer liked the respect accorded Mafia dons in the entertainment media, so he affected silk suits and cigars, even though he actually talked more like a college professor than a gangster. Posing as an ersatz mob boss was only entertaining up to a point, he reckoned, and Peter was not about to deny his education and position in polite society.

Harris and Fowler worked for D'Annunzio in unspecified categories. They were apparently paid well enough so that the headman was never formally connected with any illegal activities. It seemed Red and Magpie might even be prepared to do time rather than turn against their source of legitimate income. Peter probably thought of them as loyal soldiers.

Tagliabue thought about the pair on his way out to Westfarrow Island the next morning in a cool onshore breeze. Neither the two tough guys nor D'Annunzio seemed to be deep enough into evil to murder an innocent man, to say nothing of blowing open a boat and endangering anyone riding in it. What would be their motivation? Red and Magpie could be working for Jack Brunson, but the only point of contention remaining between Aggie and her ex was Francine, as far as he knew, and the filly's value was still unproven. Maybe Brunson had a spy out on Westfarrow. That would not be conclusive either.

Tagliabue unloaded his cargo at the town pier on the island and hopped a ride with the Pelham Island's truck to the restaurant. Agnes Ann's mother's younger sister, Maybelle Townsend, met him there and drove him over to the horse farm. She was a tall woman of a certain age dressed in a frock and sensible shoes. Maybelle drove her four-door Chevrolet carefully, her thin lips straight. She was not overtly friendly to Tagliabue, although she and he had met many times on the island and she had agreed to drive him over to see Jesse when he called her the previous evening. Maybe she was protective of her dead sister's daughter and didn't think Tagliabue was a suitable suitor. Maybe she disapproved of him working on a Sunday morning instead of going to church. Slightly uncomfortable with the atmosphere inside the car, he ventured to ask about her grandnephew, hoping that was a safe enough subject to get them through the ride.

Maybelle allowed that Jesse was no problem to board, although she thought his dismissal of academics an indicator of a faulty nature, at least.

"The boy is smart enough to do well in college, but he's not atall interested," she sniffed. "That's a shame. I told his mother so, not that it did any good."

Tagliabue was not sure how much the woman had deduced about his relationship with her niece but suspected she would not approve if she thought he was sleeping with her. He made noncommittal noises and offered no opinions about Jesse's future. After a few miles in silence, Mrs. Townsend allowed that ". . . at least Jesse doesn't seem to be part of the drug gangs that plague the island each summer."

"I didn't know there were gangs out here, Miz Maybelle."

"Well, they may not be gangs in the, er, violent meaning of the word, but they do carry on some. They drive poor Constable Fletcher crazy."

"Drugs are everywhere in the country these days, I'm afraid. I'm glad your grandnephew hasn't gotten involved with that crowd."

"No, sir. He's a good boy in that respect. Works hard and has no time for putting noxious chemicals in his body."

Agnes Ann had made arrangements for a local semiretired farmer to look after her property and the remaining horses while she and her son would be away for the summer, a man named Bill Hammet. Hammet was a friend of Maybelle's. Maybelle let him off at the mailbox and drove away. He waved good-bye; she didn't respond that he could see.

He caught Jesse as the boy was letting the four horses out to pasture. He helped him muck out the stalls and pile the manure on a compost heap behind the main barn. They talked as they waited for the iron bathtub used for a waterer to fill.

"You getting tired of this routine, Jesse?"

"I don't mind it, leastways not this time of year. It's a bitch on a cold winter morning. School's what I don't like. I like tending the animals."

"You a junior?"

"Yeah, but I won't be going back next year." The boy smiled. "I turn seventeen this summer and that's the quitting age 'round here."

"Then what?"

"I'm hoping to become a horse trainer. Mr. Collier's gonna take me on part-time, mostly to help with Francine, but I'll learn a lot."

"You already know a lot."

The boy laughed at that, a carefree sound. Tagliabue realized Jesse was having the time of his life, and things were about to get even better. They went through the house and talked about how to leave things when his exams were over in two months. Bill Hammet was going to drive Jesse to the airfield and keep the horse farm's pickup to use.

"Looks like you got it all together, young fella."

That engendered another laugh from the boy. "Yessir. You got that right. I'll drop you off at the dock on my way to town and see you on the mainland before you know it."

Jesse drove to the Town Marina and went off to a study session with a toot of the truck's horn and chirp of its tires. Tagliabue washed down *Maven* using a town water hose and let her lines go at midafternoon. He was an hour out from the neck of the Kennebec when his cell rang. Johnny Coleman asked him to meet at Joshua White's house.

"You usually work on Sunday?"

"Got a call I figure I better handle before somebody has a cow. It's been bothering White's neighbors."

Joshua lived, when he lived at all, in a converted boathouse upriver a quarter mile from Bath. Water ran under the forward part of it until the river iced up each winter. The place was cool in the summer, damp the rest of the year. The river moved actively where the boathouse was located, so bugs weren't much of a problem, but choosing to live in a place where water was part of the home environment was just one more cause of wonder for Tagliabue when he considered his mate's existence. Joshua had been different, no doubt about that.

He had a rusted woodstove in one corner next to a made-up cot and across the tiny room from a primitive galley. In that cooking area a shuddering noise emanated from a lobster trap.

"He's been howling at night and won't let me near him. I figured you might know him," Johnny Coleman said.

Tagliabue squatted and peered through the faded wood slats. A rat-faced beast lay curled on a beach towel, its bulging eyes staring at Tagliabue, a dry water bowl next to it. When he talked to the dog, the shuddering noise stopped. The animal's naked tail thumped the towel twice.

"I do know him," he said. "Damn, I forgot all about him. His name is Polly."

The little dog whined and pulled himself toward the front of his cage. Tagliabue talked to him quietly for a minute and then put a finger between the slats and rubbed his head. Polly accepted the touch without snarling, so he opened the crate and clipped a line on the dog's collar. He led him outside to the shingle beach, the detective following. The beast immediately cocked his back leg and urinated copiously on the stones. They walked down below the high-water mark; Polly hunched himself up and shat.

"Joshua never brought him aboard the boat. He was afraid the wee thing would wash over the side or get hurt when we were working."

As the two men stood watching the dog, Tagliabue realized that he had never liked its ugly face and spindly legs. He thought a seaman should own a more manly animal, if he wanted one at all, or at least a more likable one. Polly's hard, bulging body wasn't pleasant to pet or hold and its yippy voice was annoying. And it was smaller than a cat. Maybe that's why Joshua didn't bring him aboard. He knew Anthony didn't like the dog and he kept the animal away in deference to his friend's feelings. That thought made Joshua's absence a greater burden on Tagliabue's soul.

"If it's a male, why'd White call him Polly?"

The cop's question brought a smile to Tagliabue's face. "Watch," he said.

He squatted with his back to Polly and said: "Polly, up." The dog looked at him for a moment. Then he ran up the man's back and rested with its front legs over his shoulder. When Tagliabue stood up, the dog hung there like the moon over a back fence.

The cop huffed out a laugh. "He looks like a parrot on a pirate. An ugly fucking parrot." He laughed some more. Tagliabue joined him.

"Joshua was an ugly pirate," he said.

That brought more gasping laughter from the two men. The dog looked around, comfortable and unconcerned.

CHAPTER SEVEN

Anthony Tagliabue agreed to take the dog and try to find accommodations for him. Coleman also had some news from the coroner's office. He read from a notebook while Tagliabue fed the dog from a bag of Pedigree in the corner. Polly ate fast, snapping at the kibbles and spewing crumbs from both sides of his mouth. Tagliabue realized the poor beast probably hadn't eaten in days.

"The bullet in White's back was a .38 caliber. Doc Ferguson said he thinks the bullet was fired while White was still alive, but the wound was not fatal. We found blood on the pier. Not much, but the lead was in muscle and he probably had not bled a lot from his wound. According to the ME."

The detective slipped his notebook into his breast pocket. He looked at Tagliabue.

"We think he was shot on the pier at Cronk's, then made his way into your boat. Thing is, he never called for help."

"Joshua didn't believe in cell phones."

The two men were quiet for a minute as the dog attacked the dry food. Tagliabue asked, "Any idea of the time of death?"

"Naw. The body was in cold water too long, I guess. It had to of been sometime after you left in the afternoon and before you came back at one or two. I'm thinking it was after dark, when the area was quiet. Maybe between nine and twelve. That's my working hypothesis anyway."

Tagliabue looked at Polly and looked at Detective Coleman. "So I'm no longer a suspect, you're saying?"

"You never really was, not a prime suspect anyway. You do have a certain, uh, reputation in town. You killed people in the service, right? I had to look at you. Do my due diligence, as the suits say."

"I understand."

He loaded the dog food bag into the lobster pot along with the animal's dishes. He noticed Joshua's Red Sox cap sitting on a TV in the corner and put that in too. Coleman did not say anything. The sheriff's office was trying to locate next of kin for his mate, but Tagliabue guessed a stained old cap was not a valuable enough part of his estate to worry about. He put the trap in the trunk of the Jeepster. Polly went back on his shoulder and stayed there until he sat behind the wheel, then moved to the passenger seat for the drive home. The animal followed him into his apartment and seemed content to lie on the carpet as Tagliabue nuked a box of spinach and sautéed a piece of cod loin. Polly watched him with his buggy eyes the whole time. Tagliabue put some scraps of fish skin and bits of french bread in the bowl with more Pedigree; the two ate in the living room, watching television.

After a couple of hours, the dog acted as if he had to go, so Tagliabue took him for a twenty-minute walk on wet streets. Back home again, Polly went into his crate and his new master into his bed. Two hours later, Tagliabue's eyes popped open. He lay listening for whatever woke him, relaxing as he remembered he was on the beach, in naval parlance. That is, not aboard ship. He'd gone to sleep early in a small city where many people were still up and about. But the night outside his open window was quiet. Letting his eyes close once again, he drifted off. A haunting voice pulled him back. This time he got up and padded around on bare feet, listening and looking out each window, standing in the open front door. He heard rain spray against the brick siding of the house, the whisper of the tires on a car as it headed out of town. He smelled steam coming off the macadam and he smelled the mud-flats of low tide. Light seeped out of a few windows on his street and blue flickered from Tom Sharkey's TV on the second floor of the apartment building on the next block. The old man usually fell asleep in his Barcalounger and awoke at daybreak with his set still on. Tagliabue detected nothing out of the ordinary.

Sharkey was a long-retired lobsterman, permanently bent from his work hauling pots in weather both fair and foul. His face was so wrinkled that Tagliabue could never look at it without wishing he could somehow iron it flat. Sharkey's hair was wispy and white, his hands warped and knobby at the knuckles, his fingers as fat as the cigars he liked to smoke when he had an extra dollar or two.

Tagliabue remembered it was time he visited Tom with a bottle of Tullamore Dew. They'd share a drink while Tom shared sea stories, the television muted in the background but never off. Tom Sharkey was a lonely man; Tagliabue hoped not to end up like him. He sat back on his bed and rubbed some heat into his feet. Sighing, he lay back, feeling his eyes growing heavy. The sound began again.

This time he knew where it came from. Grumbling into his pillow, Tagliabue kicked off the covers and stomped to the lobster pot, remembering at the last minute that Polly's master was dead and the dog had been abandoned for days. He sighed and let his shoulders droop.

"What's wrong, buddy? You feeling lonely?"

He unlatched the cage and let Polly out. The beast wagged his tail. He walked over to the bedroom carpet and circled twice before he lay down.

"Just don't piss on the floor, okay?"

At the sound of his voice the dog came over to the side of the bed.

"And don't even think about getting up on the bed."

When a pale dawn washed through the eastern window of his bedroom a few hours later, Tagliabue woke up. He'd been dreaming of Agnes Ann sleeping next to him, her belly up against his backside, and it felt like she was actually there in his bed. The dream was so real he looked behind him. Bug eyes and a rat face peered back. The dog yawned and wagged his tail.

Tagliabue groaned. "Don't tell me that senile old son of a bitch let you sleep with him."

He felt sorry for the dog. He had been left by his owner, left without enough food or water and locked in a rotted lobster trap. Tagliabue asked himself: why would Joshua have done that unless he expected to be back that same day? The mate would not have locked his dog up without food while he sailed out to Westfarrow Island. Joshua knew the trip was planned for two nights. When he got out of bed, Polly jumped down from the other side. They ate scrambled eggs and rye toast together in the kitchen, Tagliabue thinking hard.

The dog rode with him over to Red Fowler's shanty two blocks behind Pelham East. Hannah Jones answered his knock. Her face split into a huge grin when she saw Tagliabue and his new companion.

"God knows, that the homeliest damn critter I ever seen. What you use him for anyway?"

"He puts people in a good mood, I guess. Everyone who's seen him so far laughs at him."

"Damn, Tagliabue. He so ugly he makes you look good."

She laughed and he felt himself laughing along with her. She had the door to the little house opened wide, but she was standing in the doorway, taking up most of the space with her bulk. She said: "I like to invite you in, but I don't think I want him walking in my house. My neighbors think I got rats, they see him."

"No problem, Hannah."

He squatted down and called Polly. When the dog scurried up his back and hung on his shoulder the woman doubled over, eyes watering, mouth sputtering. She tried but wasn't able to talk. She wiped her eyes and straightened up. She looked up at Polly peering at her over Tagliabue's shoulder and burst into hoots and wails. A woman pulling a shopping basket down the other side of the street looked at the pair of them, a black woman in tears and a large white man with a bony dog on his back, and hurried on.

Finally they settled in Hannah's living room. Tagliabue put Polly on the floor, where he sat leaning on the man's leg.

"Well, shit," Hannah said, wiping her eyes, "you do know how to make a woman happy now. You come here with that pup to entertain me or what? Cause if you come to be entertained, you know I ain't in the life no more, right?"

"I know, sweetie. Red has made you an honest woman. Fact is, I've come to see him."

"Well you about five hours too early then. He don't drag his ass outta bed 'til lunchtime."

"I want to see him while he's still in bed."

Hannah's eyes widened. "That ain't a good idea," she said, but Tagliabue was already making for the closed bedroom door. "Don't say I didn't warn you now."

Tagliabue opened the door. Red Fowler's massive form lay asleep on his back, his mouth gaping, releasing a sound like a rusty chain being dragged through a hawsepipe. When he inhaled after a few seconds, Red's lips quivered and whistled. The pillows and sheets that landscaped the bed were tinged gray, clothes and shoes littered the carpeted floor. Tagliabue swept open the heavy curtains covering the one window in the room and surveyed the place. Two of the drawers of the scarred and stained dresser were already open, revealing underwear and socks. He went through the drawers, feeling for a gun. Fowler's breathing rasped on. He looked in the tall chifforobe and felt the pockets of the clothes hanging in it. In a poplin jacket he discovered a cheap cell phone. He put it back and fingered through the crushed cigarette packet, change, mints, and matchbooks on the night table.

He sat on the man's chest. After a moment with two hundred sixty pounds compressing his lungs, Fowler came to with belching bluster.

"What the fuck . . ."

Sour breath issued from his mouth, filling the little room with the odor of digested alcohol and sleep. Tagliabue breasted the smell and spoke quietly only inches from the big man's face.

"I want to know what happened to Joshua White, Red. You're not the kind of man to shoot someone in the back but you probably know who did. I want to know who did it."

"Can't . . . can't breathe."

"If you can talk you can breathe. Now tell me who shot my friend in the back or you'll be breathing through a mouth without any teeth in it."

Fowler's eye widened at the threat. He growled and heaved his body. Tagliabue stepped off him and turned to face him as the redhead threw the covers aside and struggled to a sitting position.

"You invade my fucking house and try to suffocate me to bust my chops about some derelict who's probly better off dead? I wished I woulda killed him myself . . ."

Tagliabue slammed a short right into Fowler's face, knocking him back into his pillow. The meaty smack of flesh being struck rattled the open window and covered the sound of septum cartilage cracking. Fowler squealed. Tears sprang from his eyes. Tagliabue sat on him again. Blood ran from Fowler's nose and water from his scrunched-up eyes. He was gasping in pain as Tagliabue spoke in quiet, venomous tones.

"I ever hear of you talking about Joshua White, fat boy, I'm coming into Pelham and am going to beat the shit out of you in public. I'm going to pound you down and make you beg for mercy. After that, every yahoo with a few beers in him is going to try you out. Think about life after that."

Tagliabue left the bedroom, left Red Fowler bleeding and distraught, mewling in agony. He had lost his temper and was angry at himself about that, but it was too late to take it back. He'd gotten nothing out of Red Fowler. In fact, he let the big man know that he suspected something about him and Magpie. He'd been warned. Magpie would be hard to find after this. It was stupid, what he did in the bedroom, and unprofessional.

Hannah sat with her hand on Polly, both bug-eyed and silent as they stared at him closing the bedroom door behind himself. He made for the front door, massaging his knuckles.

"Hold on, big man, I'm coming wichyou. Ain't no facing him till he get right again."

They left and walked down lower Pierce Street, the little dog following along behind, stopping to check out smells on the sidewalk and piss on a johnny pump before scurrying to catch up with them again. Polly seemed content to be left off the leash. He didn't venture into the gutter.

Tagliabue looked over at the woman, who showed no emotion on her face. Her jocular mood when she first met him and the dog was gone. He took a deep breath and let it out slowly.

"Red is hurt and embarrassed. He going to take it out on you, Hannah?"

"Not likely. He know I ain't about to tolerate none of that shit. He treat me like his honeychile anyway. I do keep my own bank account, just in case."

She was a handsome woman for all her heft, Tagliabue noted as he nodded to her. She stopped in front of a corner store.

"I'm ready for a cuppa, Anthony. Don' worry none about me. Worry 'bout yourself. That Red a mean mother now. Ain't nothing worse than an old bull getting desperate."

"I know. See ya."

He walked off and the woman went into the store, a bell tinkling as she opened and closed the door. Polly stood undecided for a second then trotted after Tagliabue. They went down the hill to the harbor and *Maven*. The dog rested in the shade of the conning station while his new owner changed the oil in the twin engines and greased some fittings. Tagliabue needed to work off the nervous energy he felt after his confrontation with Red Fowler.

He was cleaning his hands and forearms with Gojo and a bucket of salt water two hours later when Polly picked up his head and snarled, his body quivering. A skinny spotty-faced teen was walking up to the boat. The dog barked and moved over to Tagliabue.

"Hey, he ain't gonna tear me up, is he?" the boy asked, laughing. "You need a real guard dog I got me a cocker spaniel up to the house."

Tagliabue smiled at him. "You're a funny man. You ought to know that size isn't everything."

"Yeah, I do know that," the boy said around a huge grin. "I know that mongrel might could bite me in the knee if he got a running jump. He's a scary cocksucker all right."

He sat on the shore power box on the pier next to *Maven* and took the reversed Wicked Weed hat off his head, releasing a burst of blond curls. Polly relaxed but stayed on his feet, leaning against Tagliabue's leg. The teenager sniffed and wiped his nose with his forearm.

"You Anthony Tagliabue?"

"I am."

"Well, Mr. D'Annunzio wants to know if you would do him the honor of visiting with him at his table in the Pelham East at about seven. He wants to buy you dinner."

"Okay, thanks. You work for him?"

"Yeah, after school some and in the summer. I'm Sean Flynn. You know my mother, used to be Heather Malsch?"

"I know her. Say hey for me. How's she doing?"

"She's okay. I'll tell her you said hello, big guy. See you soon."

As the boy started to walk off, Tagliabue said: "Hey, Sean, you want a dog?"

"No, thanks. My little sister's afraid of monsters." He sauntered off laughing and Tagliabue said to Polly: "I was only kidding, pup. You're stuck with me, looks like."

He left the animal in his apartment when he walked down to the restaurant that evening. The Jeepster was still parked near Red

Fowler's place. His blood was still boiling at the time, so he hadn't wanted to risk driving. Now he was afoot. Luckily, it was a short walk.

A tall and heavy oak door with a scene of a vineyard in stained glass opened easily into the dining room of Pelham East, blue sprays of grapes anticipating the decor of the room. The blue rug of the bar area ended at the fish tank divider. Tagliabue stepped off the oaken planks of the dining room and looked to the end of the bar. Red Fowler sat hunched on his stool, a metal cast curving over his nose, smudges forming under his eyes.

"Ol' Red's going to have some beauteous black eyes here pretty quick, isn't he?" he said to a passing waiter.

The man snapped a look at Fowler and back to Tagliabue, mouth taut. He had paused when Tagliabue spoke to him but he started off again in a purposeful stride.

"He ain't a happy camper, Anthony. I don't mind telling you that," he said softly over his shoulder.

Tagliabue went on through the dining room to the back corner where Peter D'Annunzio sat at a four-top that fit into an alcove. He was sitting in the far chair with his back to a window onto a lighted biergarten. Diners filled the outside area overlooking the eastern harbor, their voices and the sounds of a piano drifting in every time the door to the dining room opened. The door also let in cool air. Two men Tagliabue recognized as bodyguards sat at an adjoining table about four feet away from D'Annunzio. He nodded to them and took the seat next to his host, as far from the two men as he could get. Many of the other tables were occupied, conversations being absorbed by the plush wallpaper and double tablecloths.

"Hello, Anthony. Welcome."

"Thank you, Peter. Nice crowd."

"Yeah, for a Monday. We don't get much turnover during the early week, though, so we only take reservations for seven and eight. Makes us look busy."

"Nobody ever accused you of being dumb, Peter."

"What do they accuse me of?"

"Sure you want to hear it?"

"Yeah. Tell me."

"Some people think this restaurant is a front for some unspecified disreputable activity."

D'Annunzio laughed. His face pushed into a mass of glades and moguls, the fat swath below his chin wobbled, and his eyes disappeared into slits. His pointy beard bounced up and down like a matador's pigtail. Tagliabue felt the urge to swab baby oil into the rifts of his flesh.

"Anthony, Anthony. You kill me."

He dabbed at his eyes with his linen napkin. A waitress arrived then and set a hammered copper mug in front of Tagliabue. It glistened with condensation. D'Annunzio stopped laughing as quickly as he had begun.

"I hope you like this special Moscow Mule, Anthony. My barman Jeffrey over at Pelham Paris makes the ginger beer himself from his own roots and drives it over here twice a week. This just came in this afternoon. And the limes, y'know, are in season down in the Keys. Couldn't be fresher."

Tagliabue sipped the spicy drink and found it surprisingly refreshing.

"I also hope you like lemon sole almondine. It's actually flounder, but it was caught today. Our Monday chef, Alfred, has an especially delicate touch with flounder."

"It comes with *pomme frites* and curry ketchup," the waitress said. "The vegetable is steamed chard."

Tagliabue nodded to her and she went away.

"People like to eat outside even this time of year?"

D'Annunzio nodded, his chin set into motion again. "They like the view and the smell of the bay. This is about as cold as they can tolerate though. The garden will be filled every clear night from now on out."

Tagliabue drank and waited for conversation clues from his host. Since they both were born and raised in Bath there were plenty of local topics of mild interest, and that's what they talked about. Apparently the reason for the summons to dine was going to wait until after dinner. D'Annunzio had another Mule, but Tagliabue declined a refill.

"You never did drink much, did you Anthony?"

"Not much. I enjoy some drinks, like this one, and I like beer, but I want to know what I'm doing most of the time."

"That's a good strategy for a man in your position."

Before Tagliabue could find out what D'Annunzio meant by that remark, the server returned with their entrees. The fish was delicate, the fries crisp. It was an excellent meal. He only hoped that he'd be served some information for dessert.

CHAPTER EIGHT

After they finished eating and the server had swept the linen, Peter D'Annunzio sat hunched over a pony glass of Drambuie. He sipped, wiped his lips, grimaced, frowned. He leaned back, shot the brilliant white cuffs of his linen shirt and spoke. "You have caused me difficulties, Anthony."

"How so?"

"You have ruined Red Fowler's confidence. He's effective as a bouncer because people are afraid of him. If he can't, er, project an image of invincibility, drunks will begin to think they can challenge him. If that happens, we'll have fights in Pelham East. This restaurant's reputation as a fine dining and drinking establishment will suffer. You catch my meaning?"

D'Annunzio's voice took on a plaintive tone, as if he had looked into the future and saw change coming to what had been a successful and painless business arrangement. The change was not welcome; he hoped to defer such an eventuality for at least a while longer.

"It'd be tough to undo what transpired between Red and me, Peter. And no offense, especially after you just treated me to this fine meal, but I'm more concerned about finding out what happened to my friend Joshua than I am about business at your restaurant."

"I understand. Yes, I do understand. Actually, I wish to pro-
pose a possible solution that should solve both our dilemmas.
Number one, you stay out of this restaurant, in particular the bar
area, for a few months. That should give Mr. Fowler time to regain
his confidence and get back to his old, shall we say, garrulous self.

"Number two, I tell you who was responsible for the untimely
demise of your crony Joshua White. What do you think?"

Tagliabue thought the proposition was surprising, at first. The
owner of Pelham East valued Red Fowler's services but big and
aggressive bouncers were available for hire. The man was not
irreplaceable. Tagliabue surmised that Peter D'Annunzio liked to
play the role of a connected restaurateur without actually being
involved in illegal activities. He was not a gangster but cultivated
the aura of an educated yet dangerous boss. He thought people
should respect him not only because he was wealthy but because
he was mysterious and sort of on the outer edge of the compliant
and obedient masses. It was a dubious persona to Tagliabue, but
he was certain D'Annunzio wanted to own it.

If he accepted Peter's proposal there was no doubt in his mind
that the restaurant owner would tell Fowler that he didn't want
the redhead seeking retribution by beating up Tagliabue, so he
had ordered Tagliabue to stay out of Pelham East. That would
make D'Annunzio seem to have authority. It would also make
Red Fowler believe that D'Annunzio was confident he, Red, could
accomplish retribution if he wanted to. That was D'Annunzio's
interest in the bargain. As for Tagliabue, he didn't want to punish
Fowler anymore. He was also confident enough not to care if some
people thought he'd been warned off. That made his response to
the man's proposal easy.

"That sounds like a good deal to me, Peter."

D'Annunzio smiled and stretched out a hand. They shook
briefly.

"It won't shock you to learn, my friend, that Marvin Harris
was the prime mover in the bombing of your boat. Please don't
ask me his motivation. All I know for certain is that he has been

becoming more, er, criminal in his outlook lately. I'm afraid he is now what I consider to be a liability to my enterprises. At first it was small stuff here and there, shady but not evil, if you know what I mean? I pay him well and he makes more money from his side work, so to speak. He's gotten greedy, though, and I can't see an easy way to disentangle myself from him."

"What's he gotten into, Peter?"

"I'm afraid it's the hard stuff, and you can certainly appreciate that I can't afford to have even the hint of drugs in the Pelham establishments."

"So you want to sic me on him." It was not a question.

"Marv knows I'm dining with you tonight. I intend to tell him that you suspect he and Red were behind the killing of your friend and that you are looking for him."

"Was Red involved?"

"No. I can swear to that. He was in the bar all night last Wednesday and Thursday."

"But he knew about the plan."

"I'm not sure about that. He and Marv had an urgent get-together the afternoon before the killing, I do know that."

Tagliabue had already learned from Timmy O'Brien that the two had gone up to D'Annunzio's office. He decided to keep that information to himself. Not for a minute did he believe that he was being offered information so he would stay out of the bar and give Red Fowler's ego a chance to heal. Harris was becoming a liability to D'Annunzio and the fat man wanted him out of the way, so he manufactured this bogus deal in the hopes that Tagliabue would catch Magpie dealing and have him put away. That way, his hands would be clean and an odious henchman would be out of his pomaded hair. Still, even if he would be doing the bidding of D'Annunzio, Tagliabue now had a target to home in on. He nodded his assent.

"This information is between the two of us, Anthony. You will appreciate that I can't be seen to be testifying against Marvin."

"As long as the information is valid."

"Oh, I guarantee that. Fact, I made a recording of Marvin's plans to place a small bomb in your boat. He didn't specify why he wanted to, as he said, disable it. If Marvin made the hole in your boat, he surely must have killed your mate, although he might not have done it intentionally, from the scuttlebutt I hear."

"Where's the tape, Peter?"

"Rest assured I have it in a secure place."

He smiled when he said that, but it didn't quite come off. D'Annunzio was probably in over his head with Magpie's foray into the weeds, so he wanted the recording in case his appeal to Tagliabue didn't pan out. D'Annunzio started to get up, his hand reaching out for a shake.

"Put your hand in your pocket, Peter. I don't want anyone to think we're friends."

He rose to his full height. D'Annunzio's face blanched and he fell back into his seat. He cleared his throat before he managed to say, "Be careful, Anthony. Marv's carrying."

Tagliabue left the Pelham East and walked the few blocks to Red Fowler's house. Hannah Jones answered the door looking none the worse for wear.

"You left your ugly dog to home. That mean you ain't come to pound on my man no more?"

He smiled back. "Red's at the bar. I just came by to see if you're all right."

"Yeh, I'm okay. I tole you, Red don' take out his flustrations on me. I did run him to the 'mergency room to get his nose fixed. Found out he ain't too happy which you."

"I don't expect he is. See you. Take care of yourself."

"You too, Anthony."

As she was beginning to shut her front door, Tagliabue asked, "You ever see Marvin Harris around here, Hannah?"

"He come by once in a while. Ain't seen him lately."

"If you do see him, please tell him I'm looking for him."

"Uh, oh." The door closed with a loud click.

Tagliabue retrieved the Jeepster from the street and drove back to his apartment. Polly growled when he unlocked the front door, then took to slapping the floor with his tail when he recognized him. After feeding the dog, he changed to a dark T-shirt and jeans. He put sneakers on and pulled a Glock 40 in a waist holster from a work boot in the corner. At the table, Tagliabue cleaned the gun and loaded a magazine, putting another full one in his back right pocket. All this took place to the background sounds of Polly snapping and crunching his food. The apartment got quiet. Looking up, Tagliabue saw the dog standing by the front door looking at him.

"Shoot. I guess you need to go for a walk, don't you, pal?"

Holstering the automatic on his hip, Tagliabue ushered the little dog out and locked the street door. They walked into the soft night, the streets already dark. Tagliabue felt a heaviness to the air, heard the rumble and crackle of far-off thunder. He wanted to walk fast, breathe hard, and get on with the task he had assigned himself, but there was no rushing his dog. Polly bounced along with chattering steps, checking out smells and urinating his own. How does he carry all that liquid in his small rounded belly? Tagliabue wondered as he waited again for the little beast to catch up to him.

At the junction of Pine, where Patel's corner store was closed and shuttered for the night, Tagliabue reversed course and headed for home. He liked to let the dog experience both sides of the street so he called Polly close and crossed over. The houses on the far side were dark, spaced by empty lots. Something scrabbled in the weeds. Polly barked once and ran to the noise. In a few seconds he was back, having chased the something and proud enough of that accomplishment. He didn't need to catch rodents or cats to feel good about himself; he only needed to chase. Tagliabue smiled and continued his slow stroll in the dark. He carried a small high-intensity light in his pocket but felt no need to use it. No cars passed on the quiet street. Magpie was on the run, but he could worry about finding him tomorrow. Right now, all was peaceful in Bath.

Thunder clashed, closer. Polly stopped and looked down an alleyway between two four-story apartment houses. Hair stood up on his back. The tiny dog snarled, showing his teeth, then darted into the alleyway, growling and barking just as a hard rain began to pelt down. Tagliabue grinned at the little dog's sham ferocity as he paused to lift his jacket collar and take out his light. It didn't seem to him that Polly would make such a fuss over a rodent or a cat. He hoped he wasn't going to tangle with a possum or a coon.

When the dog yipped, a pained cry, Tagliabue went in after him. The peaceful feeling he was enjoying on the walk with his dog flew from him and he braced for action. He trained his flashlight on the pavement as he sprinted into the alley and thought for a second about taking his gun in hand. But he was in Bath, for God's sake, a quiet river town in Maine. One military precept he never failed to obey was, "Don't draw your weapon unless you are prepared to use it." Anthony Tagliabue was not prepared to shoot someone or something in Bath. His running presence should frighten away any animal threatening Polly.

Polly was backed against the right wall, snarling again—his growl carrying a certain fearful note this time. Tagliabue swung the light and saw shadows just as they fell on him. Something hit him above his left ear, staggering him. Flashing brilliant sparks strobed in his head. He dropped his flashlight and lashed out in the skittering glimmer it created on the ground.

He struck something, but the first blow had slowed his instincts. Hard strikes assailed him from front and back. The blows cracked as they hit, not fists then. He went down. Polly barked frantically. Thunder roared. A boot toe crashed into his forehead and more dazzling lights flared before the world went completely dark.

He woke in a cold rain, seeing visions. A grizzled, crooked man in a slicker and pajama bottoms stood over him holding a flashlight. Rain splattered off his coat, wind slapped its plastic into a rattling volley.

"Who's that? That you, Anthony? Christ boy, you been hurt. Bad, looks like. Can you get up?"

Tagliabue tried to answer but waves of nausea rolled over him and he had to fight not to vomit. Gasping and sweating, he closed his eyes and let the blackness take over again.

The next time he came to, the apparition was still there, this time accompanied by a man in uniform. The two were talking. Actually, the old man was talking, the cop listening.

"Yonder gale took out me lights, so's the television set went off," he said, his toothless gums catching and breaking suction like an octopus at work. Tagliabue recognized the peculiar diction as that of Tom Sharkey. He smiled. The old man went on, "I looks out the winder and see Anthony's new pup running in circles and barking somethin' fierce, so's I opens the winder for a gander. That's when two men come a runnin' out the alley. One kicked at the doggie but he missed. I put on me foul weather gear and come out to see what the fuss was about. Found the big boy here all bloodied and sick."

It seemed an appropriate time to spare the patrolman. Tom could be voluble when he had an audience. Tagliabue moaned. Polly whined and licked his face.

"Don't try to move, sir. We got an ambulance coming. Let them boys take a look at ya," the cop said.

Tagliabue lay still. Before long a man and a woman were putting their hands on him and training a pencil light in his eyes. The back of his head hurt if he tried to move. He heard one say "concussion" before they put a cervical collar around his neck and moved him to a gurney, the cop helping, and strapped him in. Before they slid the contraption into the ambulance, Sharkey came up to him and said: "I'll take care of yer puppy, Anthony. Don't worry about him."

He squeezed his hand and Tagliabue squeezed back.

～

"Your gun is missing."

"And good morning to you, Detective Coleman." Tagliabue was feeling considerably better after a drug regimen and a night's sleep. He had a crosshatch of stitches running from his right eyebrow to left hairline that felt stiff and sore; the back of his head was soft to the touch and ached when he moved; his left ear was cut and the temple area abraded; and his shoulders were so bruised and swollen that the hospital gown he was wearing in bed seemed made of sackcloth. But all his teeth seemed well anchored and the dizziness had abated. "How do you know it's missing?"

"There's an empty holster still attached to your belt."

"Funny. They didn't take my wallet or the magazine in my back pocket."

"They weren't out to rob you, Anthony. Thugs like this can't ever pass up a weapon. They probably didn't see the clip in your pocket. What'd they get?"

"A Glock 40, registration number Me256344."

"Shit. That the new ten mil job?"

"Yep."

"I thought your holster looked a little long. Loaded, was it?"

"Yep again, fifteen rounds of Federal 180 grams."

"No wonder they couldn't resist pinching it."

Johnny Coleman stopped taking notes and stood up. He walked around the room, pulling open the sheet surrounding the second bed to reveal an empty space and looking out the window. He closed the door to the ward and came back to Tagliabue.

"Who was it, Anthony?"

"Peter Nunz warned the Magpie I was looking for him about the shooting of Joshua White. I figure Marv hired a couple of hard cases to, er, distract me."

"We found two-by-fours with your tissue on them. You're lucky you weren't killed."

"I'm lucky they didn't catch me out on the street. The alley was a little narrow for that kind of lumber."

"Why'd you go into that alley anyway, in the middle of the night?'

"Polly heard something in there, then he got hurt and I heard him cry. I thought I'd better rescue him, although I was expecting a bigger dog or something like that. I didn't see the guys with the lumber until they were on me."

"You have your Glock out?"

"No, thank God."

"What d'ya mean? It could have saved you some flesh. They beat you pretty bad."

"I'm sure now it was some local lads, out to teach me a lesson or warn me off or something. I would hate to have shot one of them. I'm a little surprised they hit me in the head. I don't think they expected me to run at them in that alley, where I could get in a few licks myself."

"You can thank your ugly fucking parrot for that. And that grotty old neighbor of yours. Goddamn, does he ever shut up?"

"He's a bit lonely. Besides, this is the most excitement Tom Sharkey has known since Mutt James accused him of raiding his pots—and Mutt's been dead and gone for twenty years now."

Coleman laughed. He said: "Well, we're hunting the mutts who did you, Tagliabue. It ain't likely we'll find anything, but you never know. Speak to me if you hear anything, okay?"

Tagliabue tried to nod, caught himself and said, "Wilco."

"Good. Now I gotta go. There's someone waiting in the lobby to see you."

The detective left. Five minutes later, Agnes Ann knocked and slipped through the cracked door. Her smile looked forced as she stood an arm's length from his bed.

"You don't look as bad as Detective Coleman said, Tony."

"Cops always see things from the worst possible perspective."

"Can I touch you or anything?" She was using a hospital voice. Her eyes were hooded and fearful.

"My lips are in perfect shape."

She came forward in a rush and kissed him lightly. She stayed close, peering at parts of him as if he were a specimen in a lab.

"You're going to have a scar on your forehead."

"I'll look dangerous."

"You are dangerous."

"Yeah, to myself."

"Tony, you are dangerous. You have marks all over your body from all the scrapes you've been in."

"It's just the kind of work I do, Aggie. Don't make too much of this little incident."

She pulled back and sat on the chair Detective Coleman had used. She clasped her hands together and spoke in a low, urgent voice.

"I know it's the kind of work you do."

"Uh, oh. This sounds serious."

"I'm not playing, Tony. I've been putting together the last two years we've known each other. You disappear for days at a time with your boat tied to the pier. You know things a normal person wouldn't ordinarily know . . ."

"For instance?"

"You know my ex has a gambling habit. I never said anything about that."

"You ever hear of the Internet, Aggie?"

"You can't find that kind of information on the Internet, at least not on the sites available to normal people. And how come we never spend any time in your apartment? We always sleep together at my place."

"You live in a better class of place."

"The one time I was ever even allowed to enter your domain, you hustled me out in a minute, and you didn't explain why a cargo boat operator needs a Mac Pro that must have cost $4,000 and a better home security system than the Kennedy compound in Hyannis. And how come no one else lives in your apartment house? The other two floors are empty."

Tagliabue lay in bed with his eyes closed, trying to regulate his breathing. He opened one eye and squinted at Agnes Ann as she perched on the chair, her body taut, her eyes large and moist.

"I've just survived being beaten with sticks and I'm in pain. There are drugs I can't pronounce sloshing through my body. I don't think I can handle an interrogation right now."

"That's why I decided to confront you now. You're vulnerable. There's a chance you'll be truthful with me."

"I've never lied to you, Aggie."

"Maybe not, but you leave a lot out."

She sniffed, tears spilled from her eyes, but she made no attempt to stem them. Tagliabue, stiff with pain and immobilized by medications, could not hold her. He wanted to soothe her anxiety, mitigate her distress. He spoke softly: "What brought all this on?"

"I came as soon as I heard about you being hurt but they wouldn't let me on the ward for over an hour while they were sewing you up, I guess. I went for coffee in the cafeteria and saw Detective Coleman there. We talked. He said there's more to this case than a dead body. He doesn't know what. He said there are other forces, he called them, forces being brought to bear. His chief was called up to Augusta and came back all vague about the case. He told Johnny to find the guys who attacked you but nothing else without conferring with him. He and Tom Sharkey tried to get someone to let them into your apartment to get dog food. The detective said you are the only one living in that house and that he can't figure out who even owns it."

"I have long been curious about your life, Tony. There are too many things I don't know."

"You've got to be patient. We're just starting our life together. Things take time. I have to keep a little mystery about myself or you'll get tired of me."

He smiled when he said the last. Agnes Ann smiled too, wiping the tears away in an agitated gesture when she felt them touch her lips. She searched his face with her dark eyes.

"Having a mysterious stranger in my bed can be exciting, and I don't want to tie you down or pry into your private life. I just can't stand the thought that your private life might kill you one day."

"It's not all that dangerous, Aggie. My scars and bumps have accumulated over a long time, including my years in the navy."

"You haven't been around a long time."

"It ain't the years, it's the mileage," he said, trying to sound like Indiana Jones. "And I'm hoping someday you will tie me down."

"I know you love me, Tony. You don't have to say it. A woman knows those kinds of things."

"I guessed you'd figure it out. Now how about figuring out how to get me out of this place?"

It took another twenty-four hours before the hospitalist released him, and then she wasn't overly happy about the decision. Agnes Ann drove him to his apartment. He took a bottle of Percocet with him but he put it in the drawer of his night table. He swallowed four ibuprofen and allowed Agnes Ann to undress him. She kissed his bruises and cuts lightly. She kissed other parts of him, not so lightly, as the waxing quarter moon rose in the sky. While Tagliabue rested from her labors, she changed the bed and laid him between cool linen sheets. The next morning, he rose stiffened and pained. They drank coffee by the window overlooking the street.

"It's so peaceful this morning. It's hard to believe two thugs hit you with pieces of construction material just two nights ago."

"Yeah. Nothing much ever happens here. The biggest event is old man Sharkey leaving his television on all night, and he doesn't even turn up the sound."

A woman in jeans came out of Patel's with a bag of hard rolls and two containers of coffee. She strolled past Tagliabue's apartment bobbing her head to something she heard through a pair of white buds in her ears. Agnes Ann followed her with her eyes until she strolled out of sight.

She said, "I wonder how Mr. Sharkey is making out with your new little pet."

"I was just thinking the same thing myself. He doesn't have Polly's food. I can't imagine what the poor critter's eating."

"Let's get over there today."

"Yes, ma'am. We'll do it."

As was her wont, Agnes Ann changed the topic, deciding no doubt that she'd had enough small talk and wanted answers to her many questions. "How come the detective couldn't get into your apartment, Tony? Don't you have a super to take care of the building?"

"Actually, I own the building."

"The whole place?"

"Well, it's only the three floors."

"What's on the other floors?"

"Let's take a look, as long as I'm spilling my guts to you."

She said, as she helped him stand: "You don't have to, y'know."

"Yes, I do. I should have come clean, as they say, a long time ago."

They went out the front door of the apartment and took a small elevator up one floor. The door facing the lift as it opened was solid metal and painted the same pale tan color as the walls that ran from either side of it. The door was plain except for a keypad with a small plexiglass panel above it. Tagliabue punched in some numbers and placed his hand against the clear panel. The door slid into the wall soundlessly. Agnes Ann looked at everything but said nothing.

Inside, the room was undivided, lit by overhead tubes of long LED bulbs that cast the place in artless brilliance. There were no shadows anywhere. Everything was light green except for equipment; there were no wall or window treatments of any kind. Almost a third of the room was a gym with mats and weights strewn about, a heavy bag, a speed bag, and an elliptical machine. Next to it was an open shower. A corner opposite the workout area contained high-tech communications equipment in carbon pods. A large gun safe sat bolted to the floor next to the comm gear. The windows were covered from the inside with metal blinds screwed to the walls. One of the middle ones had a telescope with its objective lens pressed up against it. Tagliabue pressed a button on the wall near the scope and a circular opening whirred and appeared in front of it.

"Check out this view," he said.

The scope was fat-barreled and long. Agnes Ann sat on a stool and trained her eye through an eyepiece set at a ninety-degree angle to the barrel.

"My word. I see why you chose this building, Tony. I can make out people's faces on their boats and see clear past the harbor."

"I think of it as my crow's nest."

She continued to peer into the telescope: "While I enjoy the view, Tony, why don't you tell me how you came to own this weird place and all this equipment."

It didn't sound like a request to Tagliabue. He began to tell her how he met a mystery woman in a mysterious part of the world.

CHAPTER NINE

Images flickered among the shadows and the low-ceilinged place had about it the smell of working men exuding garlic from their pores and smoke from their mouths. They sipped tea in thin glasses as they huddled in groups of three and four and let the tiredness ooze from their bodies after a day in the souks and factories of the city. Their talk was a steady low growl throughout the room. They were dark people with flashing whites in their eyes, eyes that flashed once at a woman, not dark, who entered the bar. Giselle came in through the beaded curtain, drifting past the tables, another flickering image. She sat in front of Tagliabue, pushed the veil from her head so that it draped around her neck, and began to talk.

"We could have met at the Madinah Marriott, Mr. Tagliabue. You didn't have to go native on your first night in Marrakesh. Are you staying at this riad?"

Rather than answering her question, he said, "This is my one night in town. I'm in and out tomorrow if my hop comes through."

"I take it you want to get right down to business. Pour me a splash of that tea, please. I'm parched."

The odor of mint floated to his face as he poured. She drank and sighed.

"That's the best thing about this miserable country, I swear."

He looked at her, his face tanned and unsmiling. She took another sip, put the glass down, and leaned in. She smelled clean, as if she'd just bathed with lilac soap. Her finely lined face was powdered and dry; her short functional hairdo seemed glued in place.

"I understand you are tired of war and all the nasty little games you have to play to survive. Most of our contract personnel burn out sooner or later. You didn't last as long as most. They like the power of their weapons and the, uh, camaraderie with the other men. I have long suspected that you are a different breed of cat."

"How would you know that? I never met you . . ."

She stopped him with a thin hand raised between them.

"Don't ask wearisome questions, please. Just assume I know more about you than your poor old mother, three years deceased now. At Black Opal we seem to spend as much time and energy vetting our personnel as we do deploying them. It's the nature of the beast, if you will. People with the skills and motivation to sign on as mercenaries need to be watched constantly. I've been watching you. I'm glad you're getting out."

"That's a relief. I thought you wanted to see me to talk me into re-upping."

"Hardly, Mr. Tagliabue."

"Then what do you want, Miss . . .?'"

"Please call me Giselle. That will be my contact name if you are interested in my little proposition."

She took another dainty sort of sip and straightened in her chair. "As an adjunct to the firm that employed you for the past year or so, I employ a half dozen or so operatives, all within the borders of the USA, who do certain, uh, tasks at my behest. Some may be extralegal. All are for the good of our own country."

"How would I know that?"

The woman smiled at him, a spare gesture with her lips together. She opened her hands to him.

"That part has been taken care of for us. Just as we spent months vetting you before proposing this meeting, we spend at least as much of our energy and resources determining if a request meets our standards. You have to develop a degree of trust in me."

His teeth flashed white in the darkness of his face and the dimness of the room. He was tired of secrets and intrigue. The men he fought with knew nothing except their assignment, but they whispered constantly in the long waiting hours about the nature and purpose of their business at hand. It's what fighting men do, Tagliabue knew from his time in uniform, question authority while following it. He kept his own counsel in the field, speaking only to give orders or discuss tactics. As a consequence, he had many admirers but few close friends among the contract soldiers he worked with. He was an intense warrior, powerful, fast, and fearless, so he wasn't surprised when he received a message to meet this woman in Morocco on the way home.

If she offered him independent duty in America, he had to at least listen. Black Opal Ops, the contractor who employed him until three days earlier, had been honest in its dealings with him, paid him on time, and had never asked him to do anything he found morally objectionable. He thought BOO was probably one of the straightest of the companies that sprang up to fight America's Mideast battles when the wars in Afghanistan and Iraq had become politically out of favor. He did the same work as a mercenary with the company as he had been doing with the navy—at three times the salary.

"I don't distrust you, Giselle. I don't know you well enough for that."

"You'll learn to trust by the assignments I give you."

"Not from where they originate?"

"No. You'll never know that. We take requests from many agencies. If we accept one, it becomes ours. That's all you need to know."

He raised his eyebrows at that, nodded.

"Let's get to it then," she said. "I have a car idling outside and a nervous driver."

"I think your man in here is a little nervous too."

She smiled again, this time showing her teeth, but not looking behind her at the covered man in the corner. He admired her poise.

She said: "Your situational awareness is just one of the attributes that has drawn me to this discussion. Here's the deal. When you get settled back in Maine, you take a post office box and send me a text with the number. No names or any other identifying data. Just the three-digit number of the box. I will take that message as your agreement to work with us."

"Without knowing who you are." It was a statement of fact, not a question.

She went on, "Every once in a while, I'll send you a packet by certified mail. You read it, burn it, and send back the postcard if you accept the assignment. If you turn down two assignments in a row, you are no longer employed by us. If you accept an assignment, expense money will be wired to your USAA checking account and when you complete it, your pay will be wired. You'll receive a 1099 from one of our legitimate businesses called The Clemson Project every January. Taxes are your responsibility."

Her careful terminology meant to Tagliabue that she ran a clandestine agency housed somewhere in the bowels of the Pentagon or maybe in a special building in Langley, funded under vague national security language and unaccountable for how it spent the funds. He had always assumed such agencies existed, even in a free and more or less open society, and he had no moral objections to them in theory. Actually working for one, doing the agency's dirty work—which was surely Giselle's intent—didn't bother him either. He hoped the orders he received gave him enough information to determine that the assignment given could be at least partially open as to its moral value. He could always turn down a dubious assignment.

Giselle told him little else. She spoke the ten numbers of the phone he was to text. He memorized them immediately, repeating them silently until they entered his memory bank.

He pondered her proposition the next day as he rode in the back of a huge black C-17 as it roared across the ocean toward the east coast of the United States. He decided to use what he thought of as the Vatican Protocol to determine if any given assignment was worthy: if someone sees an apparition, a vision of the Blessed Mother, say, and it garners enough believers to warrant the attention of the local bishop, Rome appoints a priest or a nun to report on the apparition's deeds, but primarily on what it teaches or espouses. If the words of the apparition are heretical or harmful, the case is immediately dropped as unworthy of the church's approval. No further investigation is warranted.

Tagliabue agreed to consider assignments. When a package arrived from The Clemson Project he would read it carefully. If he determined that it was clean work and not harmful to any innocent person and with minimal collateral damage, he would accept it. He was anxious to learn what the company would pay.

The cargo plane landed at the Charleston Air Force Base and Tagliabue bought a used Jeepster in excellent condition that he found on craigslist. He drove it to Maine.

∽

"I had plenty of money then since I'd just been paid by Black Opal Ops," he told Agnes Ann.

She was still sitting at the telescope but staring at him instead of through the eyepiece.

"How old is Giselle?" she asked.

Tagliabue laughed. "That's the first question you can think of? I guess on the sunny side of sixty, but just. Of course, I thought you were nineteen when I first saw you."

Agnes Ann smiled back. She got up and retrieved a leather office chair from in front of the radio equipment and wheeled it across the hardwood floor to the telescope. He sank into it with a sigh.

"Comfy?"

"Yes, thank you."

"Then tell me what you can about your assignments from Giselle."

They sat on either side of the matte black barrel of the scope while he told her about his first job, a snatch. The file was detailed when it arrived at his new mailbox three weeks after he'd sent a text with its number. He locked the door and windows of his rented room and read the thing through, carefully, always aware that he had to destroy it when he knew it. The subject was a former analyst at NSA now living in the Soho section of lower Manhattan. He was suspected of passing secrets and had immersed himself in a rough crowd centering around a jiggle joint called The Blue Rathskeller in the basement of a building on a dark block of Canal Street. Tagliabue's task was to kidnap the spy and spirit him away to a safe house in the Bronx. The file gave specifics about the man but said nothing about the tactics he might use to capture him. He anticipated some violence necessary to effect the snatch; he thought he could do it without killing anyone. Tagliabue spent a week, and some of the $10,000 expense fund from The Clemson Project, setting up a surveillance post two blocks from the Rathskeller in a rented room in a fleabag hotel, and another week watching.

After he had identified the subject, a man called Arthur Blount, and his visitation pattern, he started frequenting the bar. It was a place of shadows and dark booths lit mainly by the colored spots trained on a central raised dance floor where one or two women stripped to the sounds of recorded Dixieland. The dance floor was fronted by a bar, and that was where Tagliabue sat.

"What can I get you, sweetie?" asked a bartender, a woman with a poor complexion and a big smile.

He smiled back and ordered a bottle of Yuengling.

"You rather have a draft? We got that on tap." She kept her voice raised to speak over the music. He could smell mint on her breath.

"No, thanks, a bottle's fine."

"Good thinking."

She took his twenty when she brought the beer and left fourteen dollars in change. He drank two, from the bottle, and pushed the money left over from his twenty into the scupper in front of him. During that time two dancers performed for ten minutes total with about forty-five minutes in between sets. Neither dancer was particularly energetic. They moved as if they were listening to their own music in their heads. No one seemed to care. The dancers were both young and attractive, one an Asian, the other blonde. There wasn't much of a tourist trade and the regulars treated the place as something of a local bar. Tagliabue kept to himself and no one bothered him. He was back at his hotel by midnight.

The next day he moved uptown a few blocks to a more respectable apartment hotel called The Carstairs. Barely visible down the busy city streets at ten P.M., The Blue Rathskeller proved to be no busier than the night previous. Tagliabue sat at the bar again and spoke to no one but Myra, the bartender. He did the same thing for a week, telling Myra when the music allowed that he was in town for a new job and looking for a permanent place to live.

"What kind of work you do, Tony?"

"I'm a chemical engineer."

"Wowie, zowie. You like your new job?"

"So far so good. You like your job?"

"Ah, you know. It's work and I'm happy to have it. The guys here are okay. We don't have any big problems."

"Can I ask a dumb question?"

"It won't be a first for me, pal."

"How come you have these dancers here? No one seems to pay much attention to them."

She looked around casually. Other customers were engaged in conversations or drinking single-mindedly.

"Advertising," she said in a low voice. She looked at Tagliabue expectantly, eyebrows raised. His brain tried to process the new data but nothing rational came up. His face showed his ignorance.

"The girls, man." Myra polished the bar and went to the well to wash a few glasses. She spoke without looking at him; he listened without looking at her. "The boss, Tomas, he runs a few women, y'know? He don't like them sitting around smoking dope and thinking up schemes when they're not working, so he sends them out here to advertise their wares. Make sense?"

Tagliabue shook his head, smiling. "They make any sales?"

"Enough, I guess. Lots of these guys use them. They don't want to look like they're interested but they are."

The guys Myra referred to were mostly middle-aged, dressed casually but expensively. They engaged in friendly but relatively quiet camaraderie, no yelling or fighting. One of the managers who wandered around the carpeted floor of the joint, nodding to a few of the regulars but talking to none of them, looked to Tagliabue like a bouncer. It was all very low-keyed. When he came by Tagliabue at the bar, he could feel the bouncer's eyes on him. The man said nothing to him, but he knew he was being watched. After two weeks, the attention of the bouncer seemed to wane somewhat.

"If you're interested, let me know. I can set you up," Myra said.

"What if I'm interested in you?"

The barmaid laughed. "Don't jerk me around, Anthony. I'm not for sale."

"These women who are for sale, how much are they?"

"If you have to ask, you probably can't afford one."

"Isn't that what they say about Rolls-Royces or something?"

"Maybe so, but it's right for here."

Armed with this new information, Tagliabue started paying attention to the schedules of the dancers. There were four of them altogether. Sometimes one or another would not be on the stage for an hour or more. Some of the customers went through the door leading to the men's room and didn't come back for a long time. Once, he saw his mark, Arthur Blount, go to the bathroom for almost an hour. After his second beer, Tagliabue used the men's room, and noted the stairway leading to a dimly lit hallway upstairs.

That night he went home as usual. At four A.M. he walked back down Canal Street. Dressed in soft black pants, dyed black Brooks sneakers, and wearing a pea coat, watch cap, and leather gloves against the early morning chill, Tagliabue stayed close to the buildings as he made his way back to The Blue Rathskeller. Headlights showed on the avenue. He slipped into an alleyway and stood with his back to a sooty brick wall next to an air-conditioning unit. The car rolled slowly up Canal, a black-and-white using a spotlight to check doors. Two cops rode in the squad car. He could hear them talking through an open window as they made their rounds. The spot tore away the blackness as it roamed across doorways and down into the entryway of the Rathskeller before it came to Tagliabue's hiding place. He flattened himself as much as possible and stayed still, eyes clamped shut against the blast of light as it exposed garbage cans and doorways and a shallow balcony down from his position in the alley. The cop car paused at the entrance to the alley, idling quietly as the spot probed the night. He stood against the near wall, hoped the light would be trained better on the building across from him, the one more or less facing the car. A feral cat slunk farther into the alley. The police light followed the animal for a brief minute before the car moved on. The smell of coffee lingered in the air.

Tagliabue began to breathe again. He waited otherwise motionless until the patrol moved a block away, then he opened his eyes and moved to the nearest door on his side. It figured to be the service door to the club. There was no basement door he could see. The service door was bolted from the inside, so he hoisted himself onto the a/c box and took a suction cup and a glass cutter from his coat pocket. Using a pencil flashlight, he found the pane next to the sash window twist lock. He spit on the suction cup and pushed it against the window. Holding the cup, he cut around it in a slow arc of squeak and pause, squeak and pause, pressing hard enough to cut through but not break the glass. When he finally completed a circle, he pulled on the suction cup and removed the piece of glass. He slipped the suction device from it and placed it on the a/c box. The hole in the window was wide enough for his hand, if he kept his fingers extended and grouped together, and his wrist, but not for his arm. Damn, he thought, that could have been a critical misjudgment. He could just reach the lock. It was sunk in rotted wood and turned easily.

The window didn't want to open after he twisted the lock free. He worked it slowly. Once he could get his fingers under the frame he was able to force the old window up enough to crawl in and down past the Venetian blinds. The blinds were old also, heavy wooden ones. He tightened them closed and hoped they'd keep out any passing breeze. Pausing to breathe deeply, he let the tension ooze from his chest. Sweat dripped down from under the woolen cap.

Dodging the police patrol and breaking in had taken the better part of an hour. He had to hurry now. His position was at the street side of the second-floor hallway. The doors along it were shut. A blade of light slipped from under one door. Tagliabue stood against the street wall away from the alley window he had just come through. Someone coughed quietly in the lighted room. The door opened. A blonde woman came out, hunched in a thin bathrobe and holding an unlit filtered cigarette between two fingers of her right hand. She turned left and let herself onto the balcony Tagliabue had seen as he hid in the alley. She took a plastic lighter from her robe pocket and lit up. She smoked with one arm across her rib cage holding the elbow of her other one. Each time she dragged a flare of an ember from the smoke, Tagliabue could see her face, etched with tired resignation. She was one of the strippers from The Blue Rathskeller.

After the woman had gone back to her room and put out the light, Tagliabue gave it ten minutes by his watch before he moved down the hallway and down the staircase, noting any soft spots on the stairs. He came out in the alcove with the bathrooms. To the left of the stairs a short hallway led to a door, locked and bolted. He slipped the bolt, twisted the lock, and went through the door. He was in the alley, just below the balcony the woman had used to smoke. He went back in, locked the door behind him, and climbed the stairs again. The balcony door was unlocked. It was a short drop to the alleyway from the balcony. He took it.

Dawn was coloring the eastern sky as he walked up to Sixth Avenue, stuffing his hat and gloves in his coat pockets. Since the window he had climbed through was painted closed, he didn't think anyone would notice the hole he'd cut, at least not for a while. If someone did, there might be an unpleasant surprise waiting for him the following night. He had a western omelet and a fried catfish at David Burke's Kitchen, just a short drive to the Holland Tunnel.

The next night, when Blount went to the bathroom, Tagliabue followed a moment later. His subject was clumping up the stairs as Tagliabue came through the door from the bar. When Blount stepped to the floor above, Tagliabue took the stairs three at a time, fast and quiet. He came up behind Blount just as the target reached the bedroom door opposite the balcony. Blount was already unhooking his belt.

He opened the door and turned when he realized Tagliabue was coming, but it was too late. His eyes popped open and he raised his hands, but that was too late also. Tagliabue hit him hard with a chop to the apex of neck and shoulder. Blount groaned and his knees buckled. Tagliabue pushed him into the room, kicked the door shut behind him. He stepped over him as Blount collapsed face first to the floor. He snatched the naked redhead from the bed. She froze, eyes and mouth wide. He spoke in a harsh whisper as he held her by either side of her throat.

"Don't make a sound, sweetie, and I'm out of here. If you scream or cry or anything, I'll put you out like I did him. Got it?"

She nodded. He dropped her back on the bed. She curled on her side, looking at him through half-closed eyelids. Blount's wallet contained two C-notes and another few hundred in twenties as well as a driver's license from New York State that proved Tagliabue had the right man. He dumped the money on the bed in front of the cowering woman, putting the wallet in his own front pocket. Blount's body spasmed, as if he'd been shocked with a Taser. He stood when Tagliabue hauled him up, before falling across his shoulders. Balancing him in a fireman's carry, Tagliabue left the prostitute's room and moved out to the balcony. He rolled the man over the side and lowered him as far as he could by holding his wrists. He let go. Blount hit the ground with a thump and lay in the filth of the alley as Tagliabue swung a leg over the balcony. He paused to catch his breath. The door opened behind him. The woman from the night before appeared, dressed in a thin, low-cut dress this time, a cigarette in her hand. The hand flew to her mouth.

"Oh, my God."

Tagliabue heard a male voice behind her in the hallway.

"What's wrong, Susan?"

Someone pulled Susan from the doorway just as Tagliabue swung his leg back onto the balcony. The man who had spoken was dark-skinned with a neck nearly as big around as his head. His eyebrows arched up when he saw Tagliabue rising from a crouch.

"What the fuck?" he barked as he reached for a revolver hanging in a shoulder holster. Tagliabue hit him with a straight left below the eye that stood him up. The man's hand fell away from the gun and curled open. Tagliabue slammed him with a right cross to the temple that drove him back into the hallway, his eyes rolling up in his head. The blonde broke for the door to the club. Tagliabue grabbed the back of her dress, but it tore as she twisted out of it and ran naked. He bounded after her and hit her as he had Blount.

Leaving the dark man unconscious and the nude blonde in spasms, he took the man's gun and leaped over the balcony. Dragging Blount upright, he walked with him alongside as if his friend was drunk. He even sang a sea chanty he had learned once in Belfast. Blount's legs moved okay, although they would accept little weight. Tagliabue was glad of his conditioning and strength because he needed to get away from the bar with his captive. Fast.

The nearest parking spot he could find when he had driven to The Blue Rathskeller earlier was more than a block away. By wrapping his right arm around the man and gripping his belt, Tagliabue staggered up Canal. It was late but not yet closing time. The few people about on the dark street looked at the odd couple but said nothing. One man and woman pair crossed the street rather than pass close to them. They reached the car. Blount fell across the back seat. Tagliabue secured his wrists with plastic ties before injecting him with a few ccs of GHB to keep him quiet. Sitting behind the wheel to catch his breath, Tagliabue looked around for anyone showing interest. Even the dim lights over The Blue Rathskeller seemed bright in the gloom of the street. The door flew open. A man Tagliabue made as the club bouncer looked up and down Canal without coming out. He had a cell phone to his ear. Tagliabue cranked the rental and drove west, following signs through the tunnel to New Jersey. He thought he heard sirens in the night air behind him, but one always heard sirens in New York.

Another of the dubious pleasures he learned to accept in New York was laughingly referred to as a toll—$18 for the Holland Tunnel—only on the way into the city. A driver can leave for free, glad to be shut of the overpriced place, no doubt. Tagliabue didn't have to stop for a Transit Authority kiosk as he turned onto the tail end of I-95 to the George Washington Bridge and took the lower level to the Bronx. Going off the Cross Bronx Expressway at the third exit led him and his passenger through a neighborhood of attached houses and broken sidewalks to the safe house in the middle of a gritty street. Giselle was waiting inside with two men in suits.

Arthur Blount was awake by then, moaning and trying to relieve the pain in his shoulder by rolling it. Tagliabue walked him up the front steps to the house and gave the man's wallet to Giselle. The suits took Blount off to another section of the house. Giselle patted Tagliabue's cheek.

"You'll be hearing from me, Tony."

∼

"So, did you hear from her?" Agnes Ann asked.

She was still sitting on the stool in Tagliabue's third-floor crow's nest, legs tucked under her, telescope forgotten.

"Sort of. Five days later my bank statement registered a deposit of $100,000."

"Wow. That's decent pay. Whatever happened to the guy you snatched, Blount?"

"I never heard another thing about him. I believe Giselle's agency likes to keep things compartmentalized, each person knows only what he or she needs to know. My work was over, so I didn't need to know anymore."

"You must wonder what became of him."

"Aye, no doubt. But I'd not find out if I wanted to. I try to worry about only what I can control."

"Well, my friend, you could control it by not taking any further assignments."

Tagliabue held in a laugh about her lecturing tone because she spoke with some asperity. He held up his palms.

"Arthur Blount, not his real name, by the way, was a traitor to his country. He's no doubt in prison by now and his circle of spies rounded up by, er, competent authority. Do you think I should feel guilt about that?"

"Maybe they pulled out his fingernails or something. You have no idea who this Giselle even is or what agency she represents. And, by the way to you, how come she calls you Tony?"

This time Tagliabue did laugh. Agnes Ann tried not to smile but couldn't manage it.

"I swear I never told her my name. Everyone else called me Anthony, just like here. Even my mother called me Anthony. You're the only one who calls me Tony."

"Maybe that's why she did it."

"How's that?"

"She wanted you to trust her, or something."

"Maybe. I do trust you. That's why I told you this story, although I probably shouldn't have. I am bound by a confidentiality agreement. I don't think I'll tell you about any of my other assignments. It might be illegal."

"Legality doesn't seem to be something that gets in the way of your goals."

"Legality and morality are not necessarily the same."

"Let's do something immoral then."

"Suits me. You're the one who'll have to do most of the work."

"Suits me."

"Good. Downstairs in the bedroom?"

"No. I want to be immoral on an exercise pad."

CHAPTER TEN

AGNES ANN

Ironically, since Tony is the one with bruised muscles and cracked open skin, I am the one left flattened, depleted, enervated by the pleasure we took in each other. I lie on the sticky workout mat as if my veins have been collapsed by injections, as an addict blown out by my own sort of lovely lust. I smile as I listen to his breathing catching up with his recovering blood pressure. It's a time of peace and joy.

In this weakened, relaxed state, I let my mind wander, and the wanderings immediately end the peace I've been feeling. The storm of revelations about Tony's life pushes to the fore of my thinking, upping my pulse and tightening my belly muscles. As much as I enjoy being with a man who can protect me and as much as I love his big, strong body, I was shocked to hear of his government work with Giselle—I visualize her as Margaret Thatcher—never dreaming that he was involved in those kinds of dangerous activities. It does explain a lot: the way he goes missing for weeks, especially. I thought he just needed his space, the way some people do. I am always reluctant to press him on his whereabouts or to question him about his goings-on. Jack lied so much about those things I feel better not hearing stories from Tony, even though they could not be more different types of men. I've promised to accept his schedule as it is and not try to exercise control over his life. He is exactly the same with me.

The news of his operational status with Giselle and The Clemson Project was a jolt to my system, but perhaps, on reflection, it shouldn't have been. I had long suspected that he was a mercenary—although I never attached that description to it—when he left the service. There was a time between his discharge and when he bought his boat. I suspected he used his war experiences in some clandestine manner during that time. Contract warriors became the norm in the Mideast when the US government didn't want to field a large number of soldiers in battle. Why wouldn't a competent guy like Tony want to make some money working for a contractor to the CIA or some other agency?

When he did come home, he seemed content to work the old boat. He'd graduated from The Citadel and took a commission in the US Navy, but he hadn't pursued a professional career of any kind. I just thought he liked going to sea and he liked being his own boss. Maybe he does, as long as he gets to serve his country occasionally with Giselle's outfit.

Maybe I'll leave it that way. It won't be easy. Now that I'm sure he wants to marry me I hope I can keep from tying him down, no matter what he said. A big issue will be where to live. It's going to seem strange once we're wife and husband, him living in his fortress apartment in town and me on Westfarrow Island. Maybe he'll take a post office box on Westfarrow. Maybe he'll retire from The Clemson Project and manage my farm. Jesse may not be back.

The idea of my son taking on a career before finishing high school is another frightening change in my life. I think he's mature for his age, but I'm sure many a mother of a boy in trouble feels the same way. Still there is no way to force the boy into years more at home and then college. I guess I should be grateful Jake Collier is taking him on as an apprentice. He'll be happy as a racehorse trainer someday, and I'll be proud of his work.

My mind wanders back to Jack Brunson. How did I ever fall for a man like that? My mother always told me that when things got serious to check out a prospective mate in the presence of his family. How he treated his mother, and how she treated him, would tell me a lot about the kind of man he would grow into. Jack's mother lived in California and I never got to meet her. My mother said that men who live three thousand miles from their mothers and don't see them, not even for their weddings, and who are lawyers to boot, are men to stay away from. Too bad I didn't listen to her.

My mother thought that some people in certain professions will have a hard time getting into heaven. Those professions included bomber pilots, who kill people they never see; salesmen, who talk people into buying things they cannot afford; lawyers, who defend the guilty, men and corporations. She didn't like Jack from the start, although she never said anything to me like that until he left me, and the baby, and then in effect evicted us. He turned out to be the kind of lawyer who gives them all an aura of sleaze, the kind who uses technicalities to get drunk drivers out of convictions and uses threats to ruin whistleblowers' reputations if they tried to sue the companies he represented. He was smart and amoral.

I don't see Jack anymore, but I do know that he is involved with the people at least on the periphery of the bombing of *Maven* and the killing of Joshua, people such as Peter D'Annunzio and Marvin Harris and Red Fowler. My prayer is that Tony won't have to deal with him in his investigation, an investigation I'm certain he's conducting on his own in addition to that of the sheriff's office. A man with Tony's background could never allow someone to kill his friend with impunity. The attack in the alley across from Tony's apartment house was probably an indication that someone thought he is getting too close to the truth.

I purely hated to see him banged up like that, with more scars to add to his collection. I might have to start thinking of his scars as body art, tattoos without the ink. True, they're not very pretty, but neither are most tats.

We'll be heading over to Saratoga shortly. That thought tenses my stomach too. None of us knows how Francine will respond to actual racing, if she's got what the racing fraternity calls heart.

We're not really sure how fast she can run compared to others, or what class to race her in. I know we'll keep her out of claiming races, even the expensive ones, because I am certain that Jack, or one of his reps, will claim her without thinking twice. We're trying one of a pretty good class of maiden races for fillies and mares first thing, and depending how she does there, we'll work out the next step. God knows, what if she is stakes material?

I daydream of that possibility for a while, happy enough not to be worrying about Tony's work, Jack's lack of a moral compass, or Jesse's future. I reach over and touch Tony's face. My eyes are closed but I can feel him smiling.

CHAPTER ELEVEN

Three days later, Tagliabue's shoulder swelling had eased and his cuts had healed. He was off all pain medications. Agnes Ann went back to the racehorse training facility on Heal Eddy before they found time to visit Polly and the old lobsterman. Tagliabue knew he had to resolve the boarding arrangements for Joshua's dog. Tom Sharkey surely must have spent money on dog food that he could ill afford to spend. Accepting help from a neighbor was one thing; leaving the beast with an old man for five days now was something else. He hated burdening the man.

Polly seemed happy enough to be living with Tom Sharkey, but Tagliabue wasn't certain he could tell if the dog was happy or not. His face always looked the same to him and he wasn't a face-licker type of pet.

In Sharkey's musty two-room apartment on the first morning Tagliabue was out and about since the beating in the alley, the old lobsterman and the little animal looked as if they'd been living together for years. Sharkey groaned under his breath as he knelt down to feed Polly.

"He been a lot of trouble for you, Tom?"

Sharkey looked up sharply from filling Polly's bowl. "No, no. He's not been a bit of bother, Anthony."

"Are you putting canned dog food in with that dry stuff?"

"Well, ah, the poor wee lad was looking a mite peaked, y'know. He enjoys a bit of meat."

"You've spoiled him, you salty old bastard. He won't eat plain Pedigree when I feed him next time."

"Well, er, I don't mind feeding him, Anthony. I know yer a busy man."

Tagliabue sat down carefully on one of the mismatched chairs at the card table in Sharkey's kitchen area. Sharkey was busy mixing the feed and wouldn't look at him. He likes the company, Tagliabue thought. He doesn't want the dog to leave.

He said softly: "Where does Polly sleep, Tom Sharkey?"

Sharkey's ears reddened. He spoke quietly: "On the cot with me."

"You good enough to walk him?"

The old man looked up with a glisten of hope in his eyes.

"Oh, aye," he said. "No problem atall. He follows me on the sidewalk when I go to the Paki's for me paper in the morning and we go down to the river park in the afternoon for a run. There's some other doggies down there usually. He's not a problem. Not atall."

"It was good of you to take him home for me when I got banged up, Tom. I'm indebted to you for that kindness."

"I were happy to do it, Anthony. Truth to tell, this wee beastie brightened up this old place when he came. Acted like he'd lived here all his life."

Sharkey laughed out a crackle and patted Polly's head. The dog flicked his tail once but kept on eating. "He's well-trained, don't you know, never once shat on the floor or anything and he ain't noisy or, er, demanding either. Better than having a wife around." He smiled a toothless grin at that.

Tom Sharkey had been widowed since Celeste was taken by the flu in the winter of 1988. They'd had no children. The widower lived a solitary life, Tagliabue knew. When he visited with coffee and jelly doughnuts once in a while, or with a bottle of Irish whiskey on an evening, the old man talked a lot. Even then, when he had rare company, he never turned off the television. He might mute it or turn the volume down when someone visited, but the set was never off. Now, Tagliabue noted, the TV was dark. Could this ugly little dog be lifting a long depression from an old man?

"Tom, you'd be doing me a big favor if you could look after the dog for a while. Joshua never took him on the boat and I'm afraid he may not realize he can't step overboard when we're underway."

"I can do that, Anthony. Be happy to." Sharkey nodded his head three times, quickly. "Yessir. Be happy to."

"Well, okay. Here's the deal. I'm going to give you $500 for his care. You'll need to take him to the vet to see if he needs any shots or anything, and you have to buy him food. You let me know when you need more."

Sharkey started to protest but Tagliabue held up a hand: "I'm a rich man. Don't worry about the money."

Tom Sharkey laughed. His eyes watered and he looked away. Tagliabue put a sheaf of twenties on the table, patted the old man on the shoulder and left. Polly continued to eat with snuffles and crunches as Tagliabue closed the apartment door behind him. Breathing easier, he walked down to Cronk's. He was feeling much better.

He scrubbed down *Maven* but tired in an hour. He was sitting in the shade puffing a little when Detective Johnny Coleman drove up and parked his green county car at the head of the pier. He tramped down to *Maven* with his head forward.

"Permission to come aboard?"

Tagliabue nodded.

"You allowed to work up a sweat already?"

"Well, it didn't take long."

"Even so . . . you're still in recovery mode, ain't you?"

"I'm feeling pretty good. Being outdoors again has to help."

"Yeah, you're probly right."

Tagliabue reached into a small cooler and took out two bottles of water. He handed one to Coleman.

"Anything new?"

"Matter of fact. We arrested a guy name of Henry Sanders. Charged him with assault and battery against one Anthony Tagliabue."

"Really? How'd you finger him?"

"He was drinking with some cronies down at Adolph's, showed off a new gun. Bartender called the city PD. Nervous. It was a new, long Glock. His prints are on the lumber you got hit with."

Opening his satchel, the cop took out a big baggie with a long square semiautomatic inside: "You identify this gun?"

He took a pull on the water as Tagliabue examined the weapon in the bag before taking a folded paper from his wallet. "It's mine," he said, "the serial number's on my permit." He handed the permit and the gun to Coleman.

"Why you got a permit? You don't need one in Maine."

"I'm not always in Maine."

"No?"

It seemed to Tagliabue that the sheriff's detective wanted to ask more questions. He drank water, looked at the bottle on his lap and up at Tagliabue out of the top of his eyes, his forehead wrinkled. He shook his head. He slipped the bagged Glock back in his briefcase.

"You can get this back as soon as we arraign Sanders. He's gonna rat out his partner pretty soon, I'm guessing. Plead out. There won't be no trial."

Tagliabue said nothing. The men shook hands and the cop left. As he watched Coleman's Chev drive off, Tagliabue thought about Henry "Hank" Sanders, a tough guy with meaty hands and an incipient paunch, thinning hair, and a red complexion. Sanders was divorced from his child bride at least ten years now, he thought, ten years of a steady slide down the slippery slope of malaise with a dead end at the bottom. He lived on the dole, doing odd jobs now and then with his best pal, Georgie Peterson, a bayman who owned a leaky clam boat and who worked marginally more often than Hank Sanders did. Peterson was a wiry type whose bony wrists always seemed to be longer than his shirtsleeves. Sanders and Peterson were the kind of derelicts who would mug a nun for fifty bucks.

He flexed his fists and flung his arms down, figured he'd be ready for action by the time he located Peterson. He called Timmy O'Brien at the Pelham East and asked him to pass the word that he was hunting for Peterson. Then he strolled into town and ate a steak and fries at the Bath Roadhouse.

That night his phone dinged with a text message from his cousin Maurizio: "Look for clam diggers at Jasper's early Tuesday." He slept late, exercised on the third floor, and took a long, hot shower. After lunch he walked along the river for an hour and went to bed while it was still light out. When the alarm woke him at three Tuesday morning he felt pretty limber. He drove down to the bay and parked where he could see Jasper English's establishment, Sagadahoc Seafood Wholesale. English was a crusty businessman with a certain tainted reputation. The clammers and lobstermen who sold their catch to him knew well to be alert as he was weighing and counting. If one of the hard-cut baymen with their callused hands and steeled muscles protested when he caught him at some venal act of thievery, English was quick to grovel and laugh off the complaint—and to quickly amend the tally on the tags he handed them. The baymen accepted payment only in cash and only at the time they brought their catch to him. Tagliabue was amazed that he would try to steal from men who could probably snap his stringy neck, but he'd been working his wily ways for years, maybe as long as three decades, according to some of the old baymen who hung around the docks. He thought Jasper English was the slime of the earth.

English also occasionally managed projects that evaded the fishery laws. He recruited the baymen he knew needed money and were willing to engage in some practice that was harmful to their very livelihood in exchange for some immediate gain. If clam diggers were out at night, that meant some clam farmer wanted a catch of illegally small littlenecks to stock his holdings. Or maybe some wealthy summer visitor wanted sweet undersized bivalves for a lawn party. Either way, the men raking them were threatening the natural process of growth. The state didn't like anyone taking shellfish before they were old enough to spawn. The night diggers had to complete their illegal transactions before the Maine fish and game wardens came on duty at eight.

Tagliabue sat in the silence, windows open to the brisk morning air that carried the odor of mud flats. An hour before false dawn, a light went on in one window of Jasper's fish house. Fifteen minutes later, Tagliabue heard the sound of an outboard motor at low speed. A flat-bottomed open boat eased alongside Jasper's pier and tied up. Three figures offloaded wire baskets of clams and carried them to the fish house. No one talked.

The men were still silent as Tagliabue walked in on them. Jasper English was handing out cash. He jumped when he saw Tagliabue and that made the three other men turn toward him, their eyes opening in surprise. One was the tall thin form of Georgie Peterson.

"Good morning, boys," Tagliabue said. "Don't do anything stupid."

English was the first to find his voice.

"Jesus God, Anthony," he said in a hoarse whisper. "You bring fish and game?"

Rather than answer, Tagliabue pulled his cell out of his pocket and snapped pictures of the four and their baskets of illegal shellfish as he walked toward them.

"You'll be hearing from them soon enough, scumbag. Right now I'm here to talk with Georgie."

Peterson turned to run but his rubber boots slowed him. Tagliabue snagged him by the back of his neck and slung him to the wet floor. He put a foot on Peterson's neck.

"Don't any of you try to leave while Georgie and I have a little conversation."

He hauled Peterson to his feet and pushed him ahead of him out to the pier. In the fresh air, away from the smell of water-softened wood and burlap and clams, he let Peterson go.

"It ain't but a misdemeanor, Anthony. We each only got two bushels."

"I'm not interested in your illegal catch, Georgie."

His eyes bored in to Peterson's. He moved closer, spoke in a low voice with the steel of menace hardening every word: "I'm itching to knock out a few of your rotten teeth and break a few of your bones. Don't tempt me."

Peterson's face was pale in the early light. He threw up his hands and backed to the edge of the pier.

"Don't hit me, Anthony. I can't afford to get broke up. I gotta work."

"You didn't mind breaking me up last week."

"It was Hank kicked you. We was only supposed to work you over some, I swear. Look here, we was only supposed to bang you around, no hits to the face. That little dog pissed Hank off with his yipping and snapping. He's the one kicked you when you was down. I swear, Anthony. I hardly even hurt you. Just banged you on your arms and such, I swear."

He was talking rapidly, his eyes blinking like a signal lamp, his nose running into the sweat dripping down his face. Tagliabue thought he might jump in the water if he got any closer. He spoke sharply.

"Be quiet!"

Peterson's mouth snapped shut. His hands fluttered down to his sides. He sniffed, then closed his eyes as if waiting for the inevitable. A soft whine dribbled from his mouth. Tagliabue took a step backward. He spoke softly.

"Who sent you to work me over, Georgie?"

Peterson's eyes snapped open and he broke the suction of his lips. He licked them when he saw Tagliabue had stepped away.

"The Magpie. He give us a buck apiece and said to send you a message."

"He say what kind of message?"

"No. He didn't say nothing else and we didn't ask. He wanted us to use our fists but Hank said no fucking way. Not big Anthony. We use lumber or nothing doing. We needed the money, I swear."

"Go back in the fish house and stay there, Georgie. I'll be waiting outside."

He sent the photos of the clam diggers and their catch to Johnny Coleman. When he saw the time on his phone he realized that the sheriff's detective would probably still be asleep. He called him. The man sounded surprisingly alert.

"Can you keep Peterson there, Tagliabue?"

"I think so."

"Good. Won't be long. I'll call a coupla deputies down right away."

He rested with his hip on Jasper English's van. Some conversation among the four men in the fish house buzzed out but Tagliabue could not understand what they were saying. Otherwise, the new morning was quiet until two county cars rolled up. By the time deputies arrested Peterson, a state fish and game car arrived and two rangers confiscated the illegal shellfish and issued tickets. As they were leaving, Detective Coleman drove up. He had two cups of steaming coffee. He and Tagliabue walked the empty streets to the city pier. The benches were wet from dew so the two men stood in the gray light of dawn each with a foot on the railing that lined the edge of the dock. A trio of gulls took wing from the calm surface of the bay and went off searching for food. The tide was beginning to fill the basin, covering the mudflats like snow covers a city street. The morning mist was lifting.

"The tourists'll be happy having breakfast *al fresco* today," Coleman said.

Tagliabue looked at him in mild surprise but decided not to comment on his use of language. He told him what he'd learned from Georgie Peterson.

"Marv Harris, huh? We ain't seen him around for a while now. What do you think his game is?"

"I don't know. Georgie said he hired him and Hank Sanders to warn me off. It must be somehow connected to the damage to my boat and the death of Joshua."

"Maybe. I just don't see the motive."

"Well, if I learn anything, I'll let you know, Detective."

"Yeah, you do that. Meanwhile I'll sweat these two mutts and see if I can learn anything myself."

Tagliabue drove down to the boatyard where he found Tom Cronk already in his office, having a cruller with his morning joe. He made arrangements to have the hole in *Maven* repaired permanently. On the way home, he remembered that he hadn't been to the post office in nearly a week. A familiar certified mail notice was waiting in his box.

CHAPTER TWELVE

Anthony Tagliabue locked himself in his apartment house and opened the tan polymer package the postmaster had given him in exchange for the certified notice. Inside were a New York driver's license issued to one Francis Fabris of the Bronx whose photograph looked suspiciously like Tagliabue and a credit card in the same name. It was the first time Giselle had sent him false ID material. When he read through the assignment he realized his life was about to become complicated.

He read it again. Going to the basement, he burned the papers in the incinerator, locked the card and license in the safe concreted and bolted to the floor, and placed the envelope in a file drawer with the others he had received over the past thirty months. It was the thirteenth one.

On the way to Chad's Deli, he mailed the return postcard to The Clemson Project. He picked up Maurizio when his cousin got off work at two P.M. They lunched on an outside table at The Bath Oyster House. Over clams in coconut stock and french bread, he told Maurizio what he wanted him to do. His cousin listened, asked a few questions, confirmed times, and agreed to the plan. He suspected that Anthony had some secretive side work, so he didn't ask what Anthony was up to. A week at the Saratoga race meeting was enough for him.

"I got a friend works at Belmont," Maurizio said as he mopped up sauce and scallions with crusts of bread. "He knows all them horses. I'm gonna make me some money this vacation."

He smiled broadly. Tagliabue laughed at his optimism.

"Just remember, Maury," he said. "Travel, room, and board go on my card, even if you're treating someone. Rent a car from Enterprise and leave it at the Retinue Apartment Hotel with key under the mat. You can take cabs or Uber after that. Okay?"

"Right, cuz. You need a paper trail."

"Roger that. You ain't as dumb as you look."

"Hey, don't mock the way I talk, Anthony."

He made a fist and pretended to threaten his cousin. He was nearly as big as Anthony Tagliabue but softer, and could never mount a real threat, but he looked enough like his cousin to pass scrutiny at hotel desks and such. They drank brandy after lunch before Maurizio went home for his afternoon nap. He had a smile on his face as he thought about the ponies at Saratoga and the opportunity for some legal betting.

Anthony Tagliabue decided to forgo a nap. His health was about back to normal and he had things to do. He had to work out. Having his body in top shape was paramount for any assignment and his needed toning after the beating and recovery. He also worked at getting *Maven* shipshape for her role in Giselle's plan, changing filters, oil, and belts, collecting charts and fixing electronic settings. And cleaning. He trashed the mattresses in the cabin and purchased new ones.

Tagliabue also prepped for his private, moral duty at Saratoga Race Course, meeting two more times with Maurizio in secret to go over their scheme. It wouldn't have done for people to be reminded of the similarities between the cousins. When they met he wore Joshua's old hat. It seemed appropriate, a reminder of the burden he bore to the memory of his friend.

He enjoyed the best weather coastal Maine had to offer as spring melted into summer while he waited for the race meeting over at Saratoga.

∽

When Agnes Ann called in early July to say Jacob Collier was preparing to van Francine to New York state, he was fully ready for his assignment for Giselle.

"Jesse is going to go with Mr. Collier. You want to ride down with me, Tony?"

"That's the best offer I've had all week. Is your little car up for the trip?"

"Yeah, it actually runs well. I figure I'll stay to see the boys off in the horse van and then drive over to Bath for you. I should get there for a late lunch on Friday. We can leave Saturday, if that works for you."

"Good. See you then."

By the time Tagliabue and Agnes Ann made it down the I-95 and across Massachusetts on I-90 and up the Northway to Saratoga Springs, the light was fading from the clear sky. She checked in at the Marriott Courtyard and they drove over to take Jesse to a late supper. They found the teen in front of Barn Eleven where Francine was stabled. He was talking and laughing with three other stable hands, all young. A pale girl with red hair so light it was almost pink was explaining something about hot wraps. Jesse appeared to be paying close attention to her.

"We're going out for a late supper," Agnes Ann said. "Will you folks come with us?"

All three stable hands demurred, citing early starts in the morning. It was already after eight thirty. Jesse fist-bumped the boys, shook hands with the redhead. He was smiling the whole time he walked with his mother and her friend down the shedrow to visit with the filly Francine. The horse stood looking at them over the half-open Dutch door of her stall. She moved her head up and down, nickering. Agnes Ann rubbed her muzzle and the space between her eyes.

"Girl, you're looking good," she muttered to Francine.

The animal did look good to Tagliabue, eyes clear and bright, coat glowing in the soft light of the darkening barn. Agnes Ann fed her a small carrot she had carried from Bath. It had turned limp at the tip but the horse crunched it down greedily. Jesse rolled his eyes at his mother. Jake never let anyone feed anything to his horses, not even a treat.

Over burgers at the nearby Shake Shack, Jesse was voluble about his first days at Saratoga. Tagliabue smiled and sat back, taking in the conversation between mother and son.

"Jake rents a house out of town a ways for the race meeting, but I slept in the stable for the first two days until Francine got settled in," Jesse said.

"Jake is it?" his mother asked. "I thought he was always Mr. Collier."

The boy swept aside her mild protestation. "Misters on the backstretch are owners, Mom. He asked me to call him Jake. Now I'm used to it. All the grooms and stable hands call him Jake. By the way, those other kids are just hot walkers. They got to work up to being stable hands or grooms."

"I see. Well, how is the filly? She looked good from what I could see in her stall."

"She's better than good. Still gaining weight. You going to eat the rest of those onion rings? I work her out early at a training track they call the Oklahoma. It opens at five thirty but there are guys with stopwatches there even then most days. Jake has me run her fast in the middle of an exercise run, so it's hard to get a time for any distance, know what I mean?"

"I get you, Jess. Aren't you a little big to be riding a racehorse?"

"Yeah, I'm way too heavy. For training, though, Jake thinks it's good. It's like a swimmer wearing gloves in training. He takes them off for a race and his arms feel light. Same with Francine. She's going to think no one's on her when one of those 110-pound jocks gets aboard."

"Any idea who's going to ride her?"

"Jake thinks he's got Manny Ramirez."

"He any good?"

"Yeah, one of the best. Great guy too."

They drove the boy out to the little house Jacob Collier and his wife had rented for the race meeting. Ethyl Collier, thin and lined and dressed in flannel shirt tucked into jeans, which were tucked into worn cowboy boots, put on a pot of coffee. They visited with her and the trainer. By ten thirty both Collier and Jesse were yawning so Tagliabue and Agnes Ann left and went to their hotel.

Tagliabue squatted by the floor safe in the morning and took out some cash.

"You ever hear of plastic, Tony?"

"Traceable."

"So?"

He looked up at her, the bed sheet draped over her waist as she played at her tousled hair with her free hand, one of her breasts furrowed faintly from resting on it. She looked soft-eyed, having just left the cave of Somnus, young and innocent without a trace of makeup.

"I don't want anyone to know I'm here yet."

She sat up, suddenly alert, and pulled the sheets up. Girding for battle, Tagliabue thought. He told her Maury was flying up to Albany using his ID and renting a car with his credit card. His cousin was booked into a downtown Saratoga Springs hotel as Anthony Tagliabue. He could see the light go on in her eyes.

"You're working." It was not a question.

"Small job, Aggie. You'll never even know it. I'm really here to see Francine run. Please don't worry about it."

He hated lying to Agnes Ann, although he did hope to see the filly's first race. The instructions from Giselle did not mention the track scene at all; this was personal business. Aggie could know nothing of it.

"I'm not worried," she said. She pushed at her nose with her knuckles. "Actually, I am worried. Your Giselle work is dangerous."

"This one should be easy."

She looked unconvinced. "I think I liked it better when I thought you were just the captain of a cargo boat."

"Go on now. You like a little drama and excitement."

"I get enough of that with horse racing. Anyway, does this mean you're not going to be staying with me here in Saratoga?"

"That's right. People know I'm here. Some will have seen us together. But from now on, anybody looking will think Maury is me. I'm supposed to be undercover. I'll be around, watching you and your horse."

"Well, okay. I'll be busy with Francine anyway."

"I'll sneak you into my bed once in a while."

~

For six weeks every year, the last of summer, horse racing shifted from the New York metropolitan area to the Adirondack Mountains. Belmont and Aqueduct shuttered themselves as the New York Racing Association moved its operation north to Saratoga Springs for the upstate track's only meeting. The town and the track were steeped in history; the area was tony, expensive, and popular. Tagliabue liked the ambience, liked the track more. Families could picnic under the maples adjacent to the paddock, while grizzled bettors and touts, bussed up from Queens, grumbled and finagled on the grandstand apron, more interested in their cigars than in the fact that the Saratoga Race Course is the oldest sporting venue on the continent. The meeting drew twenty thousand on weekdays, twice that on Travers Day, more than enough for Tagliabue to avoid running into Maurizio, who had agreed to restrict himself to the clubhouse environs.

Tagliabue had not been to the barbershop since June and had stopped shaving. Dressed in khakis and a golf shirt as he mingled with the serious bettors near the finish line, he now looked scruffy, almost unkempt. No one seemed to care. Maybe his look was trendy.

He marked up his *Daily Racing Form* and bet modestly. When Agnes Ann came to his new apartment-hotel for a visit on his third night in town, she grimaced when she saw him.

"What, you don't like my hairy face, Aggie?"

"Well, I don't exactly dislike it. I'm just not used to it yet, I guess. You have to admit it is different."

"That's the idea."

"You don't want people to recognize you," she said. "I knew that."

"Some people will recognize you though," he replied.

"I know. I'll just have to restrain myself from visiting."

She pursed her mouth at that, trying to figure out the implications of what he said. If people recognize her and know she and Tony are a couple, who are we talking about, she wondered. Tagliabue held up a hand before Agnes Ann could formulate a question.

"The less you know, the better, Aggie. We just shouldn't be seen together for a while."

She nodded. The Retinue Apartment Hotel was small and plain. He wanted it that way and ate most of his meals in his room. Agnes Ann went to the stables every day, spending the time with her son and her trainer, so she and Tagliabue would not have a lot of time to spend together even if they wanted to. The filly was rounding into shape. She had high hopes for Francine's debut in a maiden race for two-year-olds on Wednesday of the track's second full week of operation, only a few days away. She would be busy. There could be complications she couldn't even anticipate.

On Monday of that second week of the race meeting, Jack Brunson strolled up to Barn Eleven as his son was hosing down the horse following her morning workout. Jesse didn't recognize him.

"You know who I am, young fella?"

The visitor's voice was loud and he gestured with an unlit cigar when he spoke, making the young horse's ears twitch.

"No, sir, I don't," the teen replied as he sponged the filly's face. Francine bobbed her head and moved her feet in little clattering dance steps on the concrete bathing pad. "I think I'm supposed to. Sorry to say I can't remember exactly."

The man said "shit" under his breath. Jesse pretended not to hear it. He scraped water from the animal's back and flanks, turned off the hose, and unhooked her from the two tie-downs. He clipped his own lead to Francine's halter.

"I got to cool walk her."

"I'm your goddamn father."

The boy stopped, holding the horse close and looking over his shoulder at the man. The horse blew and shook herself. Jesse patted her neck and said, "I think I'd know my father." He led Francine away down the shedrow path.

"I have a restraining order," Agnes Ann told Tagliabue that evening as he tossed shrimp and asparagus in a sauté pan. "That bastard is not supposed to come near me or my son."

Tagliabue raised his eyebrows at her, hoping she would not ask him to intervene.

"You tell Jake Collier about him?" he asked.

"Yes. He told me to check with security at the gate, which I did. They shouldn't have given Jack a backstretch pass. They said a new guy gave him a one-day pass without checking the no-fly list. It won't happen again. Jack probably paid him off."

"That should cover it, I hope."

"It should," Agnes Ann said. "It just makes me nervous that he's even around."

The next day, Tagliabue went to the track looking for Jack Brunson. He hadn't come to Saratoga to worry about Brunson, but he was concerned that he had shown up at Francine's barn and he wanted to be sure that Jack wouldn't be in the way when he had something to do. He didn't see Brunson, though, and he began his search for his main target, the man who had murdered his friend by shooting him in the back and setting a bomb on *Maven*.

He bought a grandstand seat near the front and watched the crowd below through binoculars. Saratoga drew tens of thousands

no matter the weather, so it took Tagliabue an hour of looking and
watching races to spot someone he knew. The man was wearing a
black shirt over black pants and he had a paperboy hat shielding
his eyes from the summer sun. It was Marv "Magpie" Harris and
he was easy to follow once spotted.

Magpie walked across the track apron as if the space belonged
to him. He didn't seem a particularly impressive figure but his
confidence allowed him a certain aura. Tagliabue noticed people
gave way to him when he walked; he made no attempt to accommodate others on the move. He went straight forward and others
stepped out of the way, sensing some sort of menace in the man.
Or, perhaps, they just didn't want a needless confrontation to spoil
their day of fun. Not surprisingly, Marv had a space on the rail at
the finish line when the third race went off. He watched the race
impassively, in stark contrast to the wildly cheering mobs around
him. When the horses crossed the finish, he dropped his betting
tickets on the concrete floor of the apron.

Harris walked up the stairs behind where he'd stood at the
rail, passing within a dozen feet of Tagliabue in his grandstand
seat, looking neither left nor right, and into an open bar facing
the clubhouse. A tall dark barkeep served him a short dark drink.
He sat by himself reading and making notations in his *Daily Racing
Form*. Tagliabue could see him only by turning sideways in his seat.
It was too obvious that he was looking at something other than
the horses if he used his binoculars, so he let them hang from his
neck. He didn't dare get closer to his quarry. Ten minutes later,
Harris went back down to the track apron and again stood at the
rail. Tagliabue didn't see him place a bet. The betting lines radi-
ated out from a wall of betting windows into a large open space
behind Tagliabue's seat. Only when the time to post shrunk to less
than five minutes did the space fill up enough for Tagliabue to feel
safe in hiding among the crowds. He was growing out his beard
and wore a baseball cap, but he was afraid he would stand out to
Harris because of his size.

The fourth went off only a minute after Harris took up his rail position. Tagliabue figured him for a late bettor. Before the fifth he went up to the betting gallery at two minutes to post and spotted Marv Harris at the fifty-dollar window. He walked away through the dense concourse staring at his ticket. He didn't see Tagliabue, but Tagliabue had seen enough. He went down to the paddock and watched the horses and their trainers, riders, owners, and groomsmen for another hour. He reclaimed his car and drove back to his hotel.

"Mr. Fabris," a clerk called from the front desk. Tagliabue remembered his cover name in time to walk over to the small alcove that served as the booking area. Most people at the Retinue stayed for at least a week at a time, so there was not a lot of activity at the front of the house. That was good.

The matronly clerk handed him a pink call-back form: "Call Tagliabue."

He went outside and called Maurizio on his new cell.

"I seen the bum Brunson in the clubhouse today."

"He recognize you, Maury?"

"Sorta. He looked at me like he knew who I was, small smile, y'know, then a frown. He don't know me from Adam but he musta thought I was you for a minute. So, no problem with that, but I wondered if you want me to watch him for you."

"You sure it was Jack Brunson?" Tagliabue asked.

"Yeah, sure enough. I seen him a coupla times when he was giving Miss Agnes a hard time during the divorce. Once, when I was going over to see the new filly she just got, he got there first and they had words, y'know? I didn't want to get mixed up in their private fuss, so I held back. But I seen him good. I know what he looks like all right."

"Good, Maury, good. I don't want him to see you too much. Try to find a seat away from him, if you can. If that doesn't work, take a table at The Porch or one of those other restaurants in the clubhouse and hang out there. Okay?"

"Yeah, no problem. It's gonna be expensive though. You know what I mean?"

"I do, but you're going to bet on Francine in the third Wednesday and make enough to pay for it all."

"Francine? That Miss Agnes's horse? No shit. I didn't know she was ready. She any good, Anthony?"

"All I know is that she is a good-looking animal and Agnes Ann and her trainer think she runs like the wind. They have Manny Ramirez in the saddle, so he must think she's got a chance. Give it a shot. Spend some of your money."

"Your money, you mean."

Tagliabue laughed at that. The Clemson Project already had paid him enough to buy the filly and the other six horses in Jacob Collier's stable, had they been for sale. He was not a millionaire, but he considered himself rich. Maurizio rattled paper over the phone.

"The third is a maiden special weight, purse $83,000. She gonna be in good company, Anthony."

"Maybe we'll get some odds."

"Maybe. Two-year-olds are tough to pick. Francine will be worth a wager, for sure."

Tagliabue clicked off on Maurizio and went to his room for a nap. That evening and the next full day on Tuesday, Tagliabue spent trying to locate Jack Brunson's hideaway. He owed that much to Agnes Ann, for her peace of mind. Brunson had to be staying somewhere in the Saratoga Springs area. He tried all the major hotels first, then the motels and bed-and-breakfast houses that were popular in the resort town. No one offered to take a message for John "Jack" Brunson. On Wednesday, when the track reopened from its one dark day of each week, Tagliabue had other things on his mind than the whereabouts of Jack Brunson: it was the day of Francine's inaugural race.

CHAPTER THIRTEEN

Jesse Brunson was walking the filly, Francine, in tight circles in the saddling enclosure, a three-sided tall space with dusty clerestory windows admitting shafts of muted sunlight. The horse was visibly excited. There were other horses in the paddock, some of whom knew what was coming, having raced before, and people. People everywhere, all seemingly talking at once. The muscles beneath the young horse's red coat rippled, her head was up and moving at all the sounds of race day. She blew a few times.

"She nervous?" Tagliabue asked Agnes Ann, who stood at the entrance to the enclosure.

"More curious than nervous, I would say. This is all new to her."

"Well, that can't be bad, can it? At least we know she's got enough energy for the race."

"True enough, Tony. As long as she doesn't spend too much of it before the race starts."

"Yeah, I can see that. Well, break a leg."

She laughed. Maybe they don't say that at the races as they do in the theatre.

Tagliabue left Agnes Ann then—he took a chance slipping in to wish her luck but he knew how important this first race was to her and Jesse so he wanted to show his support. He walked out quickly, hoping no one had recognized him talking to her. His new hirsuteness had altered his appearance considerably. Even so, some sharp-eyed person could have seen through the disguise. By the time "Riders Up" sounded and the jockey Manny Ramirez got a boost from Jake Collier and settled into the tiny saddle, Francine was all Agnes Ann's son could handle. Jesse walked her out of the paddock and through the tunnel and a wall of noise from fans anxious to see the racers in the flesh. The filly's eyes were showing white, her ears were moving fore and aft and she was shaking her head as the track's bugler played the "Call to Post." Jesse handed her off to an outrider on a placid horse called a lead pony. Francine was wet along the flanks and foaming at the neck. She pranced, keeping her head close to the old quarter horse lead pony. The outrider spoke in Spanish to the jockey: "She never run before?"

"No, *nunca.*"

The bigger man pursed his lips and said something that sounded like "Oh, shit." Manny Ramirez looked as if he was ready to find a safe landing spot, but together the two experts got the filly calmed enough to get on the track and begin to warm up. Jogging a little seemed to ease her fears, but the bettors didn't like her sweat. The entrants in the third were all maidens, so none had won yet, but most of the others had run in one or two races. That seemingly meager experience gave them an advantage many experts thought amounted to 10 or 15 percent in finishing distance, so it was not surprising that Francine's fractious post parade had the punters worried. With seven minutes to post, the odds on her went up to fifteen-one. Tagliabue bet ten dollars on the nose for Agnes Ann's entrant, then settled into his grandstand seat to watch the race and Marv the Magpie. He found Harris again with the railbirds at the finish line, hemmed in but untouched.

The horses reached the starting gate. Francine went in quietly; some of the other animals did not like the idea of moving into one of the tight starting stalls. They fussed, backed, threw their heads. One even kicked out. The starters finally got them all into the gate. Ramirez was in Agnes Ann's lime silks with a darker green

WI circled on the back, so he was easy to pick out at the tumultu-
ous start, ten young beasts bolting down the chute at the bell, their
fervor accentuated by the clanging of the flung-open gates and
the yelling from starters and jocks. Francine broke well, a boon
in a seven-furlong race. She fought Ramirez for a while down the
backstretch but settled in four lengths back, still straining enough
for her rider to have to keep a strong hold on her. Tagliabue could
see through his glasses that her mouth was pulled toward her neck.

At the half-mile pole, she seemed to accommodate herself to
the race, striding easily for the first time. Tagliabue hoped she had
enough stamina left for the stretch run. She was running three-
wide and clear of other horses.

On the turn for home, Ramirez moved her in and up, two out
from the rail. The two-horse, a dun mare who was the favorite,
moved at about the same time and took over the lead. Francine
followed her up. She was boxed in by a gray filly to her left and
a horse coming on the outside, but didn't realize it, running hard
behind the leader. The five came up three deep with speed and
passed them all.

The field straightened for the homestretch, ears flat, teeth
bared, and flaring nostrils sucking in great quantities of the
Adirondack air. The roar of the crowd intensified, almost over-
powering the thunder from the horses' pounding hooves. With a
furlong left, the gray inside Francine could no longer maintain the
pace and fell back a length. Ramirez took his mount to the rail, a
dangerous decision on a new racer. Francine changed leads with
the move and surged forward, her rider's left boot painting the
fence.

The dirt was a little deeper in tight and the space to pass the
leaders was narrow, but Francine seemed to care not a whit. Her
nervousness had disappeared with the excitement of the competition itself. She was racing and that's all she cared about. Her
neck straining, her body flattening, she ate up the ground in great
flying strides. She passed the favorite and caught the five-horse

with three jumps left to the finish. She won her first race by a neck. Manny Ramirez had not touched her with his crop.

Sensing the race was over when her jockey relaxed, Agnes Ann's filly galloped around looking at the other horses with her ears up and a bounce to her step. She liked this racing business. Even the crowd noise didn't seem to bother her now. The tote lit up with the payouts for her win: twenty-eight dollars to win, twelve dollars to place, and seven dollars to show. Tagliabue had a ticket worth $140 in his pocket.

That evening, Tagliabue ended his congratulatory call to Agnes Ann when Maurizio phoned.

"Some race, eh? That red gal loves to run, don't she?"

"She does, Maury. You get down on her?"

"That's why I'm calling, plus I'm leaving tomorrow and wanted to be sure you remembered. I'm having a helluva time and hate to go, but I gotta get back to my fucking job by the weekend. Look here, Anthony. I bet fifty bucks across the board on Agnes's horse. The payout was eleven hundred and seventy-five bucks."

"Hey! Good for you, Maury."

"Yeah, thanks. Only trouble is, you got to pay taxes on anything over six hundred or something. I had to sign a form, with your name. Cause I'm using your ID."

He paused, expecting the worst.

"No problem. That's just more proof I was here."

"You don't care about the taxes shit?"

"No, not as long as you fly out of Albany in my name tomorrow."

"I'm going, cuz. I hate to leave but I'm going. Some little chicky here at the clubhouse bar is gonna miss her Anthony Tagliabue though."

"As long as she doesn't come calling at my apartment in Bath when the race meeting ends," Tagliabue said through a smile.

"She does, she's gonna be disappointed."

～

While the Westfarrow Island team celebrated their hand-ridden victory in Francine's first race, augmented by a physical exam that showed no ill effects from the contest, Tagliabue got ready for the first part of his assignment from Giselle. It required leaving Saratoga and heading back to Westfarrow Island. First, though, he had a private burden to relieve.

He changed hotels, moving farther from the track. Before leaving his old room, he shaved clean and cropped his hair short. He jammed his baseball cap on his head and left carrying his own bags. Since he had checked out earlier, Tagliabue talked to no one in his new guise. He stopped his rental in a McDonald's parking lot and pasted on a white fisherman's beard, around the jawline with no mustache, and drove to a Holiday Inn Express where he checked in as Frank Fabris. In his room he jammed a bald-head cover on his head, looking in the mirror like a bald guy—if one didn't look too closely.

Engagement day was dry and mild at post time for the first race. Marv Harris was dressed in dark clothes again, claiming his usual rail position. The grandstand was only half full. By the call for the third race, people were filling the seats, some eating sandwiches brought from home. Tagliabue worked his way past legs and bags to the aisle and down the steps to the track apron. A briefcase crossed over his chest and hung by his right side. He went into a bathroom stall, pulling the mask head from the bag. Placing it on his head, he pulled the hat over it tightly.

Back outside, it was two minutes to post. People rushed forward to the track. Tagliabue let himself be carried with the crowd until he was behind Marvin Magpie. If Marv turned around he would see him, and probably recognize him from that close. There was one person between him and Harris. The race started with a roar from the crowd. Tagliabue inched forward. There was movement in the mass of humanity, and Tagliabue felt himself being jostled. A young man next to him apologized, barely taking his eyes from the race. Someone else splashed beer on himself and cursed.

The horses turned for home. The roar intensified. Everyone on the apron, probably even the rent-a-cops hired for the month-long meeting, watched a horse move up from the back of the pack, moving so fast it looked as if he may overtake the two leaders as they raced for home. People screamed, raised their arms. Tagliabue bent over suddenly. He pulled his hat off and jammed it into his bag. Taking out a small .22-caliber revolver he turned sideways and pressed it into Marv Harris's back. He squeezed the trigger. The report barely registered amidst the concentrated tumult at the rail. He dropped the gun. Harris cried out. His voice too was lost in the crowd noise.

Bedlam reigned at the finish line. Harris was dead but his body hadn't yet fallen. Masses of people were propping it up, pushing it as it tilted, jumping and screeching as the horses closed on the wire. No one realized there was a dead body among the crowd of bettors. All eyes were fixed on the finish like laser beams. Nothing was detected in any other direction. Tagliabue peeled off his surgical gloves, stuffing them into the top of his briefcase. No one paid attention to anything but the exciting finish run. Money was on the line. The crowd surged around him as the horses reached the last pole. The noise reached a crescendo.

Tagliabue moved sideways in small shuffling steps. People had moved past him to the rail as the finish came up. He was jostled, kept moving, slowly and inexorably toward the open concrete floor behind the biggest mass of people, everyone trying to get as near the racing surface as possible as the horses thundered past. Finally, he came clear. He walked slowly under the grandstand as the crowd quieted immediately after the race ended. Someone screamed. He kept walking. A security guard started moving toward the rail to his left. The uniformed man yelled, "Make way. Police! Make a hole."

Tagliabue walked out Gate C to his car in reserved parking. It was quiet out on the concourse. It was, he knew, too early for bettors to be leaving the racecourse, so his departure would be obvious on security cameras, but he could do nothing about that. He had to get away from the scene of his crime. He walked slowly, keeping his head down and trying to minimize his height. The Hyundai started easily. Driving away, he peeled off his beard and his head mask and put them in his briefcase. He took out a hand towel and wiped the perspiration from his face and head. He breathed deeply, turned the air up, and felt his pulse begin to wane as the miles slipped by.

Back at the hotel everything appeared normal. He showered in his room and lay on the queen bed naked, willing his conscience to clear, telling himself that he had saved the state money by executing Harris and had rid the world of a blight on its culture. He got up and dressed when night came. Drinking a mini bottle of brandy, he sat by a window and watched the traffic roll down Union Avenue in a blur of red and white lights. He heard no sirens.

After breakfast the next morning, he drove his rental to Portland, Maine, and turned it in. Maurizio picked him up and drove him to his apartment. He went in quickly, fired up the incinerator, and waited for the sheriff's office to call.

CHAPTER FOURTEEN

"Where were you at three fifteen P.M. yesterday, Mr. Tagliabue?"

"I believe I was home by that time."

"You admit you were at Saratoga racetrack prior to that?"

"I do."

"When did you leave?"

"I caught Delta Flight 231 from Albany at ten fifteen yesterday."

"In the morning?"

"Yes."

"As in yesterday?"

"Correct."

Detective Johnny Coleman mashed the on-off switch on the recording system in the interview room.

"I'll be right back."

He came back a few minutes later with two cups of coffee. He didn't turn the tape recorder back on.

"You never asked why I called you in and took you to this interrogation room."

Tagliabue looked politely interested but said nothing in reply. Local police would certainly have to consider him an initial suspect as soon as the New York State Police identified Magpie as a mutt from Bath, Maine, with a sheet. Since Marv was also a known associate of Red Fowler, Jack Brunson, and Peter D'Annunzio, he wondered if they also knew that Jack was at the track. Did they manage to locate Jack Brunson? Tagliabue wanted to find out.

"Ain't you curious?"

"Of course. I think cops like to ask questions rather than answer them, so I thought I'd wait until you told me something. I figure something must have happened in upstate New York."

"Yeah, man, something happened. Maybe you can help. Marvin Harris was killed yesterday at Saratoga. Shot through the heart from behind, with a small caliber gun. Probly an assassination. A professional job. The pistol was left behind, no prints, not even on the bullets. Serial number filed off. I knew you were there, at the track, so I figured I better do my due diligence, as they say, and question you. Formally."

"Just because I was in Saratoga?"

"Well, there is a little more to it than that."

The cop fidgeted with his cardboard cup, twirling it on the plastic tabletop, squeezing the sides, watching the steam rise up unsteadily before dissipating in the clammy conditioned air of the room. He sat up abruptly and looked at Tagliabue, making a decision.

"While you were gone I was sweating that dope Henry Sanders, like I promised you. He gets nervous after a while and lets slip that Marv mighta done Joshua White. I get a warrant to search the Harris home down on the creek. Pisses off his wife. He ain't there. We find a semiautomatic in the library. Nice little Sig Sauer .38. It looks like he uses the room as his office, so we take it apart. Meantime, Jason Whitnauer from forensics takes the piece back to test-fire it. He calls me and tells me the ballistics match, the gun shot White. You got no way of knowing that, right?"

"How could I?"

"Right, what I figured. I wanted to talk to all the known associates of Harris, so I called in Peter D'Annunzio, Red Fowler, and Jack Brunson. Never got ahold of Brunson but Mr. D'Annunzio didn't like the sheriff's office, really didn't like this room. Playing the capo is okay in your fancy restaurant when you're holding court with your minions, not so much when the cops are real."

Tagliabue smiled. He liked Coleman using minions but said nothing.

"Something funny?"

"No. I just find your description of Peter being uncomfortable amusing. That's exactly the same assessment I had made of him: all show, no go."

"Yeah." The detective almost smiled himself. "He told me you hurt Fowler and, to keep you reined in, he told you Harris might of been involved with the boat bombing. That true?"

"The miserable pecker-head. Our conversation was supposed to be private."

"Like I said, the man didn't like this place."

"Well, D'Annunzio had secondhand information that Magpie might be connected with Joshua's death and the bombing of *Maven*, but he offered no proof and I haven't found any myself. Is that why you're questioning me?"

"Gotta admit it gives you motive."

Tagliabue had more motive than Coleman knew. His latest brief from The Clemson Project included a personal note from Giselle, the first he'd ever received. "Your boat," she wrote, "will probably be targeted by a known associate of a principal of this exercise, a man known as Marvin George Harris. He lives in your hometown, Bath, and you may even know him. In fact, knowing your moralistic nature, I'm all but certain you do. Harris apparently lives on the periphery of what passes for organized crime in your part of the world.

"I hate to assign you to a local exercise, but you will appreciate that I cannot very well send another agent into your bailiwick without anticipating an interaction between the two of you, so you're it.

"Besides, you must be warned that this man Harris will attempt to sink or seriously damage the cargo boat *Maven*. The attack on the boat will be incidental to your charge here, but our CI mentioned that this principal had plans to seek access to your boat for some activity unrelated to this mission. We don't yet know the identity of this principal, but he may also be someone of your acquaintance.

"Be certain to assure that you do not jeopardize this assignment by confronting Harris and allowing him to infer any leak of confidence from our CI."

Tagliabue had not allowed Magpie to infer much of anything. Giselle's confidential informant was weeks after the fact with his warning about Marv and his bombing of the *Maven*, but his assassination of Marv did apparently send Jack Brunson into hiding. Brunson must be the unknown principal referred to by Giselle. There was no one else Tagliabue knew in or around Bath who could possibly get in the middle of a secret assignment from The Clemson Project. That meant he was moving up in class, as they say on the backstretch. Tagliabue's task now was to root him out first and then complete the assignment. One good way to do that would be to discover the identity of the confidential informant, and trace Brunson through him, or her.

Since Giselle's information about *Maven* was late arriving, he probably could not rely on her team to send him updated local data on time. He had to find out who the CI was, and he had no idea about that. The CI could not be local; he would have known about the holing of *Maven* weeks ago if he was from Bath. Since he did eventually transmit the info about Marv to The Clemson Project, he must at least have a local contact. Tagliabue was betting that local contact was Jack Brunson.

Before he could cogitate further, Detective Coleman had more questions, and a few bits of information.

"Did you see Harris at the racetrack?"

"Can't say that I did," Tagliabue lied. "Saratoga draws good crowds and the weather was nice. I pretty much stayed up in the clubhouse and don't recall seeing the Magpie up there."

"We got some CCTV footage of a guy leaving the scene of the shooting. Bald, white beard. Could be tall. Hard to say with the shot from up on a flagpole. Ring any bells?"

"No, I can't say that it does. You think he's the shooter?"

"No way of knowing. Coulda been any of a hundred guys, all packed into a small area at the finish line. The race ends and everyone leaves at once. Harris falls over. Some woman screams. Nobody goes to his aid except a volunteer fireman. He tries to resuscitate Harris but the man is stone cold by the time a security guard gets there and thinks to secure the area. We don't even have witnesses to question. Even the broad who screamed because Harris fell on her shoes disappeared. All the suspects are gone and we can't ID nobody. Musta been a hit, what I'm thinking."

"I think Marv played around at the edges, so you may be right."

"Yeah. All right, Tagliabue. You can go. I'm gonna check out your alibi, just in case."

Driving home, Tagliabue went over his precautions at Saratoga. He seemed to be covered. If the New York State Police really suspected him and questioned Agnes Ann, they might come up with a discrepancy or two, minor ones. She did know about Maurizio impersonating him. She had no reason to suspect anything else. Did she?

~

"Did you hear about Marv Harris, Aggie?"

"You mean Jack's friend?" He could hear the sudden stress in her voice, as if her larynx had constricted. A second earlier she had been gushing over her filly's bounce-back from her first race and how Manny Ramirez was anxious to ride her again, her voice open and easy. Now she sounded frightened. "What happened?"

"He was killed at the track. Shot."

"My God. We did hear about a murder at the track but I don't remember hearing his name. What does this all mean, Tony? Is Jack involved?"

"I don't know. Has he been around since he talked to Jesse?"

"Not that I know of. We haven't seen him, at least."

Her voice trailed off, the darkness of fear sending her emotions into a slow spiral downward. Tagliabue had known for a while that she was afraid Jack Brunson was going to insinuate his way back into her life somehow. Nothing good could come from that. Jack had purchased the filly, Francine, thought he had made a smart deal to get her, and had recognized the potential in her breeding and conformation. Losing her to a wife he had already lost was not a slight he would forget. His bizarre visit to his son at the stable, even risking fraud at the security office by violating Agnes Ann's restraining order, even if he really had bribed someone so he could get on the backstretch, seemed menacing to Agnes Ann, some sort of prelude to a vendetta. Tagliabue felt the need to reassure her.

"Listen Aggie, I'm searching for Jack Brunson. I think he's here, but if he shows up in Saratoga I want to get back up there. Can you let me know if you hear anything?"

"Yes, of course. Do you think I need to take precautions?"

"The New York State Police are investigating Marv's murder. Have they spoken to you yet?"

"No. I haven't heard a thing."

"Maybe they haven't made the connection. You should contact them. Tell them you're frightened because Jack snuck into the track to visit a son he hasn't seen but once in his life. Tell them I said Jack and Marv Harris were up to something, I just don't know what."

"Tony, I can't do that. They'll suspect you are involved."

"They already suspect that. I've been interrogated by the Bath sheriff's office. And cleared, by the way. I want to put pressure on Jack, beat the bushes, y'know. Flush him out. He has more to worry about right now than the horse you wrangled him out of, believe me. Talking to the law would actually help me."

Agnes Ann was silent for a fat minute. He imagined her thinking of the harm she could do him. Finally, she said: "All right, baby, I'm going to the Saratoga barracks just as soon as I hang up. Is there, ah, is there anything I should not tell them?"

Tagliabue laughed at her tone, the implication that they were kids playing hooky or something and she was the good little girl wanting to keep her boyfriend out of trouble, trouble she suspected he deserved.

"Yeah," he said, "don't mention Maury, and better not tell them about us being immoral on the exercise mat."

She laughed, too, uncertainly at first and then with more conviction. She was strong, he knew, and would handle the police okay.

He hung up and drove to Pelham East. The restaurant was refreshing itself from the lunch rush when he arrived to find Red Fowler at a corner table in the bar nearest the kitchen. Fowler and a younger man, a compact black in jeans and a starched white shirt, sat in front of half-finished bowls of calamari and spaghetti. The younger man's shaved head glistened like a coffee bean. Fowler sat up when he saw Tagliabue. The other man put down his fork.

"Let's talk, Red. Send your butler away."

The man pushed his chair back, but Fowler laid a meaty hand on his arm. Fowler looked at Tagliabue's easy stance and nodded.

"Give us a minute, Beau," he said to his companion. The man walked to the bar and sat on a stool facing the table, squinting, lips tight together. Tagliabue sat down, his back to Beau.

"The sheriff been along about Marv?"

Fowler shook his head, grimaced at the mention of his dead friend. "Not yet. I been expecting them."

"They think you were into something with the Magpie. Peter may have told some tales out of school."

"I'm alibied."

"Not his murder. That's hardly your style anyway, Red. Johnny Coleman suspects you and Jack and Marv were planning some nefarious activity involving . . ."

"Nefarious? What the fuck you talking about?"

"Illegal, like the shit you guys have been pulling around here for years. He probably knows you weren't at Saratoga, but he knows Marv hired Henry and Georgie to bang me around. He probably figures it's not too much of a reach to one of you popping somebody."

"That fucking D'Annunzio. Giving us up. I'm gonna retire."

"Good idea. Living the easy life with Hannah would be better than being behind bars."

"Keep away from us, Anthony. I'm warning your ass now."

"I'll keep away from you, Red, just as soon as you tell me where to find Jack Brunson."

Fowler raised his voice: "I'm telling you . . ."

Tagliabue heard footsteps behind him and turned in his chair to see Beau standing next to him with his hands hanging by his sides. He spoke to Fowler without looking at the redhead. "Spare the boy, Red."

"Leave us alone, Beau. It's okay."

"That your new muscle? I hope he's got a clean sheet, because Coleman is going to be looking."

"He's probly clean. He's a cousin of Hannah's. Likes my style."

"Well, from the look of his tight clothes he's not carrying and he's a bit puny to be throwing his weight around."

"Naw, he ain't nothing to worry you, Anthony. Do me a favor and leave the boy alone. Hannah still ain't too happy with me from the last time you come around."

"Tell me where Jack is hanging out and I'm out of your life. You and bean head there can go on acting like you own the place, for all I care. I don't need any more punching bags."

Fowler's face colored but he made no move. His voice tight, he said: "I heard he's been seen at the Pelham Island."

"Recently?"

"Last night."

Tagliabue got up slowly and walked out the kitchen door. He waited outside for a minute, but no one followed him. Hoping *Maven* was shipshape, he motored down to Cronk's.

~

Her twin exhausts percolating quietly under the green water, *Maven* moved slowly past anchorages and buoys in the channel. She was carrying hay for Agnes Ann's horse farm. Grass was still growing on Westfarrow Island. The weather was warm and rain expected, but it had been dry. The talk of expensive hay for the winter caused her mother's sister, Maybelle Townsend, to order sixty bales from a grower in Woolwich who had a second cutting at a decent price. That gave Tagliabue the excuse he was looking for to visit the island.

When *Maven* made open water, Tagliabue snapped on auto-pilot and made a round of the boat. She had just come from the boatyard, but he felt the need to check out everything anyway, telling himself that he was just being a conscientious navigator. Satisfied finally, he sat in the conning chair and went to cruising speed.

After a smooth voyage, *Maven* made the cove that protected Agnes Ann's property. The house sat back from the sea on a wooded knoll, just visible now that the trees surrounding it were in full leaf. A red, two-story barn was off to the left and fields of grass spread out on all sides of it. Wood fencing stained dark looked to be in good repair.

Bill Hammet, the retired farmer who was caring for the farm in Agnes Ann's absence, met him at the pier in Agnes Ann's flat-bed truck. The two of them unloaded and stored the hay in less than an hour. Since the day had grown hot by the time they were finished, they sat in the shade of a leafy elm with bottles of water and watched the horses grazing placidly.

"Everything looks peaceful enough, Bill."

"Yup. No problems here. The horses stay out to pasture day and night. All I got to do is make sure they got water most days. I brush 'em out and pick their hooves once a week or so. They ain't even got shoes on."

"I know Agnes Ann is glad you're here looking after things."

"Glad to oblige. Easy money for me."

"You get any company out here?"

"Not much. It's not but a few miles from town and the beaches, but it's not on the way nowhere so tourists don't usually find their way here. Once in a while I see a sailboat or some big ol' yacht come by. The cove's not cut in enough for a good anchorage, though, so they don't usually stay. Sometimes when the weather's real calm one might hang out for a while."

"You do any sailing?"

"Nossir. The closest I wanna come to that ugly damn ocean is when we just offloaded your boat now. I like it just fine on dry land."

Tagliabue laughed. "Smart man. Smarter than many who've come to grief at sea."

The men chatted a while longer. Tagliabue asked to borrow the farm pickup.

"Sure enough, Anthony. You drop me off to home and leave the truck here when you're done with it. I'll get a ride over here tomorrow after I go shopping with the wife."

Tagliabue drove into the town called Westfarrow in the ten-year-old Dodge, a sturdy and dependable diesel that had been used often. With the windows open he could hear the right fender flapping as he negotiated the crumbly surface of narrow Ocean Boulevard, named, he thought, with the irony of country people who didn't take their brief summer tourist season too seriously. He could smell burnt fuel rumbling from a leaky muffler. The pickup suited him, blending in with other farm trucks in the crowded village. Visitors mostly flew or sailed in and stayed at the many inns and small hotels that dotted the hills around the main square. A brilliant white coastal cruise ship floated alongside the one long pier in the town marina and people in striped and splotched shorts were filing ashore from her. The Pelham Island was a half-mile along the rocky shoreline from the pier, looking over the harbor and shoals to the west. Tagliabue parked in the lot behind it and watched the place fill up for lunch.

Two hours later, he was tired of sitting in the warmth of a summer's day. Jack Brunson had not showed. Tagliabue exited the truck and stretched, letting the sea breeze air out his shirt and rolling his head around his neck. The weights and bags on the third floor of his building had him feeling fit again. He strolled around to the front of the restaurant and into the bar. The place was alive with chattering customers and hustling waitresses and the tang of the sea. Shuckers were opening clams at the raw bar barely fast enough to fill the demand. Platters of steaming shrimp and crackling mounds of hush puppies were being ferried from the swinging doors of the kitchen into the dining room and out to the beer garden.

Most of the tables Tagliabue could see were filled, but only one caught his attention. Jack Brunson was sitting in a corner with another man. He hadn't seen Brunson pull in by car; he figured he must have come by water. That was worth checking out.

When Brunson saw him walking toward his table, he pointed his beer bottle at him. His companion stood quickly. Tagliabue didn't recognize the man but he knew who he was: Jack's muscle. Thick-necked and ham-fisted, he was slightly shorter than Tagliabue. His lats bulged and didn't quite allow his hands to hang close to his body.

Tagliabue walked up slowly, looking only at Brunson. The muscle watched him, snapped a look at his boss, and caught the same tiny nod Tagliabue saw. He moved to intercept the intruder. Tagliabue banged a straight left into his nose without stopping. He heard the long bone snap. The sound did not carry past the noise of conversation and plate clatter. Blood gushed and the man sat hard. Tagliabue whipped a napkin off the table and pushed it into the man's face.

"You're messing up the restaurant, Bozo. Take a hike."

The man's eyes showed pain, not fear. He moaned when Tagliabue pushed harder. Staggering slightly, he went off, holding the napkin to his broken nose and bent over. Tagliabue sat next to Brunson. A couple at the nearest table watched the muscle leave, their eyebrows raised. Did that big guy just break the other guy's nose? The two of them had walked toward each other but the whole action was like a quick breeze. The man and woman looked at each other, shrugged, and went back to their flounder plates. The confrontation was brief, hardly disturbing the flow of the busy restaurant, and they couldn't be sure they saw what they thought they saw. Two men were sitting quietly at the table next to them now and another man had left with a nosebleed. Had he been hit? Probably not. Brunson whistled two ascending notes softly under his breath.

"You can't act like a gorilla in a nice place like this, Anthony. The Abenaki are going to start calling you Oak Tree Who Breaks Noses."

"If Tiny Tim comes back in here, I'm going to break the rest of his face and then I'm going to take that pea shooter on your hip and smash it through your teeth."

Tagliabue was speaking in a low menacing growl. Brunson smiled.

"You'd frighten me if I didn't know you better."

Tagliabue sat back. "What's that supposed to mean, Jack?"

"It means that Saint Anthony the Great doesn't attack people who are no threat to him. Or his. I know you. I'm not afraid of you. But I'm not going to reach for my piece either."

That brought a slow smile to Tagliabue's lips.

"You're smart, Jack. Evil and slimy, but smart."

"Flattery will get you nowhere, young man. Now, tell me why you felt the need to assassinate Marv. Was he some kind of threat to you?"

"Magpie was involved in the holing of my boat and most probably killed Joshua White. He deserved to die."

"True enough, I guess. I notice you didn't answer my question."

"For a smart guy, Jack, you ask stupid questions. Now answer one of mine."

"Shoot." Brunson smiled again when he said that.

"Don't tempt me."

Brunson laughed. He seemed relaxed, knowing he was in a safe place with witnesses all around. None of them were paying any attention to the two men.

"Why did Marv shoot Joshua?"

"The way I heard it, Joshua saw Marvin leaving your boat that night and confronted him on the pier. You know how he got when he'd had a few. He didn't believe that Marv had gone aboard to look for you and he told him so. I guess he got ugly to Marv. Insulting. They had words, you know what I mean? Marvin was highly pissed. The salty old bastard said he was going to look over the boat to see what Magpie was up to, then he was going to come back with the cops. My understanding is that Marv threatened him with a gun and Joshua told him he didn't have the balls to use it. Turned his back and walked away. Marv shot him, thought he killed him, and ran away."

Tagliabue looked hard at Jack Brunson. The lawyer had put on a few pounds, but it suited his image as a successful man who acted as a power broker for important, and some-times extralegal, people. Other people, businessmen and women, wanted to be represented by an advocate who wasn't afraid to find ways around onerous laws and regulations, ways that resulted from following the adage, "It's easier to ask forgiveness than to ask permission." Brunson made money. He didn't mind letting that fact be known.

In the Pelham Island, at the height of the season, he wore a straw hat with a tropical-flavored silk ribbon around its crown and perfectly fitting linen trousers over glossed golden sandals. His shirt was an Italo Mondo short-sleeved beauty in tan checks, worn outside his pants. The neck of the shirt was open four or five inches, allowing tufts of dark chest hair to grow out of it.

"The Magpie didn't look like he was afraid of the police last time I saw him," Tagliabue said.

"When was that?"

"The day before he died."

Brunson leaned forward and sipped from his bottle of Summit Summer Ale. His clothes moved with him.

"So you were at Saratoga," he said. "I thought I might have seen you but wasn't sure. Why didn't you say hello?"

Tagliabue ignored the question. "Your son was not happy to see you," he said.

Brunson's eyes moved, betraying a slip of emotion. Was it anger, Tagliabue wondered?

"Agnes Ann has a restraining order keeping you from bothering him."

Brunson grunted out a quick grimace. "Agnes, Agnes. God, she never lets it go. Can you believe it? She filed a complaint with security. I couldn't even get on the backstretch after that. It took me a fucking week to get the order rescinded and even then I had to agree not to visit their stable. She's going to ruin my reputation."

"I'm going to ruin more than that if you bother her again."

Jack Brunson nodded his head and put the bottle down with a clunk. Still leaning his elbows on the table, he looked over his shoulder at Tagliabue.

"I know what havoc you can wreak, Anthony, but I've got to tell you that Agnes worries me more. She's a vindictive woman.

Tell her, will you, that I have no more designs on her filly? She's a fine racehorse and I'm sick about losing her in the divorce, but I can see that I'll never get her back. I am going to put my money on her every damn time she runs though.

"And let her know that I won't try to see my son again. That was some kind of stupid inspiration or something, and I was sorry I did it. He does look like he's growing into a man without me, and I'm going to keep it that way."

Promises from Jack Brunson meant little, but Tagliabue knew he had done what he could to keep him away from Agnes Ann and Jesse. The muscle was out in the front parking lot, still trying to stem his nosebleed. That would be another man to keep an eye on, he and Brunson both.

Tagliabue got up and left. On the drive back to Agnes Ann's farm, he thought over what he'd learned. Jack Brunson had hired protection and was carrying. He didn't seem worried about a threat from Tagliabue and had promised to leave Agnes Ann and Jesse alone. That probably meant that hiring the muscleman to protect him had to do, somehow, with the assignment from The Clemson Project. He was now more convinced than ever that Brunson was the local guy who might get in the middle of his assignment from Giselle. Tagliabue didn't figure Brunson as Giselle's confidential informant; however, he could very well be the guy mentioned by that CI.

He had hoped to separate the two aspects of his dealing with Agnes Ann's ex and figured he had done that. Now he could concentrate on his job, fully anticipating having to deal with Brunson and Broken Nose again. He just didn't know when or in what capacity. One of the things he liked best about working for Giselle was the lack of predictability in her assignments.

Maven was at the old pier in front of the farm, a dowdy working woman resting from her labors. Tagliabue felt a tug of affection for the boat as he walked down to her and stepped aboard. The diesels started on the first try, as they always seemed to do. He let them warm up while he took in lines and coiled them on deck. The boat drifted out into the stream. When she was far enough, Tagliabue pushed the throttles forward and set sail for Westfarrow Town.

CHAPTER FIFTEEN

Tagliabue met Serge Poklov, the harbormaster for Westfarrow, halfway down the pier from where he had docked *Maven*. The men shook hands.

"How long you staying, Anthony?"

"Couple days, maybe. You got room, Serge?"

"Til the weekend, then we got some reservations. You want to stay longer, it's okay. I can work around your boat."

"She's going to stand out among all the yachts."

"Don't worry about it. Adds color to the place, know what I mean?"

Tagliabue laughed. "Okay, thanks. I'll give you as much notice as I can."

He shopped in town and brought the groceries back to his boat, settling in for supper in the day cabin and galley that lay forward and below the conning station. He had set the space up as his berth and dining area. Once on shore power, *Maven* had air conditioning and music. Tagliabue poached a piece of bluefish in scallions and chicken broth to go with a baguette and slaw as Chopin tinkled from the speakers below deck. Life in a hotel couldn't be better than this, he thought.

Tagliabue and his mate spent many nights in the same cabin, although when Joshua cooked it was more often grilled meat topside. His death was beginning to look as if it was caused by the conflation of physical men and colliding mores, lit off by alcohol and past grievances, not too unusual in Tagliabue's world. Joshua's murder and the holing of *Maven* may have been part of a plan to recapture Agnes Ann's horse, probably instigated by Jack Brunson. That scenario seemed unlikely to Tagliabue, a scheme too convoluted to work. Brunson was up to something that affected more than a boat and a horse. Joshua may have been no more than collateral damage.

That night, after the parties ended and most people were back from their dinners and drinks, Tagliabue opened the portholes in *Maven's* cabin and turned off the A/C. The only sounds were those of the anchorage: stays chiming in the breeze, fenders scrubbing against the soft wood of the dock, and oily harbor water slurping hulls. The salted air wafting into the cabin smelled fresh and clean. He sighed and lay back on a bunk.

When he woke, it was still black outside. Something had changed. *Maven* wasn't moving. The wind was quiet. What had changed?

He slipped from under the blanket and moved silently to the cabin door, pulling his Glock from the wall pin where it hung. He listened. A faint sound, maybe someone catching a breath on the main deck aft of the cabin, reached his ears. He moved forward slowly on bare feet, not wanting to rock the beamy boat, staying to the middle. Unscrewing the hatch to the fo'c'sle in slow turns, glad he kept it lubricated, he pushed it open. Hinged on the forward side, the hatch opened so that he could see down the length of the cabin roof. It also meant the back of his head would now be in the sights of any intruder behind the cabin or in the conning station.

Climbing out, Tagliabue duck walked to the conning station and jerked back the slide of his gun. The clashing metallic noise was loud in the quiet night.

"Shit," came a sharp whisper from the stern. "Don't shoot me, Anthony."

Tagliabue still could not see anyone.

"Stand up, slowly," he said.

A shadow rose up into the starlight, arms in the air.

"It's me . . ."

"Quiet."

Tagliabue listened, peered hard into the darkness. He could hear only his heart pounding in his chest and could see nothing moving on board *Maven*. He crawled down the catwalk of the port gunwale and dropped into the conning station soundlessly. The station was open to the stern, so he could see the shadow of a figure standing with his arms raised. When he flipped a toggle switch and harsh light flooded the outside of the deck, the figure cringed but did not duck.

"Kill the lights, Anthony," he whispered hard. "I don't want nobody to see me, man."

Tagliabue switched off the lights.

"Come to me slowly, Timmy. You've got me nervous."

Timothy O'Brien moved forward quietly, placing his feet with care. His night vision was shot. Tagliabue's was almost as bad, but the spots had been trained on the intruder and he had closed one eye when he threw the switch, so he could see the man approach. When he was certain it was Timmy, Tagliabue sat in the port chair in the pilothouse, his weapon on his lap, a round in the chamber. He pointed at the other chair. The young bartender sat. He left his backpack on.

"What are you doing here, son?"

"Peter sends me over in July. This joint here is packed every day and they need my help."

"What's your wife think of that arrangement?"

"Oh, she loves it, Anthony. The job comes with an apartment. It ain't much but the kids are outdoors all day anyway. It's like a vacation for them."

"Why aren't you home with them now? It'll be light in an hour or two."

"I'm the closer, so we don't shut down until three and cleanup takes me another hour at least. I don't get no days off this month, but I don't go in until nine at night. I'll take a nap when I get home, then we'll all go out for pancakes. I'm taking Frances and the boys to dig some quahogs and maybe fish off the pier."

His smile threatened to light up the cockpit as he spoke. Tagliabue took his hand off the Glock. Before he could ask Timmy why he came aboard *Maven* at four in the morning, the bartender began to speak. The words came out low and in a rush.

"I'm working the stick tonight and these two guys come in. I never seen them before. They sit at the far end and talk to each other, so I leave them alone. But when I'm serving someone close to them, I hear one guy mention Mr. Brunson. After that, I make a point of paying attention when I can. I hear the other guy, the Indian, say something about the *Maven*—at least I think that's what he said. Both guys are kinda shady-looking, know what I mean? So I figured I better warn you since your boat's tied up here and all."

O'Brien looked expectantly at Tagliabue, who nodded.

"Can you describe these guys, Timmy?"

"Yeah. The Indian is kinda tall and built. Young. Long black hair in a ponytail. Dark skin. Nose kinda like a hatchet. The other dude is older and running to fat. Greasy hair and not much of it. Needs a shave. Average height. Chews cigars and looks kinda like one of Peter D'Annunzio's boys but I didn't recognize him from the Pelham East. Talks like a tough guy. Oh, and I think he's got a gun stuck under his shirt."

"What did the Indian sound like?"

"I actually didn't hear him say much, but he sounded kinda choppy, something like old Juan in the kitchen over on the mainland."

Juan Gonzalez was a dishwasher and general handyman at the Pelham East. Everyone suspected he was an illegal but nobody cared. He showed up every day and worked hard at a job no one else wanted.

Tagliabue nodded. "Thanks, Timmy. You did me a favor telling me this. Next time call, eh?"

"I ain't got your cell number, Anthony. I didn't want to wait in case they were up to no good and you here sleeping without warning or nothing. Course, now I know they ain't about to sneak up on you, sleeping or not."

The young barman had a sheepish look on his face, a smile on his lips, and a frown in the corners of his eyes. Tagliabue gave him a card with his number on it.

"Buzz me if you see them again, could you? Don't talk. If I see your number, I'll know what the message is. Okay?"

"I'll do that, Anthony. You take care of yourself."

As he got up to leave, he turned back and said: "You know what you need, Anthony? A dog. A little dog you can carry around who'll bark if anyone comes aboard."

He was laughing quietly, in a snuffling manner, as he stepped ashore. Tagliabue was smiling widely himself as he watched his friend move quickly and quietly across the dim yellow patches that barely reached the planking as they bled from the hooded and rusted lamps of the city marina. He wondered briefly how Polly and old Tom Sharkey were making out. He promised himself that he would visit them when he returned to Bath.

A faint line of light painted the horizon between the clear gray sky and the black ocean. Daybreak was less than an hour away so he decided he'd not get any more sleep if he hit the bunk again. He went below and secured himself in the cabin. Placing the locked and loaded Glock on the table in front of him, he worked the dial of a thin paper safe hidden in his chart drawer and slid out his notes on the mission he was currently assigned. The notes were a series of marks and symbols he felt confident no one else could begin to decipher. That, he thought, covered the ultimatum from Giselle to commit to memory the details of each assignment. This one was too intricate, and too important, to rely on his brain cells alone. For the first time, written details of the mission seemed important, if not the names involved or the code phrase and reply. He looked the hieroglyphics over for the third time, reminding himself again that the go-day was forty-eight hours away. The course and speed to arrive at the target coordinates on time were penciled on the chart table, but he still needed updated data points and he had no means of communicating with The Clemson Project. He was in-harbor at Westfarrow to meet his contact, not knowing who he was or what he looked like. The contact was supposed to meet him at Pelham East and identify himself, or herself.

The daylight hours passed, a perfect summer day with brilliant sunshine reflecting off calm seas. Tagliabue worked topside on his boat, smelling the warmed tar from the marina pilings and the coconut oil slicked on holiday shoulders. He bought a tomato can of worms from a small boy for two dollars and jigged a flounder off the side of *Maven*. He grilled it whole on a hibachi and ate it for supper with a hard roll and a can of V-8 juice.

As he was cleaning up in the galley, his cell phone rang. Once. He reached for it and checked the caller's number: Timmy. He showered in the tiny head and dressed in a fishing shirt and jeans. Slipping into his sandals, he strolled down to the Pelham Island. There was a line outside the place and the bar section was full. Every stool at the long mahogany bar was taken, including one by a Latino man in a brilliant white linen guayabera. Tagliabue worked his way through the loud crowd until he was to one side of the man in the Cuban shirt. The bartender caught his raised hand and came over.

"*Una cuba libre, por favor.*"

The barkeep nodded, glanced at the Latino man with a wry smile, and reached into the speed well. The man in the white shirt said: "Tha's a good drink for theese weather, *señor*."

"Indeed," Tagliabue replied. "I think I'll drink it outside where I can breathe."

He went out to the restaurant's dock and leaned against a bollard under a string of colored lanterns and tasted the rum and limed cola. A sea breeze swept away both the mosquitos and a lot of the people noise from the restaurant. Other folks drank at benches that lined the Pelham's seaside property. Some ate fish and chips from cardboard boats. They looked relaxed and touristy. He could detect no immediate threats.

When the man in the guayabera came outside, they walked down the dock looking at boats tied up alongside.

"You are surprised to find a Mexican as your contact, *señor*? I can call you Antonio?"

"Please. I was very surprised. I thought it was going to be the guy with you last night."

"Oh, no. I came a day early to look the place over. When I see he is carrying, I figure I better see what he's up to."

"You think it was me?"

The Mexican laughed.

"Oh, no. I knew absolutely what you look like."

"That damn Giselle," Tagliabue said. "She's always one step ahead of me."

They both laughed at that.

"What's your name, *amigo*?"

"I am Carlos."

"Your English is good, much better than when you were at the bar."

"Thank you. No one expects an illegal alien to be a US spy, eh?"

"Are you really an illegal?"

"Yes. The Clemson Project recruited me from a cell in Brownsville. They look always for the unusual, in everything they do. So, here we are. Come aboard and we can finalize plans, eh?"

They were standing by a twenty-one-foot Carolina Skiff with a dark blue hull and an enormous four-cycle engine on the back. Carlos stepped aboard, the wide craft barely rocking, and stood in the cockpit under a Bimini top. Tagliabue looked at him, a dark muscular man maybe six feet tall, with shiny black hair tied in a ponytail. His Inca blood showed in his high cheekbones and chiseled face. His chiseled, expressionless face.

"This your boat?"

"Mine to use."

"The rescue vessel." Tagliabue said it as a statement, not a question. He began to see the possibilities in his mind. He boarded the fishing speedboat and sat in the stern sheets. The cushions were just beginning to pick up some moisture from the balmy night air.

"This should do nicely."

"*Sí*. She's full of pockets in the fiberglass so they can't sink her unless they get to use their big gun. We must avoid that."

The two operatives sat facing each other and spoke quietly. The plan was to hide the skiff alongside the *Maven* as they motored out to the rendezvous point, take the defector on board the smaller boat, and spirit him away in it as the *Maven* provided cover. The skiff drew less than a foot, so Carlos was to make for one of the hidden coves inland from the vast fishing grounds off Maine fed by an estuary and drive the small boat upriver to safety. They decided to work out the details on *Maven* the next day. First, they had another problem to deal with.

"Who's the man with the gun you drank with last night?"

"Don't know. He wouldn't give his name. Thinks he's a wise guy. You know, talks tough, carries a nine on his belt so I can see it. A Glock. Nice gun. Him, not so nice."

"He threaten you or anything?"

"No, no, Antonio. I just act like a migrant, you know. He treats me like a *niño*. So I let him run his mouth. He drinks too much. He says he muscle for a guy name of Brunson. I think that's a lie too. He's too old for that job. And he acts more like a *jefe*, a boss. You know?"

Carlos saw that Tagliabue recognized the name. "He involved with this op?"

"I hope not, but if he is, he's not with us," Tagliabue answered.

"Maybe I better talk with him some more."

"Maybe. Before we go tomorrow night. We don't need any interference from ashore."

"No, sir. We have our hands full with the Russian ship, I think."

"Why don't you take him for a boat ride?"

The Mexican smiled. "Good idea."

Back in the busy bar, Tagliabue didn't see Jack Brunson or the man whose nose he had broken the day before. He and Carlos had separated on the dock, so he ordered another Cuba libre and waited for his partner to enter. The bartender took his second twenty. "Thanks," he said. "You Anthony?"

"Yeah."

"Timmy's in the kitchen. He don't come on for another half hour, but he wants to see you."

"Okay, pal. Thanks."

Tagliabue knew the kitchen layout from his deliveries, so he went out the front door of the bar and worked his way around back. He found Timmy O'Brien chatting with a waitress on a smoke break near the back door of the kitchen. O'Brien slipped something into his pocket as she smiled at Tagliabue from her seat at a card table on a concrete pad under a spreading chestnut. The air smelled vaguely of wet garbage and mud flats. The waitress blew a stream of smoke straight up in front of herself. "You wanna eat with the help, big guy?"

Before Tagliabue could reply, O'Brien told her he was a friend and that they had business to discuss. She nodded and field stripped her cigarette, watching Tagliabue all the while. As she got up to go back to work, she spoke to him again. "When you're ready to eat, sit at station five. I give good service." Then she winked. O'Brien and Tagliabue laughed.

"This is a wild place in the summer."

"Sure is, Anthony. Good thing Frances is with me."

Tagliabue sat where the waitress had been. "This a good place to talk?"

Timmy looked around and nodded. They could hear a steady rattle of activity from inside the kitchen but no one was about outside. The kitchen and break area were on the town side of the Pelham Island and there was no walkway to it from the restaurant or bar. Customers would not be strolling by. The area was lit by a single hooded lamp over the back door that allowed some dark patches around the edges of the concrete pad, but Tagliabue could sense no presence anywhere. Still, he spoke softly.

"I got your call, Timmy, and met my man. Is there something else on your mind?"

"Well, y'know I told you about the guy who seems to be carrying, the older guy not the Indian? He was sitting with Jack Brunson and some big fella with a bandage over his nose in the back of a fancy sportfisherman that come by when I was fishing off Tillman's Pier earlier."

"They see you?"

"Maybe, I don't know for sure. They was pretty busy talking to each other. Anyway, I was wearing a straw hat cause I'm getting too much sun and I had the boys with me, so he probly don't recognize me if he sees me. I ain't sure if Mr. Brunson knows who I am anyway."

He knows, Tagliabue thought to himself.

"Okay, thanks, Timmy. You've done enough. There's going to be some nasty stuff come down in the next day or two and I don't want you to get involved. Don't contact me again unless it's something really critical, okay?"

"I gotcha, Anthony. I'm off to work. You take care of yourself."

After O'Brien went in through the back door of the kitchen, Tagliabue strolled across the lawns back to the bar, thinking about this new development. Who was this other character? He showed up just as the operation is set to go down and has apparently befriended Jack Brunson. Is Brunson part of this after all? Giselle's written warning to him was not specific about Brunson's role in the defector op, if he had any role at all.

There was no one he recognized in the bar until he saw Carlos enter from the far end of the dining room. He stood in the crowd finishing his drink. Carlos passed by him.

"Nobody," the Mexican said. "Midnight, eh?"

"*Sí.*"

Carlos smiled and left the bar.

Tagliabue spent the next two hours searching for Jack Brunson. He figured the man would be staying at The Commodore, the only luxury hotel on the island, but the clerk on duty would not confirm that Brunson was staying there, or if he was, what room he was staying in.

"We do not give out that kind of information on our guests, sir. You are welcome to leave a message."

"So, he is staying here?"

"I'm not saying that."

"Well, why would I leave a message for someone who may not be here?"

The front desk clerk was a young man with a deep tan, probably one of the many college students who take summer night jobs in the resort community and spend their days in play on the beaches and golf courses of the island. He was polite enough but adamant, probably doing exactly as instructed, Tagliabue thought. Rather than bully the clerk, he left to have a drink in the small hotel bar, where he hoped to probe around a tad before giving up. It just seemed as if The Commodore would be Jack's domicile of choice while on the island.

The barroom was quiet, a four-top chatting, a couple in the far corner, and an empty bar. He stood at the bar and was sipping a pony of Cointreau when the hotel security guard walked in a few minutes later. As the uniform angled for Tagliabue, the bartender caught some signal and left for the back room. The guard stood straight backed next to Tagliabue, who leaned with his elbows on the padded bar edge. He wore a white mustache with a potbelly pushing the buttons of his blue shirt. He spoke in a quiet voice that did not carry.

"I mighta known it was you, Anthony."

"Hey, Bob."

"The boy at the desk is nervous. Thinks you're here to cause trouble."

He spoke facing Tagliabue. Neither man smiled. Tagliabue did not look at the cop. If anyone was interested enough to observe them, the two did not appear to be anything more than a hotel dick checking on a stranger.

"I want to find out if Jack Brunson is staying here."

"He was. For the whole of last week. I haven't seen him today, so he may have checked out. You need to know if he's gone? I can probably find out later tonight."

"No. Tell me, though: does he usually stay here when he's on the island?"

"Yeah. He has a place in New York, down by Saratoga. He's usually there when the track is open. On some kind of lake. He stays there a lot, I hear, but usually takes a room here once our season starts. Maybe a coupla weeks in July."

"A summer house in New York?"

"Yeah, some sort of cabin. On a lake named like some kind of berry."

The two were quiet for a minute, the security guy looking hard at Tagliabue, pretending to be rousting him.

"Anything else, Anthony?"

"No, thanks, Bob. I just needed to know where he's berthed for the next day or two."

Pushing the remains of a twenty into the tray, Tagliabue left the bar. Bob followed ten feet behind, watching until he was back in the street. The clerk nodded his appreciation and Bob went back to the kitchen and his plate of *boeuf bourguignon*.

Tagliabue sat on the roof of the pilothouse on *Maven* until Carlos appeared as suddenly and silently as a wraith. The night had turned humid, a mist threatening. The air conditioning was thrumming away in *Maven's* cabin, so the two men repaired to that space to talk.

"You find out anything about the guy with Brunson?"

"*Nada*," Carlos answered. "He like disappeared. The man Brunson and his muscle too. You worried, Antonio, that they may be here to get in our way or something?"

"I don't know anything for sure, but both turning up here on Westfarrow just at this time is worrying."

"You worried enough to want to cancel?"

"No. This is really our only chance. The *Leonov* may be transiting out for good, for all we know. We'd better stick to Plan A. I do think we should get out of port ASAP. What time is your contact blast?"

"One fourteen."

"Just over an hour now. Okay. Go get your speedboat and meet me at buoy Charlie."

"On my way, *amigo*."

"Carlos."

"*Sí?*"

"Be extra careful. Time is getting short. If they're going to interfere in any way, it's got to be soon. Keep a round in the pipe and your piece in your hand. Got it?'

"Yes. I see you at the sea buoy."

Then he was gone. Tagliabue killed the air and disconnected from shore power. He eased *Maven* away from the dock and puttered out to sea. Visibility was worsening. A dirty night could help, he thought. He and Carlos had the coordinates and could navigate by radar. Anyone out to foil their plans would have to track them. First, though, he had to find Carlos and his skiff.

Barely keeping way on, with no lights showing, he maneuvered *Maven* between the green buoy to starboard and the red bell buoy to port. He had picked Charlie because there was some room to navigate on either side of it, but it was a channel marker and still inland from open water. The radar screen showed a blip that was the buoy dead ahead. There was no sign of a small craft in the area. Letting *Maven* drift to a stop, he searched with glasses and listened. The mist was thickening. The air felt suffocating and deadly silent. Time passed. Checking the radar again, Tagliabue figured he had roughly another three minutes before he'd have to get way on or risk grounding on a sandbar to leeward. Then he saw a brief flash of white light.

Answering with a click of his flashlight, Tagliabue ran low to the stern of his vessel. He had the Glock on his hip and an

AR-15 in one hand. He crouched behind the bulkhead, listening. The Suzuki on the back of Carlos's skiff was quiet at idle. If it was Carlos who had signaled with his spot, Tagliabue couldn't hear him. He waited. *Maven* drifted slowly toward shore. The lighthouse horn sounded, indicating fog. After that, it got quiet again. A form eased into sight, close enough to *Maven* that it startled Tagliabue.

"You going to have a beach party pretty quick, *señor*."

The skiff was practically alongside before Tagliabue could positively identify it. The dark hull and low profile hid it well in the darkness. It would be a good vessel for the operation, difficult for the ship to see if Carlos kept it nestled to *Maven's* side.

"You're right, Carlos. I think I hear waves breaking. Tie off and let me get out of here."

He moved forward quickly, grateful that he knew the boat so well he didn't need lights. He leaped into the conning station, noted the red blinking light on the SONAR screen indicating shoal water, and thrust the throttles forward. *Maven's* screws churned up sand beneath them as they caught water and pushed the boat ahead. In seconds, they were back in the channel and heading for the sea, the skiff bumping in their wake, bow high and made fast to one of *Maven's* stern cleats. He slowed to five knots just as Carlos slipped into the second seat.

"We got plenty of time, Antonio."

"I know. What's your latest ETA?"

The other man unzipped his briefcase and extracted a radio the size of a thick iPad. He tapped buttons and read green text.

"It's a go. Our man is bailing at 0114 local. Expected coordinates are 44°49′1.45″north and 68°12′12.8″west. Look like a few miles outside something called Georges Bank."

"Aye, that's a major fishing section just off the coast."

Tagliabue knew the area but he plotted the coordinates on the chart table anyway. They were making for the Great South Channel, which would take them past the fishing grounds and out to deeper water. They would be picking up a few night netters soon, and they hoped to be mistaken for one of them when their quarry came into radar range. Of course, the range on the *Viktor Leonov's* systems was four times as great as the one antenna on *Maven* provided. Maybe the Russians were watching them already.

"What do you know about the ship, Carlos?"

"I know more than I want to. She is a Vishnya-class intelligence-gathering ship, three hundred feet long." He sounded as if he were reading from a script. Tagliabue figured he had received his own brief from Giselle, different from his. She was always compartmentalizing her troops. "It can go about sixteen, er, knots. She has missiles but for airplanes, nothing we have to worry about."

"Guns?"

"Big machine guns fore and aft, one cannon, three inches."

"Troops?"

"She carries maybe two hundred men and at least a couple of small craft that could chase after us."

"But she's a foreign warship and has to stay in international waters."

"Right. And Vladimir Putin is not allowed to murder political dissidents."

Tagliabue chuckled sardonically at Carlos's witticism, knowing well that the sailors on the *Leonov* would stop at nothing to prevent a defection if they found out about it. This was a dangerous strategy, putting a slow, unarmed cargo boat in the proximity of a Russian naval vessel to extract a man, a communications expert, who wanted to live in a free country, in the hopes that the target warship would not suspect the wallowing *Maven* of such an activity. It was bold, maybe even workable.

But the plan could only work at all if Tagliabue had his boat on the exact spot on a major ocean, in the dark and mist, at the exact time the defector jumped overboard. The *Maven* had to appear to be part of the fishing fleet on Georges Bank, to be drifting out to sea a ways in pursuit of haddock. The Russians could not know with certainty from their course out in open water just where the Grand Banks ended. Tagliabue plotted carefully, using Loran fixes and his GPS. When they made the banks, other boats were around, showing on the radar screen as points of blurred lights, seven in all. Tagliabue had then to slow even more and move sporadically, as a fisherman might in his search for schools of fish. If he drove straight through the fishing fleet, a sharp radar-man on the Russian ship would spot an anomaly and report it, no matter how slowly *Maven* steamed.

Carlos manned the radar scope, calling out directions and distances to other vessels. Suddenly he straightened.

"Antonio," he whispered in an urgent tone. "Something is moving fast."

Carlos was tracking a bogey coming through the Great South Channel at speed, maybe twenty-five knots, dangerously fast in the prevailing conditions. It was too big a signal for a speedboat, too small for a ship. Tagliabue scanned the channel with his big binoculars but could see nothing in the dark mist.

"No running lights."

"A big boat, I'm thinking. Maybe forty, fifty feet."

"We'd better plot that sucker, *amigo*. I don't know what she could be doing out here this time of night."

Carlos nodded his agreement, both men thinking of Jack Brunson and the other two armed men in the big yacht Timmy O'Brien had seen them riding earlier in the day. Tagliabue scrubbed his face with his hand: This operation is turning out to be even more complicated than he had imagined.

CHAPTER SIXTEEN

AGNES ANN

I know Tony is embroiled in another of his secretive, and complicated, operations for that government woman Giselle. I know also that she is no competition for his affections, but I still can't avoid a little twinge of jealousy when I think about her. She's such a sophisticate compared to me, so worldly and knowledgeable, and compels so much of my man's attention. Still, he goes for months at a time without any contact with her. Now, however, he is on some sort of assignment and is incommunicado with me. I understand that he must concentrate on it—it would be unfair for me to either want to discuss it with him, as most wives discuss their husbands' work with them, or to demand his attention when he surely must concentrate it all on the task he's been assigned—but I hate the long days of no texts or phone calls from him.

I want to tell Tony about Francine's progress. And about Jesse's, for that matter. They seem a perfectly suited pair, working together on the training track as they both learn more about racing and mature into two elegant and powerful animals. Jesse is turning into a man already with the responsibilities Jacob Collier is placing on him, so much more mature than the boys I remember from high school, or college for that matter. He's probably more responsible than Jack was in college.

We're going easy with the filly. She seems eager to run but is a fragile two-year-old. Burdened with memories of other youngsters who injured themselves by coming up too fast, Mr. Collier—funny I call him that and my son calls him Jake, almost as if our roles have been reversed at the racetrack—is being deliberate with her schedule. I am the final arbiter about entry decisions, since I actually am the owner, but really all I do is listen to Jake and Jesse and affirm their opinions.

The latest of those is to run her in a Grade 3 Handicap race at Belmont in September, but we are weighing the possibility of entering her in one of the lesser races on the Travers Stakes card on the last Sunday before Saratoga closes for the year. There are a lot of races for two-year-olds at Saratoga, in fact the place is famous for that. The track features four good races before the big Travers Stakes, and one of them is the Prima Donna, for fillies. If we run Francine in that race, she won't race again until October, so I'm kind of hoping the boys decide on that one. That way, I could go back to Westfarrow after the race and let Jake and Jesse board and train, and rest, my horse.

After our big win in her maiden race, we're not going to be sneaking up on the competition anymore. So the odds won't be much good but the purse, for the Prima Donna is big enough to cover Francine's expenses until the three-year-old season begins, even if we only come in third or fourth.

If the horse herself had a say in the decision, she would opt for the race at Saratoga. She is eating well and literally feeling her oats. Jesse says she can be a handful on the Oklahoma Training Track.

"She wants to run hard, all the time," he says. "She's learning to rate but it's against her nature. She's a powerhouse."

The three of us are scheduled to have a discussion after Thursday morning's training session. I think we'll have to make a decision then. The Prima Donna is but two weeks away and entries will close Friday at noon. We could get in later, but it costs extra.

~

We meet in the tack room of Francine's stable thirty minutes after the filly had worked a fast three furlongs, thirty-five seconds, under a hand ride. Mr. Collier seems to be making an effort to contain an emotion: his face is calm but he isn't lounging in his chair as he usually does. He's a man who has suffered heartbreak and many disappointments on the track in his decades of training thorough-bred racehorses, so he has learned to temper enthusiasm and to accept discouragement. I think he has lost some of the gambler's drive that the top-line trainers possess because of the bad times he has experienced over the years, the willingness to take a chance on intuition. He has built a protective cage around his emotions, afraid to allow himself to be infected with enthusiasm.

Collier makes a good living as a trainer, mostly for the reason I have retained his service: he is a safe and cautious trainer, put-ting the animal's welfare first. He also has a secure and secluded barn on Heal Eddy, where young horses and older ones who had suffered in their racing careers can grow in strength and expertise. I think, but cannot confirm, that he dislikes running two-year-olds in races at all because of their vulnerabilities. Their leg and ankle bones, in particular, are not always ready to accept the stress of hard running with a person on board.

Before we get to talk about the results of her one hard work since her maiden race, Francine's exercise rider, and Jacob Collier's emotional opposite, comes through the door like a gale through a harbor. Jesse's face is alight, his hair in disarray and his smile splitting the bottom of his face. My son comes in fast, practically jumping into the third chair at the old, scarred table. His feelings bubble from his mouth as if they can't wait to get out.

"Man, did you see her blast by Tommy's colt? I wasn't even urging her, just sitting there in awe and letting her run. After three, I had to practically sing a lullaby to her to get her to slow down. Damn, that was fun!"

I have to laugh at his youthful enthusiasm, and even Mr. Col-lier smiles. The boy can see the stars from where he's sitting, and he doesn't want to look down into the darkness below.

"You get her cooled down all the way?" Collier asks.

"Yessir. She was so fired up it took longer than usual. That's why I'm late to this meeting. I think she wanted to go back out and run some more."

Jesse shakes his head and fans himself with some training records.

"Well," I say, "at least we know where Jesse stands about entering the Prima Donna."

"In truth, Mom! Old Francie is ready for another race. I felt her legs, Jake. No heat anywhere. She's steady on her feet and eating well. Her eyes are clear."

"Assuming your diagnosis is correct, young fella," drawls Collier, "and she shows no problems later today, I agree that she is ready for another race. The question is, do we want to run her here, and miss most of the Belmont meet, or run her twice in New York before Christmas?"

"You feel three races is sufficient for her as a two-year-old?"

"Two or three. Yes, I do, ma'am. If she rests and trains at Heal Eddy over the winter, she should be strong and fast for her three-year-old season. That's where the money is, and that's when we find out if she's really any good."

"Oh, she's good. Real good."

The old trainer looks with a squint at Jesse. I ask if her work this morning was good.

"Three furlongs under a hand ride, without asking her to run, in thirty-five seconds?" he asks rhetorically. "That's a good time, but it's only a workout, no stress, no other horses to beat, no crowd noise. I mean, it's a good indicator but only that."

"She's a gamer, Jake. Look how she ran last time out."

"That was an $80,000 race against maidens, horses who had never won before—and still haven't, by the way. The Prima Donna is a stakes race. Much better competition."

That opinion slows Jesse a bit, but only a bit. "We got to find out how good she is, Jake."

"How do you feel about this Miss Agnes? She is your horse, after all."

"If you think she's sound and can run this soon without hurting herself, then I think we should try the Prima Donna. I know it's a graded race, but we're still playing with track money after her maiden win last month. Her winnings will cover her entry fee and even winter boarding, I think, so financially we're okay."

Jacob Collier grunts.

I continue. "If you think she's strong enough, Mr. Collier, I'm in."

Jesse pats me on the back, smiling and nodding. Collier nods also, slowly.

"Okay. If she wakes up in good shape tomorrow, I'll submit her entry to the Prima Donna."

Jesse and I high-five while Jacob Collier busies himself with paperwork on the desk. I think he is secretly pleased to be running Francine again. He is one of those people who is afraid to think about too much success, afraid because the opportunity for the disappointment of failure is too great. He has suffered so much disappointment in his career that he lives in fear of optimism. Still he has a horse in Francine who has potential. Who knows how many more chances he was going to get? Not that he's ready to keel over or anything. It's just that he's getting the reputation as a middling trainer and is already attracting owners of middling racehorses. This way, if something goes wrong with my filly, he could always say, to himself at least, that Francine's owner wanted to run her in the Prima Donna.

～

I'm thrilled to have a horse in a big race and itching to tell Tony about it. He's busy with his secret agent business, however, so I didn't text him. When he can, he will initiate communications again. I already know from Auntie Maybelle that he has been on the island, his crusty workboat tied up at the city marina among the sloops and trawler yachts of the summer season.

"He's not shy about taking his place in society, is he Agnes?" she texted.

I laughed at that. Maybelle has a hard time placing Tony. He is always courteous to her and the couple of times we went to fancy restaurants or to a summer ball on Westfarrow with her, he always dressed appropriately and knew what wine to order. He's an enigma to her, but not to me. He learns as he lives, and he lives in many guises and in many locales. When he's boat captain, he acts like a sailor; when he's with the yachting crowd, he acts like a yachtsman.

I wish he were near so we could live the excitement of another race with our own horse contending, but I'm determined to live it myself so I can tell him what it was like running on Travers Day.

The hard work seems not to affect the filly in the least, but one could not say the same about the horse people on the backstretch. As she frolics about in a distance gallop the next day, grooms and hot walkers are abuzz about her time in the three-furlong work. I hang about the stable listening to their excited jabber in the many accents of the people employed by the different barns and trainers. Most seem to think that my horse had qualified herself for better company, maybe even a try at the Kentucky Oaks next spring. We would all soon see about that.

∾

Travers Day, the final race card of the meeting at Saratoga Race Course and the unofficial end to the summer season in Saratoga Springs, does not have a good beginning. Rain and mist drift in from the Hudson River and spread down the sides of the Adirondack Mountains into The Spa, blurring the dawn. I walk along the shedrow early, the drops of rain splattering off the plastic rain gear I'm wearing, sounding like minnows jumping in a pond. The other horses in their stalls, looking at me in the hopes I might be their grooms bringing breakfast, seem to be perky and alert despite the rain, or maybe because of it. It's a cool morning after a long hot season.

Francine is already chomping at her sweet feed when I get to Barn Sixteen and she ignores me completely. I feel happy to be in her presence nonetheless. She's a beautiful critter, full of life and joy. All she wants is to enjoy her health and be allowed the opportunity to run. Her stall has already been mucked, so it's filled with the fragrance of straw and horse. The experience of standing there is sublime: the only noise the grinding of oats in the animal's mouth and the thunk of her hooves as she shifts; the sweet air and the sensation of being protected from the weather combine to bring a smile to my face.

By eleven when fans start pouring through the turnstiles to the track the precip ceases pouring from the sky. Most of the clouds whisk off and a breeze blows through The Spa. The air dries in minutes, the track surface nearly as quickly. By seventeen minutes before the first race at one, forty thousand people mass all over the famous old racecourse. When the bell sounds for jockeys to enter the paddock, almost none of them can hear it. The excitement is palpable. I look at the tote board and see that the track is labeled Fast. We will have no weather excuses for the Prima Donna.

Runforfun and Mary's Grant are listed as morning line favorites at three to one; a group of three fillies, including Francine, are down at five to one. There are eleven racers entered, but one is a mudder who will probably be scratched in the drying conditions. Bettors are wary of my filly's lack of experience, so the odds go up slightly from the morning line. I get my bets down as soon as the first race is saddled. Ours is next.

Barn Sixteen is a hive of activity by then, and Francine is reacting to it. She keeps her ears pricked as she blows and stamps her feet. A horse is sensitive to its surroundings, being a prey animal in its natural state, so the filly knows it's race day for her. How could she not know? The grooms had her coat shining and her tail braided; Jesse wrapped her legs. He didn't ride her out to the training track for exercise. People came and went, their voices and demeanor telegraphing to the horse that something about today is different than every other day at the barn. She doesn't look frightened, just energetic. As Jesse maintains, she loves to run.

And run she does, too fast at first, but Manny Ramirez gets her settled quickly. She lay third down the backstretch, tucked in behind the leader, a rabbit named Social Girl. Clods of wet dirt fly up from the substrata and pepper the herd following Social Girl. Mr. Collier had anticipated that, however, with the track drying so quickly, and he had fitted Francine with blinkers in the Westfarrow colors and full eyecups. She doesn't seem to be distracted by the pellets or the crowd noise. She is focused on the animal ahead of her.

When Ramirez senses that Social Girl is but a few strides away from tiring, he goes wide around her. His timing is perfect. After drifting out evenly, Francine seems to slingshot by the leader, as an F-35 being catapulted off a carrier deck. She stretches out to a two-length lead. Ramirez hand-rides her, waiting for challenges from behind, calming her with his hands and voice. She seems to be straining even so. I can see that he's holding her tightly, teaching her to rate, to pace herself. No two-year-old is especially good at rating so early in its career on the track but my filly is less experienced than most others in the race.

They come past the six-furlong pole with Francine still holding a short lead. Plunging horses bunch up behind her. With a quarter mile to go, Mary's Grant makes a run at Francine. Runforfun is passing horses on the outside from a long way back. Mary's Grant draws almost even before Francine seems to become aware of her. Ramirez taps his ride with his stick and Francine surges back into a clear lead. Mary's Grant races gamely but cannot keep up with Francine.

At the sixteenth pole, with a furlong to the finish, Manny Ramirez lets Francine go. Mary's Grant is done but Runforfun comes on furiously. Running wide, she passes two more horses and looms at Francine's hip. By now, however, my filly is in full stride—and it is a thing of beauty, long, ground-eating leaps that no other horse in the race can match. She sweeps under the wire ahead by two lengths.

I celebrate the win with Jacob Collier and my son, Jesse, but I really want to enjoy the moment with Tony. He's on assignment, too involved with whatever he is doing, whatever danger he faces, and I know not to contact him. Our pleasure in Francine's big win will have to wait. I suspect I will have to wait for many pleasures with Tony Tagliabue.

CHAPTER SEVENTEEN

Tagliabue and Carlos watched the speeding bogey exit the Gulf of Maine and plunge into deeper waters. Five minutes later, it slowed and began circling in long reaches, as if it were a trawler looking for fish. The two men on *Maven* looked at each other.

"I don't think that no fishing boat."

"Not a commercial one, at any rate. It could be a sportfisherman, but I never heard of one fishing at night."

They both frowned as they thought of the implications to their mission of a yacht, a fast yacht, steaming in the vicinity of their planned rendezvous, but the bogey continued to drift to the south. Carlos marked it on the radar screen and began plotting a bigger contact.

"I think we may have the Russian, *amigo*."

"Roger that."

As *Maven* rolled easily in three-foot seas, the radar contact continued to close on her. Tagliabue tried to be still as the tension built, although his body wanted to pace and wander, because Carlos had to initiate contact with the defector and arrange a rather delicate maneuver in the black of night on open water. He already had his earphones on and was tuning his small tactical radio, eyes boring in concentration. Tendrils of mist curled over the gunwales, feeling cool as it brushed their faces and moistened their exposed skin. The night was suddenly very quiet. The winds were calm.

Carlos tensed, and Tagliabue knew he had made contact. He punched some numbers into his machine. Then he turned and nodded to Tagliabue. The operation was on.

Carlos spoke the coordinates in a low, flat voice. Tagliabue plotted them on the chart and turned the dial of the onboard LORAN. He sat at the conning station and put the diesels into gear. They moved toward the rendezvous point.

"I figure the *Leonov* at twelve miles an hour, 306 degrees. Steady."

"Okay, Carlos. I'm going to try to get in behind her without making it too obvious."

Tagliabue maneuvered *Maven*, altering course and speed to keep up the pretense of tracking fish, closing gradually and obliquely to stay to landward of the spy ship and far enough away not to alarm the conning officer. He knew the Russians had him on radar by now. The ship had the right of way, so he turned *Maven* to port and made a slow run for land. He throttled back so that they barely had way on and turned the boat's bows to seaward.

"She gonna pass at three miles if you don't go no farther."

"Rog."

Tagliabue moved the *Maven* seaward, closing the three-mile gap between the two vessels. He looked forward with his glasses. He thought he might have the ship in sight but wasn't sure. His own body heat was beginning to make itself felt under his sweater as he squinted to sharpen his vision. Carlos was at the radar monitor.

"Five minutes."

A gust blew up, clearing the air momentarily. The *Leonov* burst from the fog bank, big, menacing, adorned with rigging and antennae and rotating discs. She was well lit. Spotlights made her arrays glitter; the portholes down her side glowed like the eyes of a pack of hungry coyotes. A bow wake carved from her as she steamed into view. Tagliabue thought the Russian would run *Maven* over if she got in the way.

"Speed?"

"Still making twelve."

Tagliabue thought the spy ship seemed to be traveling faster than that, but Carlos's calculation was probably right: with a sixteen-knot top speed, the SSV-175 would be most efficient at twelve or so. She would stay at cruising speed if she was transiting back to the Motherland—and that's what Giselle's intel was indicating.

The defector was supposed to go over the side at 44°48'1.38" at their present longitude, a slight change from his original jumping-off coordinates. If the Russian didn't change speed, she would pass that point in three minutes.

"You better think about launching the small craft, Carlos."

"You right," he replied, closing his little radio and heading aft. "You see me take off, means he's in the water. I'll talk to you anyway."

"Rog."

The two men had their cell phones connected to each other and their Bluetooth transmitter/receivers in their ears. Carlos pulled the skiff close and took the painter with him as he jumped aboard. The *Leonov* would pass too close to see the small boat on her radar, but a sharp lookout might see its wake, white against a dark sea. Carlos was supposed to drive alongside *Maven* on the side away from the Russian, accelerating fully all the while. When he came out of *Maven's* shadow he'd be at plane and climbing swiftly to forty-three knots. If the skiff was spotted then, it would be too late to do anything. Tagliabue hoped.

The waves were big for that kind of speed. The open boat would be banging into them and could swamp if he got sideways to them. He trusted that Carlos was a good seaman.

With one minute to go, Tagliabue took *Maven* up to full speed. *Leonov* was past her now, so *Maven* matched her at twelve nautical miles per hour but would never catch the bigger vessel. Radar navigators looked forward for threats of danger, so the hope was that no one would notice what they had assumed was a fishing boat now racing at the ship's flank. At least not for a few minutes. That's all it would take, a few minutes to pull this off.

The fog was dense now. He could not see the skiff but knew Carlos was somewhere off his lee side, detached from *Maven* and under its own power. His earphone crackled.

"He's in the water."

Less than two seconds later, the small boat flashed by the cockpit to port. He saw Carlos behind the wheel, gauzy scuds of fog streaking by his head. Tagliabue kept a steady course and speed. The skiff cut in front of him, flying over one wave and crashing into the next, his big outboard motor cavitating each time then digging into the water again. The period the prop was in the air was so brief that the boat didn't seem to lose any speed. Carlos raced to a spot in the Russian ship's wake and spun the small craft as he shut the engine down. The boat spun and stopped with her bow to the waves. Water rushed over her stern before she settled in. With his glasses up, Tagliabue saw Carlos lean over the side. A sudden glare blinded him. The *Leonov* had a spotlight on *Maven's* conning station. Tagliabue couldn't see the skiff.

The light left *Maven* and started to quarter the water between Tagliabue's cargo boat and the *Leonov*. They're looking for something, he thought. They must know the radioman is overboard.

The light found the skiff. She was already south of *Maven* but underway again and moving fast. The light lost the boat momentarily and by the time it found her again she was at plane and skipping over the flat water in the ship's wake. She hit the ocean waves at full speed, heading for land and another area of heavy fog. Tagliabue slowed *Maven* to give Carlos cover. A siren went off on the Russian spy ship. Crewmen scrambled. He knew weaponry would be deployed next.

He turned *Maven* for home. There was too much water between him and the Russian for small arms to be effective, so he was not completely surprised to hear a cannon go off. A big round whistled over *Maven* rigging and splashed down not twenty yards from the racing skiff ahead of her. Their gun control radar was highly sophisticated to be that accurate so quickly. The second round landed near the skiff and blew it airborne. Carlos turned hard to starboard when he landed and began running a jagged pattern. The Russian gunners missed with two more shots but were beginning to bracket the boat again.

"Go to port!" Tagliabue yelled into his mouthpiece. Carlos did, almost broaching the boat with the rapid maneuver, but the next round missed wide. Three more rapid-fire rounds were far from the boat. Tagliabue realized the Russian radar had lost the small plastic vessel. With the mist still floating around they probably had no visual contact either.

"Head for the barn, Carlos. They can't see you any longer."

"Gottcha, Antonio. You're next."

Tagliabue had *Maven* at flank speed. He cut hard left. A three-inch naval explosive round hit on the fantail, high but with enough charge to blow away the rigging there and set on fire the small stable he had built to house Francine weeks ago. Now he was a clear target for the gunners on *Leonov*. He turned hard right, but the *Maven* was a beamy workboat and could maneuver only slowly, even at full speed and full rudder. She rolled so that Tagliabue had to hang on to his chair. The stable fire raged aft. He'd have to put it out soon. The next round hit her above the waterline amidships and lifted her partly out of the water. She was badly holed. Cold seawater rushed in.

He turned for land, knowing he was not going to make it. His only hope was to hide in the fog among the fishing fleet. He heard excited chatter on the radio, fishermen wondering what was happening out to sea. A quick radar check revealed no sign of Carlos's boat. The big bogie, *Leonov*, was still steaming north. Smudges of contacts, the fleet, were beginning to appear. Surely the Russians would not continue to fire their big gun with the trawlers so close. He snatched the mic from the PRC-25 and clicked on.

"Mayday, mayday. Navy ship firing cannon at Georges Bank."

The *Leonov* did fire one more round but she was at the end of her effective range. It splashed down far from the crippled *Maven*. Tagliabue went below to the cabin.

As he was fitting his big Glock into a plastic bag that also held his phone under the safety vest he'd put on, the starboard engine froze up with a gasp of steam that enveloped the fantail of his boat. *Maven* wallowed, even though she had reached the calmer waters of the gulf, and her steering was sluggish. He recognized that she was in her death throes. His goal was his own safety. It was too late to save his boat. She was badly damaged and the sea still rolled into her side. The pumps had given up along with electricity. Tagliabue's cell worked but he could not raise Carlos from the dark of the cabin. He went topside with flares and shot off three of them. They were hard to see in the fog even from the conning deck.

The one engine on-line was barely able to make headway as *Maven* began to founder. When that diesel expired, Tagliabue left the wheel and released the kapok lifeboat. He went over the side after it, landing next to it and pulling himself aboard. He unclipped the single paddle and worked the tiny raft away from his dying boat. *Maven* rolled, didn't come back, and went on her side. A minute later, her stern went under. The whole craft followed quietly, swallowed so completely by the sea that it was as if she had never existed.

In the sudden misty silence, he sat in the raft and let it drift. It was too far to land for him to paddle there, so he did little more to navigate than keep its nose pointed toward land. He looked and listened hard, hoping to be rescued. Someone should respond to his distress calls. His wet clothes chafed at him in places but the evening was balmy despite the wet fog, so he wasn't yet cold.

After twenty minutes of feeling alone in a nest of vapor and darkness, he heard something to his left, a motor perhaps. When he
saw running lights winking in and out through the mist, he lit off
another flare. A boat loomed out of the fog bank. It was a shiny
white Hatteras sportfisherman.

CHAPTER EIGHTEEN

He handed the painter of the life raft to the sailor who helped him aboard the Hatteras. Rather than tie it off, the man let it drop into the water. Tagliabue snapped a look at the man, but he faded into the shadow of the flying bridge without returning the look. Another person walked into Tagliabue's line of sight: Jack Brunson.

"That life raft saved my life and has a certain value in its own right, Jack. Your minion shouldn't treat it so cavalierly."

Brunson laughed, looking at home and thoroughly comfortable on a luxury boat on a foggy night when mayday calls and artillery shells had both been flying through space with abandon.

"He was not being cavalier. He's nervous in this environment and would just like to disappear, if he could. But he did hire on, so he's obligated."

"Obligated for what?"

"Obligated to disrupt your little scheme, Anthony. What the fuck are you playing at, anyway? I take it that this guy defected from the *Leonov*, which just passed by, eh?"

He stepped to one side so that Tagliabue could see two figures, one tied into the fighting chair and the other slumped to the deck next to it. The guy in the chair was someone Tagliabue had never seen, youngish despite a head of gray, curly hair and a face with the pallor of an ancient man. His eyes seemed to bulge as he watched the two men on the open afterdeck. Crumpled next to him with blood running from a wound on his head was Carlos.

"What have you done to those guys, Jack?"

"Who are they?"

"I don't know. Look here, pal. My boat was just blown out from under me while I was cruising inside the three-mile limit. I've reported it to the Coast Guard and I need to follow up with them. Let me use your radio."

Brunson smiled at that, but Tagliabue thought he could detect some uncertainty on his face. He might have discovered somehow that Carlos was going to rescue the Russian sailor, but he had no way of knowing that *Maven* was also involved. He knew nothing of Tagliabue's connection with Giselle and her agency, so he couldn't place him in the context of the defector rescue. Yet Tagliabue was out there on his old boat when the fireworks went down, so he had to be involved somehow. Brunson must have been thinking all that; his face betrayed his ignorance. What had he gotten involved in? Jack Brunson might be into something that had become bigger than he anticipated.

What was Brunson doing out there? Perhaps there was an innocent explanation for the man tied in the chair and the badly injured one on the deck of the luxury sportfisherman Brunson was riding, but Tagliabue could think of nothing that might explain it except that Brunson knew somehow that the Russian was defecting and had interfered.

"Where did these men come from, Jack? Why are they tied up? And what happened to them?" His voice was tight, maybe even aggressive. Before Brunson could answer, another figure climbed down from the bridge. It was the older man Tagliabue had seen with Carlos earlier, the man who had chatted up Carlos in the bar at the Pelham Island. He no longer had a gun at his belt; it was in his right hand.

He spoke to Brunson in a voice that sounded like a fish swimming in gravel.

"Tie the big fucker opposite the Mexican."

Tagliabue didn't resist. Once he was roped to the base of the fighting chair, the older man went back up to the bridge and Jack Brunson went into the cabin. Huge diesels took up a roar from below and the Hatteras headed north, shattering the waves as she blasted along at high speed. Tagliabue tried to rouse Carlos but it was too noisy on the fantail to hear any response. The Russian defector's mouth was wrapped in duct tape so he didn't try to talk with him.

After thirty minutes of running hard, the boat slowed. Whoever was driving turned the bows into the wave set just as she lost way. Three people came down from the bridge, the last one the older man with the gun in his hand again. The crewman lowered the dinghy and tied it off on a starboard cleat. He opened the railing and lowered an aluminum ladder. The other two watched him without speaking. The crewman and the man Tagliabue assumed was the captain climbed down into the small boat. The older man let the line go from the cleat. Just then, Brunson came out of the cabin with a shotgun in both hands. He fired a round into the dinghy.

Carlos spasmed at the blast but didn't speak. His eyes were rolled up in his head.

Tagliabue didn't speak either. He saw the shotgun load smash a hole in the bottom of the dinghy but knew that it wouldn't sink completely because it was built of air pockets like the Hatteras itself. The water that came in through the burst fiberglass would make forward progress slow for the men in the tiny craft. They would not make it ashore before daylight. If the waves grew and the winds blew, they could spend a long uncomfortable time at sea before someone found them. Turning his back to the two sailors adrift in the holed boat, the older man went up and got the yacht underway again. It was still heading up the coast, at moderate speed, in the direction of the Bay of Fundy.

≈

"You awake, *amigo*?"

Brunson had done a hurried job of tying Tagliabue and he had been able to work his head close to Carlos. He spoke softly and heard Carlos grunt in return.

"Who's the older guy?"

Carlos licked his lips without opening his eyes. His skin was gray, his eyelids dark, almost purple. Blood had crusted on his face and a bright trickle still ran from the matted hair of his head and, alarmingly to Tagliabue, from his nose. He wasn't bound, but he didn't move.

"That L. P. Cuthbert . . ."

Carlos stopped talking after that, groaning, little dark bubbles forming on his lips. As Tagliabue figured, Carlos now knew the driver of the Hatteras as L. P. Cuthbert, the man he'd drunk with at the Island Pelham, the same one Timmy O'Brien had seen with Brunson and his bodyguard riding in the stern as he was fishing with his children. Cuthbert and Brunson must have known about the defection and the rescue by monitoring Carlos's radio blips with the Russian. He didn't try to figure out what that meant or what role Cuthbert played in this operation. Carlos was severely wounded and would not be easy to move. Tagliabue had to figure out a way to live through the night.

Tagliabue tried to engage Carlos again but the man didn't respond. He didn't move. Tagliabue couldn't tell if his friend was breathing.

He worked the nylon line that Brunson had tied him with. The knots were simple double hitches, tight but not permanent, and the lines were loose enough for him to move. As he twisted and pulled to loosen the line further, the boat swept into a wide turn toward land. Within minutes he had freed one wrist. The rest was easy. He sat up against the chair and began taking off his clothes and placing his valuables in his waterproof belly-bag. As they passed within sight of the lighted fishing markers again, he brought his mouth close to the Russian's ear.

"I'll get help."

Then Anthony Tagliabue dove over the stern sheets and into the ocean, leaving his clothes in a pile on the deck of the Hatteras.

≈

The water was colder than expected, even in the middle of summer, so he was glad enough to stretch into long smooth strokes and steady kicks. He swam and stopped thinking of time. His muscles worked in rhythm, adapting to his strokes. Concentrating on breathing and kicking, he swam until he began to flag. When he looked up, the misted buoys seemed as far away as they had to begin with. Maybe he had underestimated his goal. He turned on his back and floated, kicking easily and breathing in deep draughts. The water was calm so he figured he must be inshore from Georges Bank and probably already in the Bay.

When a bout of shivers took him, he turned over again and swam. The waterproof bag around his waist pulled at him, slowed his progress, and tired his arms. Tiny waves broke over his head. He had to spew water from his mouth almost every breath now. He could no longer breathe only through his nose, but he pushed on, losing track of time, until he tired badly. His breathing turned ragged, and he knew he had made a mistake.

I should have stayed on board the Hatteras and taken my chances with Cuthbert and Brunson. Jumping overboard was a stupid move. That's what comes from relying on my body for so long, and now I'm going to drown out here on the ocean that has sustained me all my life.

His dark thoughts were interrupted when he spotted a light, faint but clear. He must have made it to the fishing fleet. That also meant animals in the area, predator fish along with the flounder and hake the boats were netting. Closing his mind to the idea of beasts in the black depths beneath him, he struck out again, willing his tired arms to pull his weight through the water. His legs felt rubbery and he knew he was no longer kicking with any rhythm. He could hear his breath and felt his heart pumping blood like a two-stroke engine at speed. His strokes slowed. Something brushed against his arm and he slapped at the water before he caught himself. He took advantage of the adrenaline jolt to set out hard for another minute. He felt something in the water again. This time he was too tired to react. He started to go under. Reaching up in desperation, he was shocked to feel something touch his hand. He grabbed at it. His hand wrapped around rough, wire-hard cord, a cord that pulled him. Big lights lit up the night suddenly as he burst out of the water.

CHAPTER NINETEEN

The timing was perfect. Adao Naños had just begun working the winch when his cousin Nicolao lit off the flood lights. The hard work of boating the net full of fish was about to begin and Adao was glad to have it begin with efficiency. The other two crewmen were coming aft then, one rubbing sleep from his eyes, the other honing his filleting knife. None was too curious about what the *Mary May* had netted; they would have to separate out the non-keepers anyway and clean the catch before icing it down. It didn't matter what was in the net, since it would all be flopping on the deck in seconds, hundreds of pounds of sea creatures desperate to escape back into the deep.

This was the last pull of the two-night voyage, though, and they would be back in port for breakfast with their families. Adao smiled at the thought as he watched the warps wind smoothly through the gantry and heard the steady power of the winch as it pulled the otter net over the stern.

"*Que diablos?*" he cried when he saw a naked human body entangled in the net. Nicolao jumped and ran to the back. Adao never spoke in the language of their fathers unless it was something serious. When Nicolao saw what his cousin was staring at, he killed the winch and yelled for the captain, waving his arms and pointing at the net. Everyone ran to see what the great ocean had brought up for them this time. When they saw the body they quieted, then burst into excited chatter when Anthony Tagliabue raised an arm.

They grabbed at him and pulled him to the deck. The feat required some effort, since he was bigger even than Big Horse Hardiman, the largest fisherman working the Eastport fleet. Tagliabue's body was puckered and pale from his time in the sea. It shivered violently. His scrotum was shriveled and wrinkled. The belly-bag left deep red creases in his skin.

The crew helped him up and walked him to the cabin. They wrapped him in blankets that smelled of fish slime and the captain gave him a splash of one-hundred-proof rum in a tin cup. It burned all the way to his gut. As they laid him on a damp and sagging bunk, he smiled. He was asleep before the net was aboard and the *Mary May* began motoring to shore. His waterproof bag was still strapped around his waist.

Tagliabue awoke when he heard the boat's engines working their way to its berth at the commercial fishing docks at Eastport. He was so tired he stayed on the cot. Ten minutes after the engines had shut down, Adao came to Tagliabue with a sweatshirt and a pair of cargo shorts.

"I borrowed these from Big Horse's wife. I hope they fit."

Tagliabue smiled his thanks and rolled from the bunk to dress. He groaned with the effort, wishing he could lie back down for another hour of rest. But he had things to do, and rest was not one of those things.

The men looked up from their work loading wooden boxes with their catch as Tagliabue walked topside, his legs a bit shaky and his arms hanging from the cut-off holes in the shirt like logs of driftwood. He sketched a salute to the men and went ashore. By the time he'd finished a piece of fried flounder with scrambled eggs and hash browns in a diner along the waterfront, the Fishermen's United Bank was open for business. He withdrew $5,000 in hundreds, asking the teller to put five of the bills in each of five pay envelopes. He taxied into Eastport proper and bought some clothes. Properly attired and looking reasonably prosperous, he rented a car, happy enough that it had an automatic transmission and did not require too much in the way of a coordinated effort to drive. Tagliabue moved cautiously during all these transactions, feeling his blood cells plumping with sugar as he slowly gained his health back. It was three hours since he'd come ashore.

When he got back to the docks, the crew of *Mary May* was sitting on boxes and bollards, sweat staining their shirts in the midmorning sun, faces shiny. Some of their families had joined them as they waited for the fish broker to bring them the cash for their harvest. Two of the men were sipping from brown bottles of beer. They all applauded when Tagliabue stepped out of the Camry and walked down to the dock, happy enough to welcome back a man who had escaped Davy Jones's locker, a fate they all feared deep in their hearts.

Tagliabue handed one of his pay envelopes to the captain, a wizened man whose face was darkened by the sun and scoured by the wind. He reminded Tagliabue of Joshua White.

"Thank you for your kindness to me, Skip."

"Y'know you ain't got to do this, mate. You'd do the same for us, more'n likely."

"I know, but it makes me feel good."

The skipper shrugged with his mouth and stuffed the envelope into a back pocket. The men slapped him on the shoulder as Tagliabue gave them theirs, smiling and wishing him luck. Children looked up at him with big eyes. He went back to his rental and drove off.

~

It was the next day before Tagliabue made it home to Bath. He had reported in Eastport that he went accidentally overboard from a big Hatteras sportfisherman, but the boat could not be located. The USCG assumed she was still out looking for her missing passenger and sent out a cutter to look for the boat. The lieutenant commander in charge of the station wondered aloud why the

Hatteras had not called in a position or a request for assistance. Tagliabue didn't wonder about that at all. Instead he went to his apartment building, showered, and called Agnes Ann.

"It was a fantastic race, Tony. I'm heartbroken that you missed it."

"There'll be many more races for that filly, I'm thinking."

"Oh, yes, indeed," Agnes Ann said, her voice alive with excitement. "She ran so well that Mr. Collier is even thinking about the Kentucky Oaks, if you can believe that. Of course, that's a long shot, but we are going to rest her up over the winter and see how she looks as a three-year-old."

"Will she run again as a two-year-old, do you think?"

"Possibly. We're thinking of a stakes race at Belmont in about five weeks. Francine has had no aftereffects from the Prima Donna. She's strong for a baby."

She and Tagliabue both knew that all thoroughbreds turn a year older on January first of every year, no matter in what month they were born. Since a horse's gestation is eleven months, owners and breeders strive to breed a mare as close to February 1st as possible. Ideally, a horse will foal early in January, so that on January 1 of the next year, when it turns one year old officially, it is nearly that in actual age. Consequently, championship stallions are in great demand during early spring. Despite the miracles of modern nutritional science, a coveted stallion can manage only a certain number of inseminations each week. Many mares have to wait their turn and may be as young as six months old when they officially turn one year. That's a major disadvantage as two-year-olds and even three-year-olds. After that it doesn't matter much, but most of the prestige races are for three-year-olds. Colts who win a Triple Crown race or a Breeders Cup often retire to stud following their three-year-old season.

Francine was dropped in March, so she was younger than some of the million-dollar babies with exquisite bloodlines. That was the nature of the competition for the Kentucky Oaks, the foremost race for fillies in terms of prestige, run at Churchill Downs during

Derby Week in May. It was important to evaluate her size and
musculature after a winter of rest and training.

"Jake got her at Heal Eddy already?"

"Yeah. Jesse's staying there too. He's his official assistant
trainer now, although he's not being paid much. There are maybe
a half-dozen horses at the stable that they're working with, including mine."

"So you won't be seeing much of your son or your horse."

"Right. Time to let Jesse and Francine grow up on their own.
He's not my baby and she's not my pet. Not anymore."

"You sound lonely."

"I miss you, Tony. I'm sorry you didn't get to see the Prima
Donna. She ran a beautiful race."

"I know. I can hear it in your voice. Where are you?"

"I'm on the road, maybe an hour out of Maine. I've got to
drop off this rental car. I've had it for months already."

"Come to my apartment first."

"I thought you'd never ask. I'll call again when I'm close."

Tagliabue walked down the block to Tom Sharkey's apartment. It felt good to be out in the sun, and out of the ocean. No
one answered at the apartment so he went down to the South End
Dog Park by the river. Sharkey was sitting alongside a walking
path that ran by the water, Polly resting on his shoulder, two young
girls talking to him. As the children left, Polly barked at them and
they turned to wave at the dog. When man and dog saw Tagliabue
approach, Sharkey raised a hand to him and Polly thumped his
tail twice.

"Have a sit, Anthony."

"Thanks."

He sat next to the old lobsterman on a weathered bench and
scratched the dog's ears. Polly accepted the gesture.

"You doing okay, Tom?"

"Okay indeed. How 'bout you? I been watching for your boat
but ain't seen her."

"Ah, long story, Tom."

Sitting there in the sun with another man of the sea, Tagliabue decided to share a sea story with Old Sharkey, knowing it would eventually become part of Maine lore that no one would ever be able to verify.

"*Maven* was shot out from under me and went down out by Georges Bank."

The mass of wrinkles on the man's face straightened some as his eyes widened with the news. He looked as if he wasn't certain if his friend was telling him the truth or was about to launch into a tall tale. Who loses a workboat to gunfire during a peaceful Maine summer in the twenty-first century? Then again, he had heard a story, confused as it was, about some Russian ship firing off flares and even discharging her cannons out to sea a few nights ago. Nobody seemed to know what it was all about, and Anthony Tagliabue was locally famous for having adventures that no one was ever quite sure about.

"Do tell."

"Yeah. Some crazed Russian opened fire for some reason and two of her rounds hit my boat and sank her."

Sharkey apparently decided to go along with his tale, since he had nothing better to do but sit in the sun with his little dog on his shoulder. Both men might as well go further down into the depths of local lore with their lifestyles and stories.

"He have something against you, now?"

"He must have thought so. I guess I was just in the wrong place at the wrong time."

"What was the Russki shootin' at, do ya think?"

"Well, nobody seems to know, Tom. He's no doubt back in Vladivostok or someplace by now, so we may never know. I reported the sinking to the coasties, so maybe our ambassador to Russia can find something out. I'll be surprised to hear anything more about it."

Tagliabue had done nothing of the kind, of course. If Giselle wanted the ambassador or anybody else to know what had transpired out over Georges Bank, it would be her decision to reveal

it. Russia would probably not admit to a defection, Tagliabue
thought to himself, and that was the main problem in his mind:
where was the defector now? Could he salvage something from
this mission by rescuing the guy? And who was this L. P. Cuthbert?
How did he intercept the communications between Carlos and the
defector?

As these questions tumbled around in his mind—now that
he was safe and not concerned with matters of life and death—
Sharkey brought up another unanswered question.

"Someone gonna buy you another boat?"

"Don't know."

It was a question Tagliabue had briefly considered before he
realized that he couldn't lay any claim for *Maven* without compromising his confidential assignment from The Clemson Project. It
also depended upon what was officially known about the bizarre
episode out on the fishing grounds. He knew he had to speak to
the sheriff's office—instead of sitting on a bench in a park with an
old friend.

"Is the little dog still working out for you, Tom? Can you care
for him okay?"

"Oh, aye. We're getting along. This wee one don't seem to
want nothing more from this here life than me. We get along. He
does get me outta the house more'n I'm used to, but that probly
ain't a bad thing either. We're just two old cronies who like to sit
in the sun."

"You reckon Polly's old? I don't know how long Joshua had
him."

"Well now, he don't jump around much and seems happy with
a walk once in a while. When he gets tired he just climbs up on
my shoulder for a ride. Ain't that some shit, now?"

He shook his head slowly, realizing how absurd it must seem
for a dog to hang on him like a pet parrot. Tagliabue smiled.

"The kids seem to like it."

"Oh, they do, Anthony. They do. Every time we come down
here some of them come by to say hey to this guy. I got to be

careful what they give him to eat is all I worry about. He don't snap or act mad or nothing. I think he likes the youngsters."

"You been to the vet?"

"Young Doc Crenshaw come by the apartment the other day. She says he's in good shape. Gave him a shot."

"Good enough. Look here, Tom, I need to go see Johnny Coleman up at the county building about this boat business. Let me give you a little money for the dog's upkeep."

"No, no. I don't need nothing, Anthony. I ain't spent all you gave me last time yet."

"Well, get to spending it then. I'm responsible for this animal and I'm going to keep paying you for taking care of him for me. You might just as well get used to it. Don't forget, you can spend it on yourself too. You're the caregiver and need to be paid, got it?"

Sharkey nodded, saying quietly, "Caregiver, eh?"

He stuffed a few hundred in the old man's shirt pocket and they shook good-bye. Sharkey's hand felt like the worn wood of the park bench.

∼

Sheriff Detective Coleman didn't offer to shake hands but he did ask Tagliabue to take a seat in his office. He sighed heavily while he looked at him.

"I know someday I'm gonna be telling my grandkids about my adventures with Anthony Tagliabue, but just now I got to say that I wish I never heard of you. My life would be hassle-free and easy if you'd never come into it."

"Somebody getting after you not to investigate too closely again, Detective?"

The baby-faced cop put his head in his hands and pressed at his temples as if he were trying to keep them from popping open. He said "shit" a few times before slouching back in his chair. He looked at Tagliabue with slitted eyes.

"No, but thanks for reminding me. That'll be next, no doubt. Right now I got the Coast Guard calling with a half-million-dollar Hatteras tied up at a broken-down pier in Northeast Harbor. There's a dead man on the back deck of the boat. An undocumented immigrant, as they say. A thirty-two-year-old Mexican national. We also got a report circulating through the system saying you went overboard from a sportfisherman. And yet another about two fishermen with a wild-ass tale about being hired on to run that Hatteras and then being marooned at sea like fucking Captain Queeg, or whatever his name was. Don't suppose you know anything about any of this shit, do you?"

"I might."

Coleman's head jerked up.

"You might?"

His voice was high with hope. He had obviously been expecting Tagliabue was going to say nothing again.

"Yeah. The Hatteras I was on when I went overboard had an injured man on it, an Indian I thought. He never spoke but I guess he could have been an Aztec or something. You sure he's dead?"

"The Coast Guard is sure. You try to treat him or anything?"

"The people who rescued me from my boat sinking were not friendlies. They tied me to the fighting chair next to that injured man. He didn't answer me when I asked him questions. I got loose, I got out of my clothes, and then I got out of there. I never saw any of them again."

The detective sat back in his chair and loosened his tie. He rubbed his cheeks with both his hands.

"What you want for dinner, Anthony?"

"What?"

"I'm fixing to order dinner for you and me, cause we're gonna be in here a long time. I want the whole story from you."

They ate fried clams and hush puppies from the Clam Basket while Tagliabue told Coleman about the sinking of *Maven*. He didn't say who fired the cannon rounds or claim he knew why, only that the world around Georges Bank turned mad for a few minutes while he was out on the high seas trying to catch a mess of haddock two nights ago. When *Maven* foundered, he went to her life raft and was rescued by a big Hatteras. He described Cuthbert and named Brunson, leaving out how Brunson had holed the Hatteras dinghy with the captain and his mate in it. If Giselle wanted the BPD to know what happened, she would tell them.

Coleman sucked soda through a straw as the wheels of the tape recorder turned. He burped quietly and asked: "Do you suppose the ship was firing at the Hatteras?"

"I suppose that's possible. I had a bogey moving fast through the South Channel that night. I was worried about all the fishing boats and their nets, with her going so fast. It could have been the Hatteras. The gunship could have mistaken me for her."

"What kind of vessel has guns that can sink a cargo boat?"

"It had to have been a navy ship of some sort. She stayed out to sea. It was a foul night and I never saw her at all."

"Maybe a pirate."

"God, I hope we don't have armed pirates patrolling the Maine coast. Things can't be that bad."

"Nothing would surprise me anymore," Coleman said. "I'm ready to believe it was a Russian warship firing at the USA, like I been hearing here and there on the street."

He looked at Tagliabue when he said this, a question on his face, an invitation maybe for Tagliabue to reveal something. The big man stayed silent.

The cop looked depressed. Tagliabue felt sorry for him but he could not reveal what he knew about the Russian spy ship, and no official in the federal government was going to tell anything of vital national interest to a small county sheriff's office. Coleman was going through the motions of an investigation with no hope of ever solving it. Based on his body language and his dull voice, he knew that all too well. He also probably knew that Tagliabue was involved in the high seas crimes, may even have caused them, but he was working for someone who pulled strings that Coleman wasn't even aware of, no less able to identify. One thing was

certain: when the county sheriff came back from talking to someone in the capital, he wanted everything to do with Tagliabue's
latest escapades kept under wraps. That could only mean that
high level federal officials were pulling these strings, and Detective
Coleman was astute enough to realize that his only option was
to let things play out and hope only that Anthony didn't start a
bloodbath in town. He also probably understood that Tagliabue
was on the right side of the nation's foreign and domestic interests,
that he was important enough to own a fortress apartment building and wield influence well above what Coleman himself could
muster. That much was obvious from the instructions his boss gave
him: "Hands off this mess, Detective."

He said: "Investigation suspended at 2112 hours," and clicked
off the recorder.

"I'll let you know what I find out about the deceased, Anthony,
and if the Coast Guard ever identifies the boat owner. If something as valuable as a big Hatteras was stolen, somebody is sure
to make some noise about it when he discovers it missing. All we
know so far is that some unknown corporation is registered as the
owner of record."

He paused. "I also know that all this has your fingerprints all
over it. But I'm not going to get in the way, because the sheriff will
get a call from some mysterious suit telling us to keep our hands
off. That's okay with me. I'm not gonna fight it. I have come to
believe that you are on the side of the angels. How's that sound?
My job these days is to cover my ass with paperwork, but I will
keep you informed. If you come across any crime I can handle,
please let me know about it."

Tagliabue left the county building feeling bad—and a bit
guilty—about Johnny Coleman. The cop thought a big boat was
stolen and somehow Tagliabue had gotten aboard it with a dead
man. Coleman had no idea of the mission to rescue the defector.
He had given up trying to solve the mystery of gunfire and murder
on the high seas. That was too bad, Tagliabue thought, because
Johnny Coleman was a good and honest lawman who was being

excluded from an adventure on his own turf, so to speak. It would have been better to have the sheriff's office along as part of the assignment, but he knew that could never have worked: cops have too many rules and regs to follow. Assignments from The Clemson Project required flexibility. Still Tagliabue hated having to lie to a good cop like Johnny Coleman.

He drove to his apartment, where Agnes Ann was waiting for him with an opened bottle of pinot grigio. His mood changed quickly. Over breakfast the next morning he told her a nuanced version of the story he'd fed to the sheriff's detective. Agnes Ann was having none of it.

"I know you can't tell me what's going on, Tony. That's okay with me, but I'm afraid the other woman in your life sounds less accommodating."

"You've spoken to Giselle?"

Tagliabue sounded shocked, and he was. He could never imagine the secretive Giselle even speaking to a civilian.

"Not exactly. Western Union sent a guy over with a message while you were in the shower. It was open, so I, er, I read it. The message said: 'Delta flight # 2178, August 28, 10:15 A.M.'"

"That today?"

"It is. I'll drive you to the airport."

After dropping Tagliabue off at the Portsmouth Airfield, Agnes Ann turned in her rental, and caught the noon hop to Westfarrow Island. Tagliabue flew to Albany, where a black Ford Expedition was waiting for him. A stone-faced driver took him to an Embassy Suites hotel and said: "Room 104." It was the only thing he said once he'd gotten behind the wheel.

Giselle let him in when he knocked and asked how he was feeling.

"I've recovered, thank you."

"Recovered, is it? Oh, my. You'd better tell me all about it, dear man."

Before Tagliabue could get started on his story, there was a tap on the door to the suite. Giselle's answer was an icy, "Yes?"

"Room service, Mrs. Hansen." The voice was female.

Giselle pulled a handgun from her purse and slid it across the table. Tagliabue took it in hand and moved to the left of the door, tight against the wall. He immediately recognized that her Walther PPQ was a striker-fired model, ready to shoot. Giselle grasped the doorknob, nodded to him and jerked the door open suddenly. A young woman in a yellow and brown uniform gasped slightly, then pushed a cart into the room without looking around. Tagliabue turned away from the waitress and stuffed the gun in his belt as Giselle signed for the meal. A silent man in a suit appeared in the hallway. As the waitress left the room the man in the hall handed her a twenty and escorted her to the elevator. A tray on the cart contained covered plates of chicken salad and a carafe of coffee.

"I liked the food in Marrakesh better."

Giselle smiled her thin smile, no teeth showing. "I didn't want to order anything too heavy. You've got work to do."

He told her what had transpired out by the fishing grounds, how Carlos had picked up the deserter and apparently had made it safely away from the Russian ship, only to end up mortally wounded on a large sportfisherman. How the *Maven* was shot out from under him and how he ended up on the same yacht as Carlos when he was picked up in his life raft. He figured time was short so he spoke briefly.

"The Russian radioman did not appear to be injured, but I'm afraid Carlos died from his injuries."

"Are you sure of that?"

"Pretty sure. The coasties reported to Bath PD that a victim ID'd as an undocumented Mexican was discovered on an abandoned fishing yacht that matches the description of the boat that captured me. Carlos was on that boat and he was barely responsive when I tried to talk to him. I'm sorry to say he probably quit."

"That's too bad. His name was Carlos Solis, and he was a good man. That explains why we have not been able to contact him. He reported the rescue and then went suddenly incommunicado. A game warden found his speedboat in a marsh, undamaged.

We had a boatyard bring it into Eastport. Cuthbert must have ambushed Carlos somehow and brained him."

"Yeah. Carlos was bleeding from the head. Who's Cuthbert?"

Giselle sighed.

"Claude Leon Cuthbert. He's a rogue agent of The Clemson Project. Went over to the dark side two years ago, for money apparently. He may own the yacht that picked you up. We'll call the USCG and confiscate it, but the main issue is our defector. Cuthbert is no doubt going to try to sell him back to Mother Russia for a million or two. He's not in any of his usual haunts. He seems to have disappeared. We've got to find him but I've no idea where to even look."

"He has teamed up with a local lawyer, a mobster-wannabe named Jack Brunson. Brunson, by the way, probably owns the Hatteras, not Cuthbert. I'm thinking Cuthbert used Brunson."

"Kin to the estimable Agnes Ann Brunson?"

How did Giselle even know Aggie's last name? Tagliabue had never listed her as a relation or mentioned her to anyone outside of Bath. Maybe Carlos passed on a tidbit. It didn't matter if he did. Tagliabue just had to get used to the idea that this woman knew everything about everybody, all the time. Her sources must be phenomenal, to say nothing of her memory. He had never seen her refer to anything, paper or electronic. It was all inside her skull.

"Her ex."

"Ah. How is that obvious fool tied to Cuthbert? Wait, he must be our mystery man, the local source we were warned to expect. Right?"

"I'm guessing affirmative on that. I don't know how Jack got tied up with Cuthbert. Carlos saw them together in a bar and then a friend of mine saw them on the Hatteras. Brunson is also money oriented, but I don't see him getting into something this deep on purpose. He did hole the dinghy the hired crew was in, but he probably knew it wouldn't sink. He was just buying time by slowing them down. Killing Carlos is probably more than he bargained for. He's not known for getting involved in murder."

"What about your mate, Joshua White?"

"I believe that was a mistake. I don't think *Maven* was meant to sink. Maybe Jack Brunson wanted my boat disabled to keep me out of the way while he worked this deal with Cuthbert. He didn't know that I worked for you. Maybe he still doesn't know. Maybe he just wanted to bust my chops for taking over his wife. Maybe the holing of *Maven* went haywire when Joshua interrupted Magpie planting the bomb."

"That is Marvin 'Magpie' Harris?"

"Yes."

"The same Magpie who was assassinated at Saratoga?"

"Yes."

"Did you kill him? Is that why you wanted the false ID?"

He didn't answer.

Giselle peered at him but said nothing else about Marv Harris. She put her hands flat on the coffee table and sat up straight.

"Okay. Let's see if we can salvage something from this fiasco. Cuthbert probably still has the defector. He can't have negotiated a transfer this quickly, but it's not going to be too long. Brunson is probably sticking to Cuthbert like mayflies on a honey jar. He's the only one who knows what he's doing. Where do you think they might be?"

"Brunson has a summer cabin on a lake just outside Saratoga Springs. He's a major horse racing aficionado, wants to be an owner . . ."

"Hence the disputation over the phenom Francine."

Tagliabue nodded at her. "The cabin is not common knowledge. I only found out about it last month and I've known Jack Brunson awhile now. The sheriff is looking for him in Bath and on Westfarrow. It's the only other place I can think of."

"You know where it is?"

"Not exactly. On a lake with 'berry' in the name."

Giselle picked up her phone and said into it. "Find me a lake house in Saratoga, New York, in the name of John Brunson. The lake has the word 'berry' in it." She put the phone down and looked at Tagliabue.

"The sheriff know about our defector?"

"No."

"How many men are we talking about with Cuthbert?"

"Three, I think. Maybe only two. Brunson has hired some muscle."

"Okay, you can handle that. If it turns out to be an army, contact me immediately. Meanwhile I'll be searching for communications and other signals indicating the Russkies are dealing. Cuthbert may have a hidey-hole of his own we are going to try to locate. Here's a burner cell. Use it only to call me, once. Then destroy it and its card. If I use it to call you, same deal. I trust the one time you call me will be to say it's over and ask what to do with our defector. If you make a mess, tell me about it then and we'll take care of it. Got it?"

"Yes."

Her phone pinged. She looked at it and said, "It's Loughberry Lake."

"Got it."

"If I don't hear from you, I'll see that your assets are transferred to Agnes Ann."

Tagliabue opened his eyes at that.

"You can do that?"

"It would be easier if you two were married, but we'll take care of it."

"How do you know we're not married?"

Giselle only smiled, her enigmatic smile, showing no teeth. "Take the car that picked you up. The keys are in it."

"I hope you can eat two salads," he said as he rose to go.

"Don't worry, Tony. I have friends."

Tagliabue left immediately, taking Giselle's 9 mm with him. He didn't think for a minute that she had forgotten she gave it to him when the food arrived in her room. In the hotel parking garage, he checked the fifteen-round magazine. It was full.

Interstate 87 north of Albany, the capital of New York State, is also known as the Adirondack Northway. Tagliabue took it out of the Hudson Valley and farther into the Adirondack Mountains. He hadn't eaten lunch but his belly didn't want food. It wanted to settle things first with Brunson and Cuthbert.

His charge from Giselle was to rescue the defector, assuming the Russian was still alive. The Russian Navy might be just as happy with proof of the defector's death. Either way, Tagliabue's gut was tight, his mind running the reels of possible scenarios.

By the time he made it to Loughberry Lake an hour later, the GPS in the big Ford's dash blinked on a location on the southeast shore. Giselle had located Brunson's house on a tax map of the area and sent it to Tagliabue. He drove through the locale, noting that Brunson's cabin sat on wooded acreage that seemed endless. It fronted a narrow road and the lake on the other side of that. There was no other structure in sight. The place looked quiet. He stashed the government SUV on a leafy dirt track a mile away and walked the graveled shoreline road back toward the cabin. When he came to the curve of a small shallow cove, the manufactured lines of the cabin's front porch broke the symmetry of nature. He ducked into the woods.

CHAPTER TWENTY

THE ADIRONDACK BUSHMAN

A man named Hoyt Ballard came to realize that even living on the streets of western Queens County with other homeless people was too demanding socially. His stay in a shelter on one August night left him in clean clothes and with a full belly, but it had also caused the left side of his face to droop with Bell's Palsy. It had happened before. It was caused by pressure, the demands of life. He didn't want to talk to people. He didn't want to act polite and pretend to be grateful for a cot and an overcooked stew once a week. He wanted to be left alone.

The other vagabonds in the Fifty-Ninth Street Bridge camp wanted to know about his face once he came back home. When they realized he couldn't speak clearly, some survival-of-the-fittest reflex kicked in and the men began picking on Ballard, the way chickens will peck at an injured member of the flock. These men, who were outwardly friends of Ballard, weren't thinking about survival of the fittest, but their minds had become so attuned to the base level at which they existed that the instinct to take advantage of a less fit individual, one who presented less than a serious threat, prevailed without them thinking much about it. Soon they were pushing him, then getting no response or seeing no defense reaction, they began pummeling him. If guilt requires both consent to, and appreciation of, an evil, the homeless men beating Hoyt Ballard may not have been guilty. It made no difference to Ballard, however, who covered his face so that the pain they inflicted would be less noticeable. He knew he was going to have to find an alternative home after his former friends finished beating and robbing him.

They eventually pushed him into the garbage pile and wrangled over his bedding while he struggled to his feet and scrabbled away into the dark and noisy night. He curled up on a slab of concrete broken from an abutment pad, but was afraid to sleep until the entire camp finally gave out of energy. With the slap and whirl of car tires droning overhead, he slept fitfully, snapping awake every few minutes in fear of the hoboes who had once been his friends and who had now drunk his sweet wine and smoked the remains of his stash.

As he shuffled along on Queens Boulevard the next morning, Hoyt came across a bus chartered by the New York Racing Association parked at the curb in front of a corner store. Clumps of men, and a few women, were boarding, most carrying paper cups of coffee and white bags containing a bagel with a schmear or a buttered hard roll. Their faces were buried in racing forms and newspapers. None were young and all appeared phlegmatic, serious about their business. They were a bit rumpled. This was not a holiday excursion, although a few were vulgar in their enthusiasm about a winner or two the day before. These were serious bettors going upstate to feed their semi-addiction. Hoyt Ballard figured he'd fit in, even though he had never placed a bet at a track in his life. His immediate goal was just to find alternative living accommodations.

The busload was heading up to the Adirondack Mountains, to Saratoga Springs, for a day of racing. He wasn't sure where Saratoga was but decided it was probably better for him than the city streets. He melded with the crowd and found a seat in the back of the bus, away from the groups who drank and ate—and talked. He was alone, the nearest bettors more interested in their racing forms than in one rough-looking man sleeping it off. Hoyt rubbed the side of his face as the door closed with a hiss and the bus drove off in a burst of oily smoke. Once they crossed the Tappen Zee and rolled along the thruway at a steady rumbling speed, he dozed.

Everything was fine for a few hours, until Isaac Fishbine lit up a cigar. He had moved to the empty seat next to Ballard to catch a few winks before they got to the track. The New York Racing Association rep ambled back and said, "You know you can't smoke on the bus, buddy."

"It's for medicinal purposes," Isaac said, flapping a hand up and down in Ballard's direction.

A few other men turned around to Ballard's seat to watch the action. They knew what a homeless man smelled like, and said so. One bettor suggested they leave him be so as to not stir up the stink by his movement, but the racetrack man was having none of it. This bum had infiltrated his big, clean chartered Trailways, threatening the very tradition of honest betting men by sneaking into their midst. He prodded Hoyt Ballard awake.

"You got a ticket for this bus, buddy?"

Ballard looked around frantically, not having had enough sleep and with his numb face disorienting him further. His expression was wild, like a possum in a trap. When he tried to talk, a sound akin to gargling issued forth from his crooked mouth and a string of spittle meandered over his lower lip. The racetrack people leaned away from him—except the association man. He turned red in the face, furious that someone would be shifty enough to board one of the organization's buses without paying ahead of time like everyone else. It made a mockery of the honor system that enabled the transportation arrangement to function smoothly.

He yelled forward, "Jack, pull this damn bus over soon as you can."

Minutes later, Hoyt Ballard was deposited on the side of the Northway, watching the men watching him out the back window as their bus roared back onto the highway, spraying gravel behind itself. Ballard turned away and shuffled into the deep woods. He forced himself to keep moving until the sounds of the road were but a hissing murmur in the background. The scene on the bus had raced his heart in fear and embarrassment. The official on the bus could have called the police. A stay in a jail cell with other malefactors was more than he could bear to think of following his abuse of the night before. He felt weak in the knees, wobbly, so he lay down to rest. It was cool in the woods, and remarkably quiet. He slept.

A rumble woke him. It was his belly, talking to him and telling him that it had not seen nourishment in nearly twenty hours. Hoyt Ballard realized he was not going to find a street to panhandle here in these dark woods of the Adirondack Mountains, so he began walking. Afraid to encounter any other representative of officialdom outside the city, he kept to animal trails when he could find them, following alongside a moving creek other times, always angling away from the highway. He walked until the woods got dark at sundown, late on a summer's evening. When he burrowed into a pile of leaves beneath a massive oak tree and became still, animal sounds began to signal the start of the hunting hour. For some reason, they didn't worry him. Maybe he didn't know that black bears were common in the forests of northern New York State, and that they could injure or kill a man. People were the danger to a man like Ballard, not an animal he had never seen.

The hours of traveling through rough terrain had tired him so he was soon asleep. Shafts of light were knifing through the trees when he woke. He started to walk again. The energy he had regained by sleeping soon drained away: he needed food. He forced himself to forge onward, stopping to rest at ever-shrinking intervals, his thighs chafing and his feet beginning to blister. He moaned in agony. Breathing in with a hiss, he let the pain out with every exhale. Finally he could walk no more. He sat next to the creek and removed his cracked boots, cardboard lining showing in places, and plunged his burning feet into the cold, flowing water. Resting while the sting of his open sores ebbed away as his feet turned numb, Ballard looked up from the stream and blinked in surprise. Was that the back of a house jutting out from the trees on a rise above the stream?

He'd hoped to avoid all contact with fellow humans, but he was weak from hunger and knew he had to cadge a meal. Carrying his boots, he trod barefoot through the shallow water and started to climb the slope. His feet couldn't take the coarseness of the forest floor; he had to sit and wrestle on his blooded socks and boots. When he pushed his creaky body up to the cabin, no one answered his knock. There was no vehicle on the rocked road out front.

Desperate for food, his mind driven to find something to eat, Ballard checked the doors and windows. He was panting by the time he found a bedroom window unlocked and climbed in. He ate crackers and a jar of strawberry jelly from a cupboard. The fridge was empty and off, the door open. The electric baseboard heaters were warm. The water from the kitchen faucet dribbled weakly into a stain on the sink. Sitting on the linoleum of the kitchen floor, his back to the cabinets, his legs stretched out in front of him and his belly bloated from all he'd eaten, Hoyt Ballard tried to make sense of an empty house with electricity on and water left running. Eventually he came to the realization that the people who owned the cabin had left it for the coming winter and would probably not be back until at least late spring. It was a summer house. The mountains in winter might hold some attraction for the owners once snow blanketed the area, but he didn't know about that. He did know that the nights were even now beginning to cool down and September hadn't arrived yet, so he figured the summer people had left.

Someone local would be watching the place for them, however; he was sure of that. He didn't want to attract attention, so he slept the night on the floor and left in the morning. When he passed a mirror in the bedroom he was using to leave the way he had come into the house, he knew instinctively not to look in it. If he had, he would have seen a straggly man in stained and torn clothing. His face was roughened and marked with permanent dirt, pimpled with sores, and flaked with dead skin. His teeth were discolored, his lips cracked. The body odor which wept out of him like the effluent from a sewer pipe he recognized as his own. It was a familiar smell.

Ballard took the empty jelly jar and cellophane wrappings with him, stuffed into the pocket of his coat with a clutch of hard candy and half a box of raisins.

Thus began a lifestyle for Hoyt Ballard that he eventually worked to near perfection. He trudged through the woods day after day as fall settled on the area until he came to a lake ringed with houses on large lots. Slipping back into the deeply forested wilderness, the grizzled man set up a cave by closing the entrance with boulders and logs, leaving enough of an opening for smoke to drift out from the fire he lit every night and extinguished every morning. On days when he was needy—about once a week on average—he closed his cave and set out in a prescribed direction, south one week, east the next and so on. He visited empty houses, trying for a different one each time. Keys were almost always secreted in a planter or under a stone in the shrubbery. Foodstuffs were his usual targets, but he also stole a blanket here and a winter coat there, trying, though, to leave the burgled cabin as if no one had visited. The local caretakers were interested in storm and freeze damage more than robbery so they never noticed anything missing, as long as there were no broken windows or doors. Owners sometimes wondered about tins of veggies or a bag of candy bars they remembered leaving, but it was never enough to bother the local police about.

Rumors drifted around about a mysterious figure glimpsed occasionally by someone fishing or hunting in the woods. The figure always disappeared before he or she could be identified. He became known as the Adirondack Bushman, but no damage or violence was ever reported. The Bushman became a rural legend no one worried about, and that added a touch of spice to north woods living.

Ballard may have been antisocial and irresponsible in his choice of lifestyle, but he was not stupid. He realized that residents of the sparsely populated woods surrounding Saratoga Springs would never summon the animosity to launch a campaign against his presence if he did no harm to them or to their property. At night he raided their garbage cans when they were visiting their summer homes, but always put the tops back on to keep the raccoons out. If he used a hidden key to enter a house when no one was home, he cleaned up after himself and stole only what he assumed the owners would not miss. Venison, for instance. Local friends often gave owners of summer homes gifts of processed and frozen deer, but they found that tastes, evolved in the cafés and bistros of downstate cities, did not easily tolerate the gamey, fatless flesh of wild animals, so Ballard dug out ice-rimed chunks from the bottom of box freezers and lived through the winters. He provoked no confrontations with dogs and picked only a few apples from each tree when they ripened.

Most homeowners in Saratoga knew of the Adirondack Bushman only from tales and rumors. But Anthony Tagliabue would have reason to recognize his survival techniques. Tagliabue discovered his signs because he was looking. He needed to know who was in the vicinity of Jack Brunson's cabin. Some people could be in the forests to do him harm.

First, Tagliabue noticed signs of someone moving through the area. Large animals would never scar the forest floor as a man would because their feet were soft and unshod. Ballard didn't much care if anyone saw his markings as he walked. No one was looking for him and not many people were in the woods, and those who did walk the woods would assume the prints were made by another hunter. The trail of prints left by Ballard to and from the Brunson cabin appeared to be weeks old. Tagliabue noted them and then pushed them to the back of his mind as he worked his way to the back of the cabin. Daylight was failing.

CHAPTER TWENTY-ONE

Yellow light issued from the windows of the cabin. Tagliabue could smell smoke and saw it being pushed around by the evening breeze as it floated out of the chimney. Wishing he'd worn a warmer coat, he willed his body to ignore the dropping temperature as he lay in the deep shadow of an old pine and watched. He saw one man walk past the kitchen window. It was Brunson's bodyguard, the one whose nose he had broken in the Pelham Island. He was a man, Tagliabue assumed would be driven by thoughts of vengeance and used to violence, a man he would have to pay special attention to when he breached the perimeter of the house.

The bodyguard had not been on the Hatteras. Tagliabue figured that he had been sent to the cabin to assure the area was safe enough to hide the defector if Cuthbert and Brunson were able to capture him. Maybe he even drove them to the cabin when they abandoned the boat.

The rest of the windows of the cabin were covered in curtains but when he circled the house he could see silhouettes he recognized as Jack and the older man, Cuthbert. He saw no one who could be the Russian. It was important to know where he was—if he was even in the cabin—and if he was alive. After reconnoitering slowly and quietly for another fifteen minutes, he came to realize that the defector was probably in the one room in total darkness. A bedroom, he figured.

At about nine thirty, when the sun was fully gone from the sky, the kitchen door opened and the bodyguard came out to the small back deck for a smoke. Through the opened doorway before the back door swung closed, Tagliabue could see Brunson and Cuthbert sitting in the living room, one room back from the kitchen. Broken Nose looked around as he smoked, a rifle hanging from his left shoulder. When he ground out the butt on the sole of his hiking boot and started back in, Tagliabue came up fast behind him. The man turned, reaching for the Ruger tactical rifle already slipping toward his hand. Tagliabue shot him in the face with Giselle's Walther from two feet away. Blood and bone and brain tissue were still spraying from the back of the bodyguard's head as Tagliabue lunged past him in a crouch. Cuthbert had leaped to his feet when Tagliabue's first shot sounded. He moved with remarkable agility, but the attack was almost instantaneous and he had no chance to defend himself. Cuthbert was drawing a gun from a shoulder holster when Tagliabue fired at him. The first round missed but made the older man flinch, ruining the smoothness of his draw. The second caught him in the chest and the third tore open his neck. Thrashing, he crashed into a flat-screen television set and went with it to the floor, his Glock flying from his hand, the TV still blaring a ball game.

Tagliabue's momentum carried him fully into the living room; by then, Jack Brunson was kneeling on the carpeted floor behind the recliner he had been sitting in, with a big pistol out. Tagliabue had a quick thought of talking to him, but it was too late. The .357 Magnum in Brunson's hand boomed. Tagliabue felt the impact turn him and twist him off his feet. He landed on his right side. The front door slammed open seconds later. He could feel the cool night air drifting through the cabin as he lay on the floor in a sudden silence, trying to assess his situation.

Brunson's bullet had caught him just below and to the left of his diaphragm. His belly hurt and it took him a minute to get his breath back. His Kevlar vest had prevented any mortal damage but he was bruised by the powerful bullet. The bodyguard was dead and Cuthbert was sprawled on the TV, eyes wide, hands empty. As Tagliabue's ears recovered from the noise of guns firing, he could hear the sounds of the late-season Yankee game and a wet, gurgling noise coming from the turned agent. He could not hear Brunson.

Getting to his feet slowly, tracking with his gun, he toed Cuthbert's handgun out of the dying man's reach and stuck it in his waistband. Bent over like a man with stomach cramps, he moved through the small house until he found someone tied by the wrists to a bed in the second bedroom. He whispered to him.

"You hurt?"

The man shook his head. Tagliabue slipped a knife from his belt scabbard and sliced the plastic ties.

"Get ready to move fast."

"Da."

"I'm going to check out the rest of the cabin. I'll be back for you in a minute."

"Da."

He found no one else. Cuthbert had become silent. Aaron Judge was facing a 2-2 count in the fifth. Tagliabue searched the corpse quickly, the Walther never leaving his hand. He found keys on a Land Rover fob and a wallet. Leaving the car key, he stuffed the wallet into a big leg pocket of his cargo pants. He took a wallet and the tactical rifle from the stiffening bodyguard and turned out the lights. Standing in a corner, upright by now in the dark, Tagliabue could hear nothing. Jack Brunson must have left the cabin. Was he waiting outside?

Leaving the remains of the two dead men for the cleanup crew, he shuffled along a wall to the captive's room. He led the Russian to the back door. The man would not look at the bodyguard and his ruined skull. Tagliabue spoke in a whisper.

"I'm going out now. You wait for me to whistle, then come out fast and go behind the first big tree. You understand?"

"Da."

"Repeat the instructions to me, please."

Panting hard, the man said, "Go out fast. Go behind big tree."

Tagliabue nodded and patted the man's back. Then he shot out the door, leaped off the deck, and ran into the woods. No gunfire. He waited. The woods were silent. He waited some more, listening hard for any movement. When he whistled once, short and sharp, the Russian came out of the house at a run. He crashed into the woods and fetched up behind a tree near Tagliabue. The two of them waited in the dark forest.

Tagliabue had thought of taking the Land Rover parked in front of the cabin, but worried about Brunson lying in ambush. With a road and parking area in front, there were a lot of shooting lanes. Jack Brunson was a lawyer, not a soldier, and he was probably halfway to Saratoga Springs in his own car by now, but Tagliabue could not take that chance with the radioman from the *Leonov*. There could be other associates of Cuthbert and Brunson in the area. Brunson could have called for help. Deciding it was safer for him and the defector to make their way back through the forest to his government Ford, he punched Giselle's number on the cell she'd given him.

"Yes?"

"I'm out of the cabin with our man. Cuthbert and one other inoperable inside. Brunson on the loose, armed and uninjured."

"We'll remove the debris and clean the cabin. Get back to base with your friend."

She clicked off. Tagliabue took the phone apart and slipped the card into his pocket. He smashed the phone underfoot and put the pieces in another cargo pocket.

"What's your name?"

"Alexis."

"Okay, Alex. Here's the deal: I work for the US government. We have to get to a hotel in Albany. I have a car but we have to go through the woods to get to it. That means we have to wait until it gets light out so we can find our way through the woods.

And there's one bad guy left and he could be hiding in the dark. Understand?"

"Da. We should go away from house."

The Russian's voice was pitched a little higher than Tagliabue expected, but was steady. He was young, despite his gray hair, and slender, needing a shave. Life under Putin might be making Alexis show the aging effects of stress, but his mind still worked. Putting some distance between them and the house, where Brunson could still be lurking, was Tagliabue's idea as well.

"Good idea. Let's move."

They worked their way through the woods for ten minutes, pausing often to listen for pursuit. Tagliabue hoped they were heading in the direction of his government Ford but the main goal was to put distance between themselves and any possible danger. He tried to keep the lake to their left but it was difficult to see any-thing clearly much of the time. When they stopped for the night, both men took cover at the base of trees. Tagliabue thought of giving Cuthbert's automatic to Alexis but decided against it. God only knew what the defector's mind had cobbled together so far, after being kidnapped from the small boat Carlos had used to pick him up. As a radio operator, the young man could not be familiar with the level of violence he had experienced in the last twenty-four hours. Did he have any reason to think Tagliabue represented any safer an escort than the three who had him imprisoned in Brunson's cabin?

He settled into the pine needles and listened for movement as he kept an eye on Alexis, who sat with his back to a tree, his chin on his chest.

First light was just beginning to color the waters of Lough-berry Lake when the Russian suddenly lunged toward him. At almost the same instant, bark blew off the tree above where Alexis had been sleeping and the crack of a long rifle echoed in the woods. Tagliabue scooted around his tree, pulling Alexis in close.

"You see him?"

Alexis pointed into the woods in front of them after touching his ear. The Russian must have heard something but it was deadly quiet now. Tagliabue had the bodyguard's rifle in his hands as he scanned the area ahead of them. The gun was a Mini-14, the new 5847 that fired standard NATO-caliber bullets. It felt like a plastic carbine to Tagliabue, but he knew the magazine held twenty rounds and was full. He had checked it automatically when he snatched the gun from Broken Nose and was glad to have that many shots available now, in the middle of a sniper attack. The rifle was light and short and quiet, probably the perfect gun for hunting a man in the deep woods.

The man who shot at Alexis was a pro, no doubt about that and little doubt that he had at least one partner to spot for him. Now that his prey was alerted, the assassin was satisfied to sit still and let his target move first. To the assassin's disadvantage was the daylight creeping in among the pines and up the side of the rocky hill behind his two targets. Alexis lay next to Tagliabue like a dead man, his jacket covering his head.

Five minutes passed in silence. Tagliabue could feel sweat forming at the small of his back, despite the coolness of the mountain air. Something moved in a tiny glade some two hundred yards to his left. His sight was obstructed in that direction so he listened carefully. More cautious movement, faint rustling in the undergrowth. Tagliabue trained his rifle in the direction of the clearing. He took in a breath and held it. Something brown ambled into his line of sight.

"Don't shoot the deer. He's my friend."

The voice behind him startled Tagliabue. He spun around, the Walther in his hand, a round up the chute. A man squatted in a patch of sunlight on the side of the hill facing Tagliabue and Alexis, ten yards from them and maybe ten feet above them. His arms rested on his thighs and his hands hung loosely over his knees. Eyes and mouth both popped open when he saw the handgun but he didn't move. Tagliabue couldn't shoot an unarmed man who was no apparent threat to him or Alexis. This one with a lopsided face and scraggly white beard looked . . . incompetent somehow. Tagliabue couldn't be specific about his reasoning at that tense moment, but he didn't sense danger from him. Maybe it was the blank look on his face. He barked a harsh whisper at him.

"Get out of the sun, man. There's someone shooting at us."

"Not no more."

"What the hell do you mean?"

"I seen 'em both head off."

"Which way?"

Hoyt Ballard pointed to his left, away from the lake. That meant, if the forest man was right, that there were two shooters for certain and they were in the process of circling around to flank him and Alexis. The Russian's head was out from under his jacket by then; he was looking back and forth from his rescuer to this strange creature in the sun.

"Get down anyway. They're not leaving, just changing positions."

The strange man, who seemed to blend in with the foliage around him, worked his lips as he appeared to consider the advice. He said, "I'm going home."

With that, the Adirondack Bushman stood up and walked across a section of flat gray rock and disappeared into the side of the hill. There must be a cave in the rock there, Tagliabue surmised, a cave with a hidden entrance. He told the Russian to follow the forest man, and then he made a decision he hoped he wasn't going to live to regret—if he lived at all. He gave Alexis the Glock he'd taken from the knotted rug in front of Cuthbert's body.

"It's ready to shoot, Alex. All you have to do is point and pull the trigger."

The Russian nodded and took the gun. He didn't look comfortable handling it, but he put it in his pocket.

"Just don't shoot me by accident. I'll shout out when I come back."

The Russian nodded again and then climbed to his feet and went off the way their visitor had gone, running bent over. He too disappeared into the side of the hill. Tagliabue crept off to intercept the two gunmen.

CHAPTER TWENTY-TWO

He moved at a crouch, trying desperately to make as little noise as possible. The thick layer of pine needles helped, just as they'd helped the two assassins begin their flanking exercise, but now visibility had improved markedly. The sun slanted through the trees, glistening off the dew that glazed low grasses, throwing shadows and striking the eyes of anyone or anything facing east. The men who had fired a single shot at Alexis and who were seen leaving the area by the Adirondack Bushman were somewhere out there, cautious men who had observed the destruction their enemy could wreak.

Tagliabue was at a disadvantage in this kind of warfare, and he knew it. He was too tall to be inconspicuous and too big to be as agile as a true jungle fighter. He had trained in special ops, so he could move quietly and quickly, and he could shoot well, but he'd done his service in the rocky wasteland that was Afghanistan and had never fought in a jungle or a forest. And he didn't hunt for sport. Hoping that the assassins were city men, he moved forward.

The trees became thicker and more closely spaced the farther he got from the lake. When he determined he was far enough from the Bushman's hideaway, the place on the rock cliff where he had disappeared and the place he called his home, Tagliabue slung the Ruger over his shoulder and climbed a fat aspen plugged deep into the rich soil. Deer had been snacking on the tree's suckers, so there was a small clearing around the tree. He found a big limb about ten feet up and straddled it, his back to the trunk. Knowing that hunters tended not to look up as they hunted, he waited. The leaves were fat and green, some were translucent where the rising sun hit them on its passage up. Not many had fallen yet, so sight lines were few. But they also protected him from anyone wise enough to search for a deer stand on the perimeter of clearings. That was how Tagliabue spotted the first of them.

The man was on one knee, peering through the scope on his rifle, slowly rotating the weapon through the branches of trees to the east of a clearing some hundred yards from his own perch. The man knew enough to watch for moving shadows, to pass on pines and spruces which offered no branches thick enough to bear a man's heft. The gunman stayed in the penumbra of a thick tree, barely visible, a patch of sunlight on his shirt creating a tiny target and only the barrel of his gun protruding into the clearing. He moved it so deliberately that it looked like just another thin branch, but Tagliabue had seen its brief reflection off the low sun. Tagliabue's line of sight was marginal, and he had to shoot through a leaf below and forward of him. He fired a single shot. The Ruger's crack was almost lost in the open air. The target's gun fell into the clearing and his shadow disappeared.

The Ruger was a quiet rifle. Even so, the report startled Tagliabue and drove a thrush into the air from the aspen that hid him. He slung the rifle quickly and dropped down from the tree. It was a noisy dismount, but his cover was blown and he didn't know if the second man had seen his muzzle flash, or the spooked bird. Crawling slowly on his belly, he moved toward the man he'd shot, hoping the second hunter would try to go to his aid. It took ten minutes to spot him. He was curled on his right side, his left arm sticking out. He was still breathing, red bubbles forming on his lips with each labored exhale. The woods were silent except when the wounded man spoke.

"Tommy, I'm hurt, man."

His voice was cast low, each word punctuated with a gasp. Tagliabue waited. A second man burst from the trees in a short run and dove to the ground. Tagliabue saw him but there wasn't time to aim and shoot. He held his fire. The three men lay on the forest floor, each twenty yards or so from the other, only the wounded one moving. He clutched his gut with one hand and pulled himself forward with the other. A piteous moan twisted into the air.

"God . . . help me."

Tagliabue heard his partner start to move to his aid. The second gunman moved, then stopped, listening. He moved again. He was suddenly at the wounded man's side.

"Lemme see where he got you, Joe." His voice was muted. It barely carried through the dry morning air to Tagliabue's location. He had to hold his breath to hear what the man was saying.

"Ah, fuck, it hurts, Tommy."

"Okay, man. It's gonna be all right. Lemme see."

Tommy rolled Joe over and unbuttoned his shirt. "Shit, you been gut shot."

"Am I gonna die?"

"Naw. If I can get you outta here we can get it stitched up. Keep some pressure on it so's it don't bleed so bad."

"Okay, Tommy." Joe was still breathing hard but his voice seemed calmer than before, as if his partner's presence had eased his fears.

Tommy slid off Joe's belt to tie a tourniquet. As he raised up a few inches with the belt in his hand, Tagliabue shot him in the head. It was an easy shot from the short distance. The wounded man wailed. Tagliabue put one in his head too. As the gunshots echoed away, the forest turned silent again.

He slung the Ruger over his shoulder and worked his way back to the spot where Alex had almost been shot, the last place he had seen him and the Bushman. Now he had to be careful that he didn't get shot by the man he was trying to rescue. When he arrived at the bottom of the long flat rock that Alexis had walked across before he disappeared into the Bushman's lair, he called out.

The Russian answered, "We are okay."

"Good. Don't shoot. I'm coming in."

Tagliabue blew out a breath. He had to trust someone, so clenching his abdominals he stepped up on the flat rock and walked to the hill. He found tree limbs and small trunks closing off the face of a cave, a cave he hadn't seen even from the bottom of the rock. The trees still had leaves on them. Two pairs of eyes looked out at him. The tree door opened and he walked in.

"How often do you change the trees?"

The Bushman answered, "I change one pretty near ever' week."

The cave was about five feet deep, lined with a dried grass bed, a flat stone stove, and an open fireplace fashioned from rocks braced in place with parts of a bicycle, an old heater box, and pieces of aluminum framing. A section of rusted stovepipe vented the fireplace. Tagliabue spoke as he kept watch on the woods outside the Bushman's cave.

"You comfortable in here?"

"Best home I ever had."

Tagliabue nodded at that. "Where'd you used to live?"

"Under the Fifty-Ninth Street Bridge, mostly."

"You need anything from us?"

"Don't think so."

"Okay then. Thank you for warning us about the bad guys moving off. And thank you for accommodating Alex here while I took care of some business."

"Alexis."

"Beg your pardon?"

"His name's Alexis."

"I know. I call him Alex because we're friends."

The former homeless man said nothing to that. Tagliabue told him he and the Russian were leaving. He said nothing to that either. Alexis went over and shook his hand. He and Tagliabue slipped out onto the flat rock and walked through the woods to the road fronting Lake Loughberry.

"Are we friends, *bolshoy chelovek?*"

"That depends on what a *bolshoy chelovek* is," Tagliabue responded with a smile.

"It means large man. I don't know your name."

"I'm Anthony."

"I'm Alex."

They laughed at that, both relieved to be safe finally, and walked down the graveled road until they came to Giselle's big Ford SUV. Driving past Brunson's cabin, they saw a gray Hyundai stashed in a copse of pines. The assassins' car, Tagliabue figured: Jack Brunson would never drive something so mundane. He went on into Saratoga Springs. He stopped at a CVS and bought a cell phone. He called Giselle and told her about Tommy and Joe in the woods.

"And there's a guy near there living in a cave."

"Ah, yes, that must be the famed Adirondack Bushman, part of the local lore I've been reading. What about him?"

"He did the right thing for us. I don't want him hurt or hassled."

"Roger that. These guys are a cleanup crew, not operatives like you. They just now got to Brunson's cabin. I'll tell them about your Bushman friend."

"I appreciate that."

"What do you know about Brunson?"

"Nothing. I'm thinking he's on the run. We're watching out for him anyway, in case C. L. Cuthbert taught him enough to make him come after us. I doubt it though. He shot me in my vest and didn't try to finish me off. If he thought I was dead because of a single body mass shot, he must still be an amateur. I imagine he's in way over his head."

"Okay. Watch for him and get the Russki here safely."

Tagliabue drove through the McDonald's on Broadway for some road food and then out to I-87, the Northway, heading south. On the road to Albany, the Russian asked about the two colleagues of Cuthbert and Brunson.

"They're not in the game anymore, Alex. Forget about them. Brunson, now, he's a different story."

"He still playing your game?"

His tone made Tagliabue look over at him.

"Look here, Alex. You're a brave guy, doing what you did. You knew it was a dangerous move. You're lucky to be alive. These guys after us and the ones that kidnapped you and killed Carlos were either going to give you back to Mr. Putin and his torture chambers or kill you. They were probably just waiting for word to filter back to them from Moscow. Put these guys out of your mind. Put me out of your mind. Life is going to get a lot better for you real quick. Think about that, instead of worrying about a couple of mutts who are better off dead."

Alexis was quiet for a few highway miles. Then he asked, "What about Brunson? Will he not kill me if he can?"

"He's a lawyer, not a gangster, although I admit it's hard sometimes to tell the two apart. I don't know how he got mixed up with Cuthbert and his crew. I suspect Cuthbert sold him a story about how much money he could make by snatching you. Jack's not a good guy but he's never been involved in dangerous stuff like this before. So he's a wild card, all right."

"He will come after us, do you think?"

"Possibly. I think he probably believes he killed me or at least put me out of commission in the cabin and is on the run. But then again, he did shoot me. We know he's armed. He probably doesn't know about the two thugs sent to kill us in the woods, so maybe he's out looking for us. Or for you.

"Jack Brunson's a nervous cat by now. He stepped into an alley for a little fun and profit and got into something so dark he never imagined it could happen to him. Now he's part of that darkness. That's what I think."

After a few more miles, he asked Alexis who killed Carlos on the Hatteras.

"The other *bolshoy chelovek* with the, um, plaster over his nose. He hit him with his gun, in the head." He shook his head at the memory. "It was terrible, the way it sounds, the way he falls."

"I'm sorry you had to witness that, Alex. Carlos was a good guy. The guy with the broken nose has paid for his sins."

They were quiet until the big car pulled into a parking place outside the entrance of the Embassy Suites. Before he left the car, Alexis turned to Tagliabue and said, "I'm glad we're friends, Anthony. Thank you."

In Suite 104 Giselle took the wallets Tagliabue handed her and gave them to a suit.

"There are two more in the woods."

"Roger," Giselle said. "Our cleanup crew will get them if they haven't already."

She turned and spoke softly to Alexis in what sounded to Tagliabue like Russian. The young man nodded and replied. Before he went off with another suit, he turned to Tagliabue, and shook his hand. "I will remember you," he said, "no matter what you say."

Giselle and her agent sat down at the same table they had used to discuss the hunt for the Russian. She sighed.

"You broke the back of Cuthbert's ring, Tony. They were a serious thorn in the side of The Project. For a long time now. You also got our defector back. I guess I should express my thanks."

"You never have before."

She laughed, her teeth-showing smile. "I don't mean by saying thank you. I mean to give you a bonus."

"That would be timely."

"I know. You mean to leave the game, marry Agnes Ann, and live out on Westfarrow Island, mucking stalls and breeding. Mares, I mean. Although I suspect you'll be doing some hominid breeding as well."

"How could you know I want to retire?"

"You've been at it for a long while, and you came back different from this one. I can see it in your eyes, big guy. Everybody with a working conscience has a limit. You've reached yours. Know that you've done a lot of morally good things for the human race, and I hope you'll take some comfort in that."

He nodded in reply.

"George will drive you back to the airport. You can catch the two fifteen to Boston."

"George? You mean your minions have names?"

"Please forget I said that. He won't answer to it anyway."

He smiled at her and reached for the doorknob. Giselle spoke again.

"Tony." He turned to her. "Don't forget that Jack Brunson is still out there. He's no concern to The Project, but he might not know that. The state constabulary will be seizing his assets once we tell them about his activity in the murder and kidnapping, so I expect he'll be somewhat desperate for money after a while. I don't know how that might affect you and Agnes Ann. Just take care, eh?"

He nodded.

Giselle continued, "And I'll take my Walther back."

CHAPTER TWENTY-THREE

Anthony Tagliabue flew to Boston, thinking all the while about Giselle's parting admonition. Jack Brunson was somewhere out there. He might think he had killed Tagliabue in the cabin, in which case he might think he could escape legal repercussions from his part in the kidnapping of the Russian defector and the murder of Carlos Solis. He might be able to claim he wasn't in the cabin when the criminal enterprise took place, although he probably could be placed on the Hatteras. If he had learned enough about Giselle's agency from the turncoat Cuthbert, he might even realize that most traces of his latest criminal activity would be erased by her cleanup crew. At least from his cabin. The boat might be a different story, since the Coast Guard already had found Carlos's corpse on board, but who knows what strings Giselle or her boss could pull to smooth over that episode also?

Brunson was probably in hiding somewhere, trying to establish an alibi for whatever charges the police might try to bring against him. Eventually, though, he would represent a threat to Agnes Ann and her son, if not to Tagliabue himself. Tagliabue wondered if he should hunt Brunson down.

The question was rendered more or less moot when he found Agnes Ann waiting at his apartment. She hadn't heard from her ex-husband, but she did have important news for Tony: her diocese had transmitted word from its tribunal that her marriage to

Brunson was considered nullified on the grounds of his early and often unfaithfulness and his abandonment of their child.

"The canon lawyers found that he couldn't have taken his marriage vows seriously, based on his actions after we were married."

"So, no commitment, no marriage?"

"Right. It's as if I was never married."

"They think like that, these canon lawyers?"

"They do. Fortunately, we don't know any of them."

"What about Jesse? If there was no marriage, what does that make him?"

"Not a bastard, if that's what you mean. This is just a decision of the church; it has no legal standing. As far as the State of Maine is concerned, Jack and I were married and divorced. But it was never about legalities for me. It's about my faith. Clear?"

"Clear enough. You made a vow and you were sticking to it. Now the vow has been voided. I'm thinking this means we are free to wed, you and me."

"If we agree to, yes."

Tagliabue grew quiet. He knew he had a lot to learn about this woman.

"So, you mean, ah, if I ask you and you say yes?"

"Right again, big guy."

"Agnes Ann, will you marry me?"

"Just as soon as you get me a ring."

"A ring?"

"Yeah, an engagement ring. That's how humans pledge their troth in this country."

"Pledge their troth," he said. She waited peacefully, drinking a cup of coffee at his dining room table. She smiled at him.

He said, "I need to take a nap."

Afterward he did go to Bingham Jewelers and purchase an engagement ring. Agnes Ann put it on and looked as happy as he had ever seen her. Her eyes were wet when she told him she would, indeed, marry him.

They did that a week later in a short ceremony during the noon mass. They had a celebratory lunch, along with the priest, Jesse, Tom Sharkey, Maurizio Tagliabue, and Timmy O'Brien, at Boncoddo's Oyster House. If Carlos had survived, Tagliabue would have invited him.

The newlyweds flew out to Westfarrow Island, where Anthony got to work at the horse ranch. He fixed fences and cut firewood; he schmoozed Auntie Maybelle. He tuned farm vehicles and hauled broken ones to the repair shop; he mucked out stalls and composted the manure. The weeks drifted by. October brought a change of leaves. They did not hear from or about Jack Brunson. When they drank coffee on the front porch and watched the sun go down over the Atlantic, they did not speak of him.

They did speak of Agnes Ann's filly, Francine.

"She's developed a little softness on a bone in her fetlock," she said to her husband. "The vet thinks a few months rest will make it calcify and become stronger than before, so we're not going to race her again until the spring."

"I hope it's not something serious."

"I don't think so, and neither does Mr. Collier. I think he's happy not to risk running her again as a baby."

"Well, one other good thing is that we won't have to leave the island again to go racing in New York."

"There's that, Tony. Maybe we'll have a spell of peace and quiet."

They did, but it was a short spell.

◦∾◦

Two weeks deeper into the month, after Tagliabue watched condensed breaths of the horses wreathe their heads like cirrus clouds as they clopped in from the meadow for their breakfast, Johnny Coleman called. Tagliabue agreed to meet him at the town marina. When they drove up an hour later in Agnes Ann's F-150, they saw the detective standing on the dock next to a familiar white sportfisherman.

"You joining the yachting set, Detective?" Tagliabue asked.

"Not hardly. One ride out here is enough for me."

"You drive this thing?" Tagliabue gestured to the sixty-footer at the pier. Coleman laughed. He said to Agnes Ann, "Your old man thinks he's funny."

Sagadahoc County agreed to ferry a charter captain home to the island if he would pilot the Hatteras. Tagliabue thought he knew why but he asked anyway. Coleman sighed.

"Somehow, this evidentiary property ended up titled in your name, Anthony. I suspect it actually belonged to Mr. Brunson before it became property of the US government when it was used in a federal offense. You know anything about that?"

"How could I?"

"Course not. Well, some goddamn federal—excuse me, Mrs. Tagliabue. Some agency I never heard of asked the sheriff to deliver it to you after we were done with it. The Coast Guard found a dead body on it, some undocumented immigrant named Solis. The FBI did a forensic scan of the boat and then handed it over to us. We didn't find anything much on it except traces of you and one John 'Jack' Brunson. The sheriff went down to Portsmouth to raise hell about federal interference. When he got back, he told me to deliver it to you. Same as before."

Coleman sounded frustrated.

"Johnny, I'm sorry they're being so high-handed. I'm not allowed to tell you anything more, except that the case is done with. Over. Jack is sort of a loose end, but he seems to have disappeared."

Coleman sipped on his paper cup of coffee. He hadn't offered any to Tagliabue or his wife. "You hunting Brunson?" he asked.

"No. The case is done and I've retired. I hope never to see Jack Brunson again."

They drove the detective out to the airfield where he caught the noon shuttle to the mainland. Afterward they lunched at the

Pelham Island, open post-season only on Friday, Saturday, and Sunday. They sat in the main dining room and watched the bartender lay logs in the fireplace. There were customers at four other tables, none nearby.

"Was that wishful thinking? About Jack?" Agnes Ann asked.

"I've asked myself that, Aggie, many, many times. I'm still not sure. I believe he got into this, er, deal with some bad characters. He probably thought he could handle them, but his idea of bad guys is the Magpie or Red Fowler. He had no idea how vicious and remorseless these international gangsters can be. He's probably hiding under a desk somewhere far away."

"But he can't just leave his business here. He's bound to show up again."

Tagliabue nodded to her as the waitress arrived with their bowls of she-crab soup. She poured small carafes of sherry in them and left.

"He might. I don't think you or I are ever going to hear from him again. His law office is probably worthless now that his name has been besmirched by the state police and the sheriff's office . . ."

"Besmirched?"

He ducked his head and colored a little. "It seems to me, Jack got in over his head, wanting to be a mob lawyer and make piles of dirty money. He found out how dangerous that life can be. I doubt he wants any more of it."

"Did he also find out how dangerous you can be, Tony?"

He smiled at her.

"I thought you liked having a dangerous man around."

"Oh, I do. I'm not complaining. I know you'll have to go off now and then, even though you're retired. I just wanted you to know."

She spooned some of her bisque as she looked at her husband, as if her view was through a mist somehow. He looked back and ate quietly. After lunch she asked him how he came to be in possession of such an expensive boat.

"In my last conversation with her, Giselle intimated—"

"Intimated?"

"Suggested. She led me to believe that her agency was going to grant me a bonus, for my years of service. The Hatteras was it, I guess."

"She might be mysterious, but she's generous."

"Amen to that."

"What will you do with her, the boat, I mean?"

He laughed, shaking his head. He knew what she meant, still fighting off some latent jealousy over Giselle, who had taken up so much of his time and energy in years past.

"I'll clean her and get her shipshape and then sell it when the season starts back in."

"Maybe we should buy another cargo boat, for hauling hay. We're going to need some every year."

"Good idea. Maybe I can teach you to be my mate aboard ship."

"I'd like that," she said.

He put on Joshua's old Red Sox cap and they left together to make arrangements to berth the Hatteras at the marina until he could prepare their dock to keep her over the winter. On the way back to the horse farm, Agnes Ann noted darkening clouds west of the tree line and the bite of the wind through the pickup's windows.

"You might be a rich yachtsman, sonny boy, but you'll have to start feeding hay to the horses once the fields frost over."

"I'm ready for that," he said and powered up the windows.

CHAPTER TWENTY-FOUR

A week later the first frost arrived. Tagliabue went out to feed the animals before dawn. Along with the four horses—two geldings for riding and two brood mares—Agnes Ann kept two scrub goats who lived in the stalls with the horses at night and went out to the pastures with them every day. The goats picked their own stalls for the night and spent their days grazing. They were companion animals only and she thought they calmed the horses' nervous dispositions. They ate whatever the bigger beasts ate. All six were moving around, stomping and shaking their heads, the goats bleating. The horses put their heads out over the half-door and watched as Tagliabue hauled a bale of hay off the nearest stack and cut the baling twine with his pocket knife. They nickered at him, hungry, since the fall grass was no longer adequate and they wanted hay.

The bale sprang open. He took a slice for each horse and shook it out in his or her manger, looking for dust or any suspicious-looking growth. He let the goats out in the barn and fed them on the floor. When everyone was munching contentedly, Tagliabue picked up the half-bale remaining to put it back on the stack, piled off the floor by Jesse on a platform just tall enough to keep the goats from reaching it. Jesse always stacked the hay as it came in, newest to the back, so it occurred to Tagliabue that the day's feed he had just given the animals was from the shipment brought over on *Maven* the day she had been holed by the Magpie. When he set the half-bale on the platform, something foreign pushed out from what had been the center of the intact bale. He pulled the hay away to see what it was: a baggie full of yellow capsules. Each was stamped with the legend: "IG322 300mg." Tearing the bale open, he found ten quart-sized bags hiding inside; all were filled to bursting with pills.

Tagliabue felt his stomach clench and he looked around him quickly, suddenly filled with anxiety. He had closed the barn door behind him when he entered, in case one of the horses got out of his stall. The lights he had left on low. Now he switched them on high and pulled his knife from his jeans. He opened hay bales at random. There were bags of pills hidden in every one he opened.

When Anthony Tagliabue went around the acreage of his wife's horse farm, caring for the animals, fixing, feeding, and cleaning, he carried his big Glock in a holster on the left side of his belt, the butt facing forward. There was a bullet in the pipe and the magazine was stacked full with more of them. He and Agnes Ann argued to each other that the gun was for varmints or maybe even to euthanize a badly injured farm animal, but they both were on edge because Jack Brunson was unaccounted for. Brunson was a dangerous loose end that was flapping around and distracting them from their happiness. Once Tagliabue realized the stacks of hay concealed some kind of drugs, he jacked a round into the handgun's chamber. He let the animals out to pasture and walked to the house.

Agnes Ann had a pot of coffee perking and was pan-frying a few herring fillets she had smoked the day before. She snapped a look at Tagliabue as soon as he walked through the door.

"What's the matter, Tony?"

"How do you know anything's the matter?" he asked as he reached for the landline telephone on the table.

"You've finally learned to pace yourself and now you're back to moving like you're fighting a gale. What's up?"

"I figured out why Joshua was killed and the *Maven* holed."

⁓

Constable Ian Fletcher arrived within the hour. He accepted a mug of coffee and agreed to stand guard in the barn until Detective Coleman arrived from the mainland. Agnes Ann took him out a plate of fried herring and cornbread for breakfast. It was lunchtime before Coleman arrived with two lab people and a satchel of equipment. The pills were gabapentin; there were four hundred sacks of them in the hay.

"They're prescription narcotics?" Agnes Ann asked a female tech named Debra, a short, stout redhead with a friendly smile.

"Actually, no. Gabapentin is a drug for nerve pain, but junkies say it increases the high when you take it with an opioid."

"How much are they worth?"

Debra looked at Coleman, who raised his eyebrows at her. She went on.

"I'd say, on this island in the summer, when it's wall-to-wall tourists, maybe a buck or two each capsule."

"So, somewhere between $1,500 and $3,000 per bag, and there are four hundred bags, right?"

Debra smiled and nodded.

Agnes Ann rubbed her temples with her fingertips. "How much is that, Tony?"

While Tagliabue was working the arithmetic in his head, Coleman spoke, "Between $600,000 and $1.2 million, street value." He held up his phone with a shy grin. "Calculator."

"Jesus God. You think Jack would shoot someone and try to sink a boat for another million dollars? That's obscene," Agnes Ann said.

"That's also a lot of money," Tagliabue said.

"Well, ma'am," Coleman replied. "We don't think he meant to do either thing. Now that we know he owned that fast sport-fisherman, we think he meant to move the drugs out of Bath on the *Maven* . . ."

"Why would he do that, if he's got his own boat?" Agnes Ann asked.

"Well, we're speculating here, but maybe his boat couldn't carry all the hay. Maybe an expensive new boat would have been too noticeable in town. Maybe he didn't want to be seen tearing apart all the hay to get to the stuff. Maybe it was just a crappy plan. We don't know. We do think the idea was to disable *Maven* and rescue Anthony at sea on the Hatteras, then come back to retrieve his drugs before she sank. The plot was foiled when Anthony didn't radio for help. Maybe the drugs weren't even destined to end up on Westfarrow Island; maybe Brunson was going to run them up to the Canadian Maritimes or down to Boston. That there boat . . ." He pointed behind him. "Your husband's new vessel, can go a long ways in a hurry.

"The victim, Mr. White, was what we call collateral damage. We're pretty sure Marv Harris messed up when he let White find him on Anthony's boat."

She shook her head slowly at his reasoning but said nothing else. Agnes Ann and Tagliabue agreed to vacate the house while Coleman set up a surveillance. Bill Hammet would come to feed and water the animals once each day at noon. The horses would remain out in the fields.

"We'll try it for a week and see how that works out. If you hear anything from Brunson call my cell right away."

The Tagliabues flew to Portsmouth and from there to Saint Croix. Four days later, while Agnes Ann was examining how the sun didn't seem to tan her napping husband's scar tissue, Coleman called, waking him.

"We got him. You can come home."

Even with the poor reception, she could hear the excitement in the detective's voice.

"Good for you, Detective Coleman. Did he come to the farm?"

"No, he bought a ticket to Westfarrow using his own credit card and driver's license. The ticket agent had a BOLO and called my guy at the SO. We picked him up at the airport on the island."

She didn't know what the acronyms meant, so she asked Tagliabue, who was by then sitting up on his deck chair rubbing his face.

"BOLO is Be On the Look Out and SO is the sheriff's office. I guess Jack decided to just brazen it out."

"He is a crafty lawyer. I hope he doesn't get away with it."

"It's probably going to be a long trial. They're charging Jack with selling class-three narcotics without a license, conspiracy to commit murder, two counts of conspiracy to kidnap—that's Alexis and me—and using a gun in the commission of a felony. I think they may even try to tie him in with Marv in the bombing of *Maven* and the killing of Joshua. There could be a federal connection, for all I know, since the Hatteras was at sea when they beat Carlos to death. It probably won't even start for months. Nobody's going to rush things."

"Agree," she said. "No sense wasting the rest of this vacation by hurrying back, is there?"

"No sense at all. I'm going to wake up in this pretty lagoon we're staying in front of."

"Okay. I'm going inside to get bare and wait for you."

∽

The next call from Detective Coleman advised Tagliabue that Brunson had been let out on bail, having pleaded not guilty and ignorant of all the crimes he was alleged to have committed. Coleman ruefully admitted he had been optimistic earlier about the evidence against Jack—but he was still enthusiastic.

"We didn't get any prints from the bags or the hay, so we're going to have to rely on witnesses to place Brunson with the drugs.

D'Annunzio was in the room when Brunson, Magpie, and Fowler were plotting to smuggle them to the island. Red claims he didn't take part in the scheme, but he at least knows about it. And knows Brunson was involved."

"What are your prospects?"

"Well, the solicitor is optimistic. We do have his prints on the Hatteras and in the vicinity of Solis's body."

"But it was Jack's boat. Of course his prints are on it. I doubt a jury is going to put much stock in that."

"Er, right. So it's gonna be a process to tie it all together. We got work to do yet, but let me tell you that we are still investigating hard. We feel we're gonna come up with something else. It's too bad the magistrate let Brunson walk. That's the biggest problem we got right this minute. I wanted you to know that Jack Brunson is on the loose. You probly should consider him armed and dangerous."

"I do appreciate that, Detective. I'll keep an eye peeled."

Tagliabue decided not to warn Agnes Ann about her ex-husband's release until they returned home, for her temporary peace of mind. His own mind was whirling with the possibilities the news generated and with what action he should take. He and Agnes Ann were heading back to essentially the same predicament they faced before they left Westfarrow: Jack Brunson was still hidden from them and was still an existential threat to them.

CHAPTER TWENTY-FIVE

Winter settled in on Westfarrow Island. Ten inches of fresh snow kept most of the residents indoors and muffled the sounds of nature. Anthony Tagliabue stood on the porch of Agnes Ann's farmhouse observing the land as the sun struggled over the trees to the east, scattering its watery light on the pastures and reaching for the barn. His boots had scoured out a rough trail to the barn when he had trudged over to feed the animals, but the snow was otherwise soft and pristine. A rabbit sat on the lawn and twitched its nose as it tried to detect predators in the new day. It bounded under a bush when Tagliabue turned to reenter the house.

Two months had passed since Jack Brunson gained his freedom and they had heard nothing. Christmas was now on the horizon. Jack had not contacted them, and neither had Coleman or any other official in authority. Both Tagliabue and Agnes Ann went about armed when they left the house, and a loaded deer rifle lay in a sling over the front door. He didn't think that was enough.

"We need a dog."

"You're not bringing that snarly little critter on our property, soldier. Ol' Mr. Hammet would probably think it was vermin if he ever saw it running around, and then all the neighbors would think we had an infestation. Besides, that dog probably wouldn't like Auntie Maybelle."

"No kidding? I was thinking Polly's kind of small for a guard dog, but if he wouldn't like Maybelle . . . Hmm. Maybe I should reevaluate the little guy."

"Very funny."

He took the mug of steaming coffee she handed him, smiling at her.

"What would you say about a real guard dog?"

"I'd like to have a dog. Can a guard dog be a pet too?"

"I don't see why not. Let me look into it."

Tagliabue called for an appointment at Island Kennels and Guardians. The business was located out of town and inland from the sea, a private home on a large lot fenced in cyclone wire. The owner was a trim man with a firm handshake.

"This island is such a peaceful place, we don't sell many animals to local residents," Brad Gentry said. Tagliabue refrained from commenting. "Most of our sales are to the mainland. We breed and train the dogs here."

"People have to fly over here to see the dogs?"

"Some do, when they've come to the island for vacation. Mostly they order them by phone or e-mail and they don't see their new guardian until we bring it to them."

Tagliabue pondered that, so Gentry continued. "There's a four-day indoctrination period before we transfer a dog to a new owner, so that's usually taken care of at their home on the mainland."

"So, how long does it take after a dog is ordered?"

"We usually have a few dogs about ready to go to a home. It's all we do. We don't prepare dogs for show or for businesses. We only train dogs for personal protection. Even a house protector needs to be out of the puppy stage, however, so our Schnauzers are about two before they're ready to go to work."

"Schnauzers? Aren't they a little, uh, small for protection?"

"These are giants. They look like regular schnauzers but they have dane in their blood and are as big as shepherds."

Tagliabue was so intrigued by the idea of giant schnauzer guards that he ended up spending an hour with Gentry learning about the dogs. When he returned to Agnes Ann and the horse farm, he filled her in.

"I'm so sure you'll love this female they have that I tentatively bought her. We have to go to the kennels for three hours a day, four days in a row, so the beast will get to know us. And so that Gentry can train us."

"Really?"

"Yeah. She's a push-button dog. Comes when you call her, walks next to you when you tell her. Attacks on command . . ."

"Housebroken too, I suppose?"

"Oh, yeah. She just needs to transfer her allegiance over to us."

"What's her name?"

"Ethyl. It means noble."

Ethyl the giant schnauzer was soon part of the Tagliabue family. She substituted for Jesse in the food consumption department and was an engine of energy. She toured the farm with her new owners, playing with the goats while Tagliabue and Aggie did their chores. She ran alongside Aggie when she exercised her horses and slept on a blanket outside their bedroom door. No one could come on the Seaside Stables property without Ethyl growling low in her throat and coming to attention.

Jack Brunson wasn't interested in getting on the Tagliabue property, however. He had a more sinister plan in mind.

～

When Case #2319 of Sagadahoc County Superior Court convened in Ol' Woody, the famed knotty-pined courtroom in Bath, the county seat, on February 15th, the big question fueling interest among the curious attendees—dozens of them having whetted their appetites for drama on the stories circulating about Big Anthony's exploits and Jack Brunson esquire's chicanery in the matter of drugs and murder and the sinking of the well-known cargo vessel *Maven*—was whether or not Brunson would show up for his own trial. Opinions were divided among those who thought he had long ago debunked for warmer climes and those who thought he now swam with the flounder and haddock in the cold deep of the Atlantic Ocean off the Maine coast. None of the opinions was educated in the least way, but that fact had no bearing on their durability. After all, validation was everywhere in the courtroom on opening day of the trial: bailiffs looking open-mouthed at the defendant's door, thumbs hooked under their gaseous bellies within range of their police specials; three lawyers in fitted suits and layered haircuts whispering frenetically among themselves at the defense table; Anthony Tagliabue and his luscious bride chatting with their heads together.

"I guess Jack's expensive lawyers have been retained but not yet paid," Agnes Ann said in an aside.

Her husband nodded in what he hoped was a sage manner. He knew he should have smiled at her witticism but was too apprehensive to do so. The sheriff's office had just finished up a long investigation, but the results seemed tenuous to him. Tagliabue was anxious about the prosecutor's case. Jack Brunson was up to something, that was certain.

More people pushed in through the oak doors of the courtroom, filling the old space to capacity. A buzz of murmuring swarmed high to the dusty ceiling and back down to the shiny pews in a constant ebb and flow of voices. The room was fusty with the smell of wet clothing.

Into it all strode Jack Brunson, resplendent in a fur-collared greatcoat and merino wool felt fedora. Two bailiffs rushed up to him as spectators looking for seats moved to let him pass. He patted the bailiffs on their shoulders and smiled at them, saying their names. They apparently could not refrain from returning the smile, even though their boss, Judge Andrew Conyers, was waiting in his chambers with ill-concealed fury at the delay to proceedings. The guards led the defendant to the defense table as though they were escorting the prince consort to the altar.

Jack was folding his overcoat on his chair when everyone's attention shifted to a commotion in the front of the courtroom. The judge burst into view with a flourish of bellowing robes and waving arms. Someone spoke loudly, people clattered to their feet, and sat just as abruptly. Judge Conyers took the dais.

"Are we ready to proceed while it's still light out, ladies and gentlemen?"

"Yes, your honor."

"Then let's get at it. I got me a hot date waiting on me."

People tittered at the idea of this old curmudgeon with the glistening bald head going out dancing at one or more of the supper clubs squatting in the dust of Portsmouth's Tan Town, where slick-haired trumpet players wailed the kind of jazz that had been popular in Manhattan a half-century ago. Judge Conyers was a known aficionado of the late Louis "Satchmo" Armstrong.

Daniela Martin presented the case for the prosecution. She was a brassy public servant whose ringlets bounced as she barked out the state's case against one John C. "Jack" Brunson: "Murder, attempted murder, conspiracy to commit murder, felonious assault using a deadly weapon, conspiracy to smuggle and/or sell a regulated substance without a license to do so, and transporting an injured person without providing medical care. The state will prove each charge, your honor, with an array of credible witnesses and forensic evidence to authenticate their testimony. We intend to put this rogue attorney away for the rest of his natural life."

Martin's heels clacked back to the prosecution table and one of Brunson's team slouched up to the podium. He stood there, shuffling a few papers in the folder he held in one manicured hand but saying nothing. The judge's head began to redden.

"You have an opening statement, counselor, or are you going to stand there posing for a picture?"

The lawyer looked up slowly, maybe even insolently.

"I am rendered speechless by the eloquence of Assistant District Attorney Martin's statement, Judge. I thought you might want to let it seep in, so to speak."

"Well, you thought wrong, Meathead. Proceed, or one of these fine bailiffs will provide your sleeping accommodations for the evening."

The lawyer smiled, and brushing an imaginary hair from his forehead with one hand, he held up a few papers in the other. The judge glared at them.

"In that case, your honor, we ask the court to accept this filing, outlining our demand that this fishing expedition against our client be dismissed without prejudice."

"On what grounds, if I may be so bold to ask?"

The lawyer ignored the sarcasm and spoke plainly. "On the grounds that the state no longer has any witnesses to its overreaching charges. Moses "Red" Fowler and Peter D'Annunzio have just advised this legal team that they will not testify against Mr. Brunson."

The courtroom burst into an excited collage of chatter. Conyers banged his gavel. Without Red and D'Annunzio verifying that Jack wanted to disable *Maven* and take from her the bales of hay that contained the drugs, the DA's case against him would be no more than Tagliabue's sighting of Brunson on his Hatteras with Carlos's dying body. The state had no hard evidence. Cuthbert was dead and the Russian defector was off in the bowels of official Washington and would never be allowed to testify against Brunson. His knowledge of Russian communications was too valuable to expose him to any court proceedings. Brunson could be placed on the Hatteras by fingerprints and DNA traces, but the boat belonged to him at the time, so that forensic evidence meant only that Brunson had been aboard his boat at some time in the past. The state's accusations against Jack Brunson were reliant on the testimony of the men who had been in the room when he and the Magpie plotted to disable *Maven* and steal the cargo of hay bales. Red and Peter had been granted immunity for their testimony, but apparently that was no longer enough. The district attorney's case had just fallen apart, and the look on Daniela Martin's face indicated that she was suddenly aware of that reality. She looked as if she had just discovered the head of a toad in her Starbucks cup. Then she looked down at Tagliabue and whispered, "I was afraid of this. They were starting to become uncooperative with us."

Over at the defense table, contrariwise, smugness was the order of the day. The lawyers managed not to smile broadly, but Brunson could not prevent a thin grin from brightening his tanned face. He might have money difficulties in the short term, but he was about to be released as a free man.

The judge turned his stare at the prosecution. It took the prompting of another DA office lawyer to haul Martin's attention to his unstated question: Do you have enough left to continue trying Jack Brunson? She stood stiffly, rummaging fitfully through the papers in front of her.

"Well, uh, your honor, I, er, am caught off guard by this sudden turn of events. Er, we request an overnight stay."

"I guess you do," Conyers growled. "Okay folks, we're going to pause these proceedings until tomorrow at nine A.M. We will continue to conduct this case then. If the state of Maine cannot mount a stout prosecution at that time, I intend to dismiss all charges against the defendant."

He banged his gavel once, hard, and fled the room in a flurry of black robes and shiny head. By the time the chief bailiff called for everyone to rise, the judge was gone from sight. A roar of voices filled the courtroom once the door to his chambers banged closed. People were on their feet talking to each other and gesturing. Brunson and his team held an impromptu press conference at their table. The prosecution team alternatively rubbed their foreheads and thumbed their smartphones madly. Martin had hers to her ear and was working her mouth rapidly.

"This must be what's known as a study in contrasts," Agnes Ann said.

Tagliabue sighed. "Somebody got to Red and Peter. We should have anticipated that."

"Who could it be?"

"I'm thinking it's probably the people who financed the drug deal. They wouldn't want Jack to cop a plea, which he might have done if Red and Peter agreed to testify."

Sheriff's Deputy Johnny Coleman made his way over to their seats and suggested a meeting at Tagliabue's apartment. Once there, he apologized to the Tagliabues for the collapse of the state's case against Jack Brunson.

"We had Red and D'Annunzio sewed up, but something happened. Some new players got involved, some group with enough juice to make Red and Nunz more afraid of them than they are of us."

"It's got to be the mob, don't you think, Johnny?" Tagliabue asked. "They're afraid if Jack senses he's going down, he'll strike a deal with the prosecution to save his own backside. Jack's drug deal probably leads back to them."

"No doubt. The Portland mob don't want Jack Brunson pointing any fingers. Shit."

They sat in silence around Tagliabue's kitchen table, letting cups of coffee grow cold as the heat leached from their own energy. They could feel themselves deflating. Coleman spoke again, in a voice that sounded as hopeless as a treed coon's cry.

"I don't guess there's any chance the feds might bail us out, is there?"

Tagliabue thought about Giselle and her Russian defector, Alexis. She had what The Clemson Project wanted, and they were probably gathering data as fast as they could translate it. She might be willing to help Tagliabue in what to her was a local matter, but never at the risk of compromising her source. He already knew he wasn't even going to ask her to assist.

"I'm afraid that's not going to happen, Johnny. We're on our own."

"I kinda knew you were gonna say that."

~

The prosecutor from the DA's office, Daniela Martin, met with Tagliabue, Agnes Ann, and Detective Johnny Coleman at eight the next morning in a gritty-floored conference room in the old courthouse. Jack Brunson's trial was due to reconvene in sixty minutes, but Daniela was not hopeful that it would last long.

"I'm afraid ol' Satch Conyers is going to throw out the case when I tell him that we have not been able to convince either Peter D'Annunzio or Red Fowler to testify against Brunson after all."

Agnes Ann asked into the mournful silence, "Why do you call the judge Satch?"

The prosecutor smiled, relieved to be able to say something that wasn't pure pessimism. "The judge plays trumpet in juke joints all over the northeast. Can you believe that shit?"

Tagliabue could not envision Conyers, who seemed devoid of a sense of humor, playing jazz in his spare time. Detective Coleman seemed not to hear the explanation.

"Somebody get to D'Annunzio and Fowler?" he asked.

"Looks that way. They both told me and my investigator again last night that they could not remember anything about any meeting or collusion between Brunson and Marv Harris. They had a lawyer with them. Joel Blanton."

The detective reacted to the name with a groan. Tagliabue looked at him with his eyebrows raised in a question.

"Blanton is Alphonso Delgado's main lawyer, his *consigliere*, if you will. For your information, Mrs. Tagliabue, Delgado is suspected of being the crime boss of Portsmouth, maybe of all Maine. We've never been able to nail him on anything serious, mainly because of guys like Blanton. He's got legal representation on everything his syndicate touches. Delgado is better protected than the pope."

A uniform from Coleman's office handed some papers to the detective as the rest of them sat in the plastic chairs, Agnes Ann working on a sticky spot in front of her with a tissue from her purse. After a minute of depressed silence, Tagliabue asked, "We have nothing without the testimony of those two mutts?"

Martin's face was fallen, her mouth a thin line curving down into the sag of her cheeks. She shrugged her shoulders. "You got anything, Detective?"

"As a matter of fact, I do have something."

They all looked at Coleman in surprise. He looked half his age when he smiled sheepishly. He was holding a few papers in his hand like an offering to a goddess.

"Over at the stationhouse just now, the forensic department had left me a report. They actually got two partials and one whole fingerprint from the pills Anthony found in the bales of hay. They're one partial of Magpie, and the other two are Brunson's."

The room erupted in noise.

"My word, there were thousands of them," Agnes Ann exclaimed. "You folks looked at every pill?"

"Musta' been a slow month in the lab," Coleman said around his grin.

Prosecutor Martin was transformed into a new vision of herself with the detective's news. Her posture straightened and she had a glint back in her eye. Coleman handed her the forensic report. After looking it over, she said, "Let's get back into court and unload our surprise on Jack Brunson."

When she told Judge Conyers she had verified that D'Annunzio and Fowler were suddenly reluctant witnesses, the old man growled. Brunson and his legal team sat back in their chairs, trying hard not to look overly satisfied. Jeffrey Magnusen got to his feet. He was the second of Brunson's lawyers, not the one who had infuriated the judge with his attitude the day before. Apparently the team had decided overnight not to press their luck any further with Conyers.

"I'm sorry to hear that the prosecution's case has collapsed, your honor, although we never thought they had enough to commence this trial in the first place. We ask the court to dismiss the charges against our client and let us all go home to our families."

Conyers looked at the lawyer as if he was surprised that the man had a family to go home to, but he directed his next question to the state's attorney.

"Do you have anything to prevent me from agreeing to that request, counselor?"

"I have forensic evidence that will place Mr. Brunson in contact with the confiscated drugs, your honor. We may not be able to prove the other charges against the defendant, but we believe we have more than enough to convict the defendant on conspiracy to smuggle and/or sell a regulated substance without a license to do so."

Magnusen jumped to his feet.

"This is the first we've heard of this evidence, Judge. We need time to process it and arrange our defense."

"Have you never heard of discovery, Ms. Martin?"

"We just now heard of this evidence, your honor. The sheriff's office released its forensic report last night on the drugs they seized and I received this report before court this morning. I haven't even had time to make copies yet."

Conyers rubbed his face and spoke to the jury. "We will suspend proceedings now and reconvene on the day after tomorrow, Thursday. We will complete the trial expeditiously then. I'm sorry for these delays. I know you have lives to get back to, ladies and gentlemen. There will be no more delays, I promise."

Before the judge could vacate the courtroom, Jack Brunson walked up to the dais quickly and spoke to him. Conyers's eyes popped open at this breach of court etiquette. His two lawyers were in the process of leaving the courtroom themselves; they reversed and got to the bench just as Conyers nodded to whatever Brunson had said. The three stood with their heads together in earnest conversation as the judge beckoned to a bailiff and spoke to him. The bailiff hustled after Daniela Martin and asked her to meet in the judge's chambers with his honor and the defense team. Martin shrugged at Agnes Ann and Tagliabue and went off with the bailiff. They waited for her on the courthouse steps.

When she returned ten minutes later she was smiling.

"Jack wants to cop a plea. I agreed to accept unlawful possession with intent to distribute for fifteen months in the state pen, revocation of his license to practice law, and that he agree to be a witness against the crime boss Alphonso Delgado as party to the transaction."

"I can't imagine his lawyers are happy about that deal," Coleman said.

"They didn't find out until after Jack told the judge he wanted to plead out. They are, to coin a phrase, pissed off to beat the band. When I heard what he told Conyers, I made a plea offer."

The four of them laughed and agreed that the bargain Martin had offered was a good one. She told them she would meet with the defense team and the judge in his chambers on Thursday morning.

"I'll call you on the island and let you know what ensues. I think Jack will take it. He could be out of prison in less than a year."

～

The Tagliabues stayed in Bath overnight, treating Johnny Coleman and his wife to dinner to celebrate their win in court, and took the early plane out to Westfarrow. They caught up on farm chores in the afternoon and went to bed early, Ethyl curled at their door. Daniela Martin called them at lunchtime the next day. Agnes Ann listened and put the receiver down gently.

"Bad news, Aggie?"

"Jack was a no-show at court this morning. No one has seen or heard from him."

They sat and cogitated. Was Brunson changing his mind about his plea bargain? Had he decided not to risk any prison time and gone to ground? Skipping a criminal court proceeding is a serious offense for the defendant. The sheriff's office was no doubt out hunting for him. Agnes Ann was worried about his legal system truancy; her husband was more sanguine.

"He probably cached his remaining funds somewhere offshore and is lounging on an island in the Caribbean getting ready to spend them. I can understand why he wouldn't want to be behind bars for even a year."

"I know you've been around the block a time or two, Tony, but you don't appreciate the evil nature of Jack Brunson like I do. He will want to get even with us. I guarantee it."

Her frown disfigured her face and her shoulders sagged. She shook her bent head slowly from side to side, her hair framing it in a curtain of concern. Tagliabue was pained by the look of her, wanted to ease her worry.

"Look, Aggie. We have the dog. We go around carrying. And I'm sort of a protection expert."

She looked up at him, folding her hair behind her ears.

"I've never shot at anything or anybody. I'm not sure my little gun will do me any good if he comes seeking his revenge."

"Well, we stay together until this is settled. After lunch, let's go out and shoot a few magazines in the ravine. The more you shoot, the more confident you'll become. I promise. And I promise not to leave you alone."

She offered a mellow smile to her husband. "I know you want to be my hero, Tony. My protector. But you can't spend your life looking after me."

"I can—and will—until this deal with Brunson is finished."

"When I go to the bathroom, you will not stand outside at attention."

"I'll be hiding behind the shower curtain."

They took the Jeepster in four-wheel mode down into a small basin, reversing it at the bottom and opening the tailgate to lay out their ammunition and weapons. The side of the ravine opposite their entry path was a pronounced rise, ensuring that bullets fired at it could not escape the perimeter. Tagliabue had fixed a strip of chicken wire between two trees. He clipped paper targets to the wire with clothespins.

He watched his wife load rounds into her .38 Smith & Wesson revolver. She leaned forward, arms outstretched, concentration written on her face. She squeezed off rounds smoothly, not jerking the gun or moving her body. Her aim was accurate at five yards.

"If you can hit something at this distance, you will be able to defend yourself."

Agnes Ann popped open the cylinder of her gun and let the empty brass fall into her other hand. She rested with one hip against the fender of their old car, looking long, slim, and competent. Sitting next to her on the tailgate was a new gun Tagliabue had purchased just for home protection, a deadly looking Remington twenty gauge that was just more than two feet long, with a pistol grip instead of a stock like a normal shotgun. This Model 870 TAC-14 was designed specifically to repel a home invasion. Agnes Ann pumped a round into the chamber like a mountain man. She leaned forward and fired the shotgun from her hip. It boomed—and shredded one of the paper targets into confetti.

She smiled. "Now that's more like it," she said.

That night they rested easy, each with a handgun in reach. The shotgun was cradled over the bedroom door. The dog circled her blanket a couple of times before settling in to guard their room.

The wind blew after midnight, keeping Ethyl on alert but quiet. Hours passed. The wind fell off. When she detected movement not caused by the wind, she was no longer quiet.

Tagliabue slipped out of bed and into his jeans. The black dog growled low in her throat. Agnes Ann's eyes went wide.

"What is it, Tony?" she whispered.

"Something's bothering her. Sit on the floor with your piece. I'll let you know it's me before I come back through the door."

So, she thought to herself, if someone comes in without announcing himself, I just shoot him. It was a frightening thought. She pulled on her robe and sat on the carpet at her side of the bed, the far side from the door. She cleared her throat and waited. The door clicked closed.

Tagliabue and the dog went downstairs.

They left through the sliding doors on the bay side of the house, the big schnauzer quiet now that the hunt was on. They stopped in a shadow. The two blended in immediately, the man in dark clothes and his black animal. The moon was a waning quarter, the sky cold and clear.

They looked at the Hatteras floating on a steel sea. Tagliabue could detect no movement on the white boat and the water was perfectly calm. No ripples. No bubbles. He touched Ethyl's head and started around the back of the house. When they slipped through the corral gate, they could hear the horses moving their feet. One snorted. It was late; they should have been asleep in the moist warmth of the barn. Something had disturbed them.

Tagliabue got down and crawled forward on his elbows. The dog stalked beside him. The horses had tramped most of the snow in the corral to mud. It was frozen hard now and he could feel its furrows and ridges on his chest. They crossed the fenced area by moving a few feet, then stopping. They made the back door of the barn. It was closed. The outside latch was set. Tagliabue squinted through a crack between bottom boards. The burning night-light was small, the interior of the barn dim. His field of vision was narrow. He could see Hat Rack with his head over the half door of his stall. The gelding was quiet, but he raised and lowered his head as he peered out.

The horse was looking at something Tagliabue couldn't see. After his heart rate slowed, Tagliabue raised up an inch at a time, one hand on the dog's head, thigh muscles straining. He slid the latch bar through its staple. Pulling on the heavy door, he tried to remember if it creaked as it opened. It didn't. At least, not for the first ten inches, and that was all he needed. Peeking in, he still couldn't see what the horse was curious about. He sent the dog in with an attack command. Ethyl bolted silently, a black streak through the center of the barn. She erupted into a snarl when she reached the other end. Someone screeched. Scuffling sounds rose in the building and horses started snorting and stamping their hooves. Tagliabue went in at a run.

He found a man up on a mound of hay bales, pointing a handgun at the big dog lunging below him. Tagliabue bellowed and fired his 9 mm at the ceiling.

"You shoot that dog, turkey, and you're a dead man."

Horses whinnied in fear and bucked around their stalls. Their goat companions bleated in complement. Tagliabue flipped the main light switch, throwing into stark outline a vision of young Timmy O'Brien with his hands raised high, one holding a black syringe case. He was wild-eyed, open-mouthed. Ethyl barked. The barn was in an uproar.

∼

"I hope you can explain yourself, sonny boy."

This time Tagliabue kept his piece in his hand, pointing in the general direction of Timothy O'Brien. When he had caught him on *Maven* the summer before, he had relaxed his gun hand in the presence of a man he considered a friend. The younger man now pressed his back against the wall of an empty stall, his eyes never leaving Ethyl, who sat watching him, her backside flexing silently, her mouth tight and wet.

"Plea—please, Anthony. Call off your dog."

"You don't move, she won't move."

"I ain't gonna move. Not a damn inch, I swear. He's making me nervous, like he's ready to attack."

"Getting caught on someone else's property with intent to harm valuable racehorses is what ought to make you nervous," Tagliabue said.

He had picked up the syringe case with his handkerchief when O'Brien dropped it. He could feel the syringe in the case. The other animals in the barn had quieted now that they recognized him, and now that his dog had settled into watching mode. The horses were looking out into the passageway but had stopped kicking the ground and whinnying. He pressed Agnes Ann's number on his cell and told her: "Everything's okay. Call the constable and tell him to get over here. We have an intruder in the barn." He clicked off. O'Brien licked his lips.

Tagliabue called Ethyl over. She sat next to him, watching the young man, her muscles hard as stone, vibrating. O'Brien sank slowly to his rear. His face was crumpled.

"It's all a fucking mess, Anthony. A real fucking mess."

"Tell me about it."

"I shouldn't a done it. Shouldn't a done it. I done bad things before. This is the worst. I'm really sorry."

O'Brien began to blubber. Ethyl whined. Tagliabue waited. He had always liked Timmy O'Brien, thought he did remarkably well after the disaster his father, Bronc, had turned into. Timmy was the only bartender he knew who didn't drink. He had a pleasant wife and two young boys he doted on, spent time with them. Worked two jobs. What could make a man like him go off the rails and do something so dangerous and illegal as this? In a voice so weak Tagliabue could barely hear him, Timmy answered him.

"I'm addicted to pain pills, Anthony. I can't get by without 'em."

Tagliabue felt heat rise into his face. His muscles hardened, his pupils dilated. He clenched his teeth before he exploded.

"Is that the best you can do, O'Brien? Whine about how you can't live without eating some fucking chemical? You've got a family, children. You're supposed to be a man, for God's sake. You're supposed to be responsible for them. You're not supposed to be some Mary who can't control his appetites!"

His voice had risen, his body also. A roar of anger and profanity was something rarely heard from Big Anthony Tagliabue and O'Brien cowered under the assault, as if he expected Tagliabue to hammer him with his fists as well as his bellowing. He didn't reply. His face was ashen and his mouth hung open. But Tagliabue's fire died as quickly as it had risen in him. He sat back down, breathing hard. He had learned years ago not to release his bile. He had learned that he was so strong and fast that he could do serious damage if he lost his temper, so he trained himself to always control any rage that threatened to fill him. The training had worked, but he was so disappointed in this young man he considered a friend and a good person, so dismayed at Timmy's failure to act responsibly, that his fury momentarily overcame his training in the barn that cold night. Timmy O'Brien moaned. His pain sounded real. Tagliabue forced himself to speak quietly.

"You get your pills from Jack Brunson?"

O'Brien nodded, sniffling and crying.

"You came on my boat last summer when she was tied up near the Pelham Island, doing something for Brunson?"

He nodded again. "I . . . I was supposed to plant some pills, but you heard me."

Tagliabue exhaled. "Tell me your story and hurry up. Ian Fletcher is on his way."

O'Brien began to talk. He told Tagliabue how he got addicted and how Jack preyed on his addiction. He told him how he was supposed to medicate Francine on Brunson's orders. It all came out in a rush.

"I swear to God, Anthony, this is the end for me. Frances will help me get clean. She's a good wife and she'll help me. I'll work this out. I'll never do you wrong again, Anthony, I swear. Give me a break, man. Please give me a break! I'll rat Jack out if I even see him again."

Tagliabue raised his sidearm.

"Get your sorry ass out of here, Timmy."

Tagliabue holstered his weapon. Timmy O'Brien scrambled to his feet and ran out of the barn. Ethyl whined again. She looked from her master to the fleeing felon, but she stayed seated next to him.

"You did a good job, girl. Let's go tell Aggie what transpired here tonight."

~

"You let him go, Tony?"

"Yeah," Tagliabue sighed. "He promised to get help. He promised to let me know if Jack contacts him again."

Agnes Ann was silent.

"I know, Aggie. I'm a sap."

She turned to him as they stood outside in the cold waiting for the island constable. They both had on their lined jackets and wool hats. The air turned their breathing to ice clouds.

"You're not a sap, Tony. You're a good man. Good men prove they're good by their behavior. I think you behaved well just now."

He smiled and wrapped his left arm around her.

"So Timmy snuck over here because he had to feed his habit. Jack sold drugs, you mean?"

"Not directly, at least, not at first. The Magpie was the dealer who found out Timmy wanted pain pills after he recovered from a hospital visit for shingles. He probably had an aide or a nurse at Bath General who tipped him off. After Marv died, Jack took up supplying a few guys who could help him. Timmy said Jack wouldn't take any money. He just wanted favors now and then."

He told her that Timmy O'Brien was supposed to inject "the red horse" with the sedative in the syringe, to slow her morning work so that Agnes Ann would consider selling her back to him. Brunson apparently didn't know that the racing filly, Francine, was over on the mainland with his own son, Jesse, being trained and worked for her three-year-old season. O'Brien was trying to find a chestnut among the herd when his searching around made the horses nervous and alerted Ethyl. He didn't think that a sedative would harm Agnes Ann's horse. Two days later, she and Tagliabue found out that Jack Brunson had lied to his addicted helper. Neither of them was surprised.

CHAPTER TWENTY-SIX

"The needle was full of botulism," Johnny Coleman said. "I'm sure glad Ian Fletcher didn't open the case. He told me it was a poison, so I gave the whole deal to forensics. I didn't touch nothing but the baggie it was in."

The sheriff's detective was speaking on a video conference call with Tagliabue, Agnes Ann, and the DA's Daniela Martin two days after the intruder had run from the main barn at Seaside Stables. Town Constable Ian Fletcher arrived at the horse farm just after three A.M. and took the plastic syringe case the intruder had dropped in his haste to vacate the premises—the constable's words. Tagliabue still felt washed out from the incident. He had witnessed the perfidy of people he liked many times in his life, but finding Timmy engaged in an attempt to harm him and Agnes Ann left him with an empty feeling in his chest.

"It's too bad you didn't grab the jerk with the needle, instead of just chasing him off," Johnny Coleman said. "Constable Fletcher didn't find no sign of the intruder except for blurred footprints in some snow and tire tracks. A car did pass him going the other way as he was coming to your property, but he didn't recognize it. It didn't stand out or nothing."

O'Brien had been wearing gloves, so his fingerprints were not found on the case Tagliabue had assumed was a gun at first. Partials matching those on file for John "Jack" Brunson had been lifted by Coleman's lab tech. The syringe contained enough *botu-linum toxin* to kill an animal the size of Francine, the detective told them, almost 460-nanograms. The bacteria were dissolved in a fluid and had apparently been stolen during a big compounding pharmacy heist down in Boston over the summer.

"The stuff was part of a stock that the pharmacy was watering down for treating wrinkles in old ladies, like Botox. No offense, Daniela," Coleman said with a laugh.

Martin huffed and said, "Little old ladies aren't the only ones with wrinkles, Detective. I heard Satch Conyers gets Botox to keep his head smooth for the ladies."

Everyone on the phone laughed, a short-lived break from the serious nature of their conversation. Tagliabue opined that a major robbery was well out of the expertise range of a bent lawyer like Jack Brunson.

"I suspect he was given the poison by the Delgado organization."

"Why would a gangster want to kill my horse?"

"Alphonso Delgado doesn't give a damn about Francine, Aggie. Jack asked for the toxin to exact revenge on you. Delgado owns Jack and his twisted legal mind and favors rendered are how guys like that keep a tight hold on guys like Jack."

"How can Jack help him if he's in hiding somewhere?"

"Don't know, but I would guess that he had the toxin for months, long before all his troubles with the law began. This was probably his last best chance to use it."

"What befuddles me is why anyone on Westfarrow would agree to kill a horse," Martin said, not knowing that Timothy O'Brien was the intruder. "It's not as if there are hardened gangsters on the island."

Coleman had an answer to that apparent conundrum.

"Probly didn't realize it was going to kill the horse. We know that the pills in Mrs. Tagliabue's hay belonged to Brunson. He may have been using an island guy. The perp here might of needed the pills. Who knows?"

"Our defendant was selling him drugs?" Martin asked.

"Brunson probly got them from the Magpie. Marv Harris. A small-time crook who shot Anthony's mate. Dead now, but him and Brunson were buds. Could be Brunson's got a few other guys doing odd jobs for him lately and getting pills in return. Now he don't have Harris anymore."

Martin murmured to herself as she digested that information, no doubt trying to calculate how she could rearraign Jack Brunson on drug dealing charges, Tagliabue thought. She asked Coleman if the police were looking for Brunson.

"We're looking okay, but we ain't seen hide nor hair of him."

If Brunson had gone to ground as they suspected, Tagliabue said, his gangster friends must not be happy with him. "Otherwise, I don't see why he ran off after asking for a plea deal. He made at least some kind of bargain offer with the judge. Jack's not going to get anything better from the state, is he Ms. Martin?"

"Not likely. So, you're assuming Delgado didn't like the plea bargain and told the defendant as much? He's afraid Jack was going to implicate him in some nefarious activities."

"When Jack heard of your proposed plea deal from his lawyers and realized he was going to have to testify against the Delgado cartel, plus spend time in prison, he must have figured it wasn't such a good deal for him after all."

"And," Johnny Coleman said, "prison's not a safe place for snitches. Brunson musta figured he'd be better off on the run than in the clink."

Tagliabue nodded. "It's the only reason I can discern for Jack to go into hiding."

Agnes Ann mouthed "discern?" to him as they ended the phone call. He smiled at her playful mockery.

Less than two months later they found out that Jack Brunson had not gone into hiding as Tagliabue thought he must have done.

∾

Toby Walsh was raking quahogs from his scarred and roughened clam boat off the Doubling Point lighthouse in a thin spring sun, working hard enough on a fertile bed to have removed his lined jacket. He was still wearing his Carhartt overalls and his forehead was shiny from his exertions. He worked the long handle to dig the tines of his rake into the bottom mud and scratched loose into the attached basket enough bivalves to have almost a bushel of legals in the bottom of his boat. It was a decent harvest for so early in the season. He was enjoying the labor, the feeling of being in rhythm with the sky and water as his muscles oiled themselves after a long winter's rest. In a few more pulls he would have caught enough and would motor into port before the sun got too low in the west. The salt air still got icy after sunset.

The tempo of his work was interrupted when the rake caught on a snag. He pulled to loosen it. Walsh's muscles were hardened from his years of bay work, so he was surprised when a determined yank didn't dislodge the obstruction. There wasn't much debris on the bottom here and he hadn't expected this problem. He pulled on the handle, drawing his beamy boat to the rake. He gripped the pole of his rake as if he were removing a fence post and pulled straight up, grunting in effort and dipping the gunwale. When the rake came suddenly loose, a rush of gas bubbles came with it. They smelt of rot when they broke on the surface. He extracted the rake hurriedly: in the catch basket were a few clams, a single oyster shell, a wriggling shiner—and a bone enshrouded in white cotton. Walsh swallowed a few times, threw a buoy over the side to mark the spot, and reached for his cell to dial harbor patrol.

∾

"The coroner's office ID'd the remains as those of one John C. 'Jack' Brunson," Johnny Coleman told Tagliabue. The detective was speaking formally because he hoped this find would tie up the loose ends of his investigation, so he was experimenting with the verbiage of his final report. He wanted to be shut of it; he hoped to get back to work on cases that didn't involve interference by a secretive federal agency that seemed to have more juice even than the sheriff. Coleman had come to like, and admire, Big Anthony Tagliabue, but he wanted nothing else to do with the man's complicated assignments. The demise of Jack Brunson would also free Agnes Ann Tagliabue of the fear of retribution by her ex-husband that had darkened the last winter months on Westfarrow Island.

Anthony Tagliabue felt the relief also. He wanted only to work Seaside Stables and accompany his wife as she raced her fast filly and watched her son grow into manhood. The lurking danger Brunson represented had kept him alert, unable to completely relax. Their guard dog seemed to relish the prospect of a constant job, but neither of her owners had enjoyed what should have been a time to rest and recharge as nature did when the land froze over.

Agnes Ann was continually grateful during those past fretful months for Anthony's training and experience in the world of violence. His proficiency in war and crime fighting was a comfort to her. Tagliabue referred to his government work in the past tense whenever she mentioned it. He told her, and himself, that he was done with Giselle and her Clemson Project. She smiled and patted his cheek when he made that impossible promise to her.

AUTHOR'S NOTES

Dear Readers:

I was assisted in the creation of this book by the contextual editing
of Judith Shepard, co-publisher of The Permanent Press, and by
the deep line editing of Barbara Anderson, who ended up knowing my manuscript better than I did. I also thank the famed crime
writer Chris Knopf for the benefit of his wisdom and experience
in the craft of writing and my critique partner, Tim Bryant, author
of the hilarious *Blue Rubber Pool*, for his sage advice about life and
weaponry.

If you notice any literary or factual blunders as you read this book,
you can assume they occurred because I did not always follow the
advice offered to me by these generous folks. Sometimes a fella just
has to stumble along on his own path. It helps that I always have
the shoulder of my wife, Joan Lee, to fling my arm around when
I have trouble navigating that path.

There is no Westfarrow Island off the coast of Maine, but there
could be. There is no Clemson Project, but there could be. All
the characters in the book are likewise fictitious. The Russian ship
Leonov is real, but she never had a radioman defect out at sea—as

far as I know. The town of Bath is real also, a jewel of coastal Maine, but my place settings there are but loosely connected to the actual features of the town and her riverine environs.

Thank you for taking the time to read this book.

Peace and good to you.

Paul A. Barra